The prisoner turned eyes like tombstones on Zavala

The guard stopped short of taking a step backward and putting his hand on his pepper spray. Barnes sighed. His spiel would be just as ineffective.

"Listen, you're here for a reason, but while you *are* here, I'd like your stretch to be as easy as possible. If you're in real trouble, I'll do what I can to help you."

The prisoner turned to stare at Barnes. "Thank you, Officer. I'll keep that in mind."

Barnes hit the button and the bars clanged shut behind him and the guard. Hoots and catcalls erupted from the tiers of inmates. Horrific offers and suggestions rang out. Bets were laid. All eyes were on the new prisoner.

This was a maximum-security facility, and it was overcrowded with murderers, rapists, hit men and assorted cons. For the first time in the jail's history, an Executioner had walked in.

MACK BOLAN ®
The Executioner

The
Don Pendleton's
Executioner®

PRISON CODE

A GOLD EAGLE BOOK FROM
W🌐RLDWIDE®

TORONTO • NEW YORK • LONDON
AMSTERDAM • PARIS • SYDNEY • HAMBURG
STOCKHOLM • ATHENS • TOKYO • MILAN
MADRID • WARSAW • BUDAPEST • AUCKLAND

First edition May 2013

ISBN-13: 978-0-373-64414-8

Special thanks and acknowledgment to Charles Rogers for his contribution to this work.

PRISON CODE

It is said that power corrupts, but actually it's more true that power attracts the corruptible. The sane are usually attracted by other things than power.
—David Brin

How does a man become corrupt? How does a man lose his soul? I have my theory. Those who hold the lives of others in their hands have to toe the line of decency or face my wrath.
—Mack Bolan

THE
MACK BOLAN
LEGEND

Nothing less than a war could have fashioned the destiny of the man called Mack Bolan. Bolan earned the Executioner title in the jungle hell of Vietnam.

But this soldier also wore another name—Sergeant Mercy. He was so tagged because of the compassion he showed to wounded comrades-in-arms and Vietnamese civilians.

Mack Bolan's second tour of duty ended prematurely when he was given emergency leave to return home and bury his family, victims of the Mob. Then he declared a one-man war against the Mafia.

He confronted the Families head-on from coast to coast, and soon a hope of victory began to appear. But Bolan had broken society's every rule. That same society started gunning for this elusive warrior—to no avail.

So Bolan was offered amnesty to work within the system against terrorism. This time, as an employee of Uncle Sam, Bolan became Colonel John Phoenix. With a command center at Stony Man Farm in Virginia, he and his new allies—Able Team and Phoenix Force—waged relentless war on a new adversary: the KGB.

But when his one true love, April Rose, died at the hands of the Soviet terror machine, Bolan severed all ties with Establishment authority.

Now, after a lengthy lone-wolf struggle and much soul-searching, the Executioner has agreed to enter an "arm's-length" alliance with his government once more, reserving the right to pursue personal missions in his Everlasting War.

1

Lancaster County, Pennsylvania

MACK BOLAN, AKA the Executioner, scanned the decrepit Holstein barn through his night-vision goggles. Nothing moved. Bolan had learned of the fallow farm's existence within the past two hours, and he decided to make his move against this group. He'd had his eye on them for some time. He had gotten a satellite window just as he had begun making his approach through the orchards below twenty minutes earlier.

The soldier didn't care for what he was looking at.

Dairy cattle barns in this part of the country were often built into a low hillside. Their forebays overshot the foundation, and that left the area beneath the overhang a pool of darkness. Holstein barns were big. This one could easily swallow up half a dozen vehicles if need be. Their lower levels were made of stone and the barns usually had basements. If a person was misbehaving in Lancaster County, an abandoned dairy barn on an overgrown farm that the forest was busily reclaiming could be a fortress of evil.

Bolan had very actionable intelligence that someone was misbehaving in Lancaster County this night.

It was a beautiful summer night, cloudless, with a full moon. Fireflies winked through the scrub trees encroaching the fields, lighting up their willingness for love. The soldier's phone was currently fastened by Velcro to his wrist. He spoke into it now. "Bear, do we have anything on satellite?"

Aaron "the Bear" Kurtzman came back. "No, nothing, and right now I have my hands on a high gain thermal-imaging NSA bird. You'd think if something was really going on in there, there would be some light leakage."

"Unless it's in the basement."

"Right, but then where are the lookouts up top?"

It was a good point, and one that Bolan had already considered. He pushed the selector on his Colt submachine to full-auto. The weapon was a DEA special with a built-in sound suppressor. The Colt had further modifications by John "Cowboy" Kissinger at Stony Man Farm, including a 40 mm grenade launcher mounted beneath the barrel, a Taser unit to port and a high intensity flashlight starboard. Bolan glanced over at the farmhouse. The roof had caved in. The windows were missing and the remaining walls listed at sharp angles. The farmhouse had gone to wreckage.

The barn looked dilapidated, but in comparison it was clear that someone was maintaining it. "I'm going in." Bolan stepped out into the overgrown, waist-high grass between him and the barn. He got three steps in before Kurtzman's urgent message came across the link.

"Striker! I have two heat signatures coming at you fast from your eleven o'clock! Straight out of the farmhouse!"

Through his NVGs Bolan saw the grass rippling and leaving a pair of wakes as two somethings plowed toward him faster than a human could run. They were arrowing in from the house rather than the barn. Bolan faded back into the trees a bit to give himself a clear shot. The mastiffs exploded out of the grass, looking to be over the 150 pound mark. The huge dogs weren't barking, which told Bolan they were bred to attack rather than guard. Their owners most likely triangulated on the victim's screams.

Bolan put his hand on the Taser's trigger and squeezed twice. The weapon chuffed and dogs twisted in midlunge as the probes hit them. The soldier held the trigger down and gave them the juice. The mastiffs skidded out and fell, twisting and convulsing in the leaves beneath the trees. Bolan cut the current and yanked the barbs. He quickly cut lengths of paracord and hog-tied the two shuddering beasts.

"Dogs are down," Bolan reported. "I'm thinking someone's home."

"The dogs came out of the house, but as of now I'm still detecting no movement."

Bolan pushed two fresh wire and probe cassettes into the stun gun's double muzzle and armed them. "I'm thinking the dogs kennel or den in the house and are let off leash at night to blindside anyone approaching the barn, just like they did to me."

"So you would think someone would be watching from the barn and have reacted by now?"

"If anyone is watching, all they saw was the dogs running off into the woods. I'm going to hold tight a minute."

"Copy that."

Bolan was rewarded within ten seconds. Kurtzman came back. "Two contacts, coming out of the barn."

"I have them."

Two men walked out of the shadows of the Holstein barn's overhang. They found the wakes the dogs had made in the grass and then walked in the mastiffs' footsteps toward Bolan's position.

"Shit," one muttered.

"Don't hear no screaming," the other replied.

Bolan watched the sentries approach. The two Caucasian males were dressed in civvies and armed with surplus ComBloc SKS carbines that had been dressed up with folding stocks and optics. One was a skinhead and one had a mullet.

"Well, hell, Dale," Skinhead said. "If it was a man, they would have run him down by now."

"What if the Feds shot 'em?" Dale replied.

"Feds don't use silencers, Tucker. There would've been gunshots and screaming and a ruckus."

"Maybe it was a pig."

"They do like pig," Dale admitted. "Almost as much as human."

"Naomi!" Tucker called. "Wynona!"

Bolan suppressed a small smile beneath his NVGs.

Dale spoke into his cell. "Kurt, the girls're off chasing something." Dale recoiled as he got an earful and clicked off. "Kurt ain't happy."

"Kurt ain't never happy," Tucker stated.

Bolan was fairly certain that if Kurt survived the next ten minutes he was going to be unhappy for ninety-nine to life. The Executioner rose and squeezed the stun gun's trigger twice in rapid succession, then held it down. Tucker and Dale contracted like burning insects as the electricity ripped through their nervous systems and toppled them to the leaves. The stun gun pumped more juice than was legal for law enforcement, and the two men made little more noise than a few groans and some speaking in tongues as they short-circuited. The soldier cut the juice. He cut some paracord and hog-tied the men next to the dogs. He was running out of paracord and down to his last stun gun cassette. He took two strips of duct tape and gagged the two men.

The Executioner gave his captives a few seconds to recover, and while he did he linked their cell phones to his and began transmitting their contents back to Kurtzman. Bolan reloaded his slightly less than lethal weapon. "Tucker and Dale, is it?"

Tucker and Dale twitched as they strained against their bonds and glared over their gags. Bolan pushed the safety off the stun gun. "Guess I'll just have to juice you and keep juicing you." He leveled his Colt. "Tucker and Dale, is it?"

Tucker's mullet bobbed in acknowledgment.

"You make any sound I don't ask you to, and I'm going to Taser you in the face. The juice goes straight through the optic nerve into the brain. You don't know the meaning of heartbreak until the day you've had that done to you. You read me?"

Tucker nodded, then flinched as Bolan stripped the tape away. "How many inside?"

"About twelve?"

"About?"

"Twelve."

"You're sure?" Bolan probed.

"Twelve!"

The soldier stripped Tucker's weapon and cleared it. He cut the man's ankles free and hauled him to his feet. Bolan hung the empty SKS across Tucker's chest.

"Are you a Fed?" Tucker asked.

"Nope, worse."

"Worse."

"Oh God, you're black helicopters and shit!"

"Worse," Bolan said.

"What does that mean?"

"It's means I'm worse. I'm me."

"What are you going to do to me?" Tucker asked.

"Don't know. Maybe let you go if you cooperate."

Dale snarled behind his tape.

Tucker looked at Bolan hopefully. "Really?"

"Sure, shooting man and beast with a stun gun, taking down the Lancaster County Regulators?"

Tucker flinched. The Lancaster County Regulators were a rural, northeastern white supremacist group who vaguely modeled themselves after the "regulators" from New Mexico's Lincoln County Wars.

Bolan shrugged. "Letting people go? I pretty much do whatever I want. Now what's going on in that barn?"

"They're having a meeting," Tucker whispered.

Dale thrashed.

"And?"

Tucker gave Dale a leery look. "It's something important."

"Forget him," Bolan advised. "Go on."

"A guy drove out from Harrisburg. Someone high up, a suit." Tucker nodded meaningfully. "He drives a Town Car."

Dale actually managed to rock himself up onto his knees. Bolan aimed his weapon at his face. "As God is my witness, both probes. One under each eye."

Dale sagged back to the ground. Bolan put his boot on the back of the man's shaved skull and pushed it down into the crackling summer leaves.

"Town Car's a sweet ride," Bolan admitted. "What are they talking about?"

"I don't know." Tucker cast his eyes down. "I'm only second tier."

"An Outrider." Bolan nodded. He'd done his homework on the Lancaster boys. "Not yet a Regulator."

"Yeah…"

Bolan believed it. Tucker was barely sentry duty and managing the man-eating dogs material, and that was only because the Regulators were short on manpower in Pennsylvania. "So who's minding store besides you, Dale and the dogs?"

"We pulled sentry duty. Dale was in the National Guard."

"And you?"

Tucker hung his head. "I washed out."

"I'm sure you have other talents."

"You think so?"

Bolan was pretty sure Tucker was about as useful as bird droppings on a pump handle. "The Regulators saw something in you."

Tucker beamed. "Thanks, do you really think—" He suddenly caught himself. "What do you want me to do?"

"Get me to the barn without getting shot."

Tucker looked down at his boots. "Okay… That's it?"

"That's it."

Tucker looked up hopefully. "You'll really let me go?"

"I give you my word."

Dale was literally crying beneath Bolan's heel. The soldier sighed. "Sorry about this." Tucker jumped as Bolan shot Dale between his shoulder blades and stunned him hard. He snatched the Pittsburgh Penguins cap from Tucker's head and settled it on his own with mild distaste.

"Let's walk." Bolan and Tucker headed through the tall grass toward the barn. "Anyone likely to be watching us?"

"Maybe, but that was, like, our job and stuff."

"Who's Kurt?"

Tucker started as they passed an old stone well. "Kurt's the district Regulator. He used to be a Marine."

Tucker was turning out to be a minefield of knowledge. "Which one's he?"

"Oh, Kurt's easy to spot. He looks like Thor."

"Good to know."

In the gloom beneath the upper barn overhang Bolan made out a newly installed steel security door. The overhang flooded with light as the door flung open and a reasonable facsimile of the Norse god of thunder in a wife-beater and jeans thundered forth his wrath. "What the hell are you assholes doing out there? You know we got—" Kurt's eyes flew wide as he made out Bolan. "Jesus!" The steel door slammed shut and clicked.

Bolan leveled his weapon at Tucker. "Sorry about this."

"Oh, God…"

"Run, when you can." Bolan fired his last stun gun probe and juiced Tucker to the ground. The soldier broke open the breech of his grenade launcher and pressed the button on the base. Inside the launch tube the grenade clicked like a switchblade as the five-inch standoff probe extended. The U.S. military used door busting rifle grenades of Israeli design, but they were two feet long and had to be attached to the muzzle of a rifle. Bolan's munition was a Cowboy Kissinger special. The grenade detonated when the probe touched its target. That meant it exploded against the obstacle rather than through it, killing everyone behind.

Bolan pulled down his goggles to shield his eyes, and fired.

The security door flew backward off its hinges in a pulse of smoke and blast. The soldier pulled a flash-stun from one of his pouches as men within the barn shouted and screamed. He pulled the pin and tossed in the grenade. Light flashed and sound cracked and Bolan stepped into the firefly swarm of pyrotechnic aftereffect. Kurt lay beneath the blackened door moaning. He gasped as Bolan walked across the door. The rows of stone cow stalls lay empty. Sawdust sifted down from the wooden boards above as men shouted and ran about upstairs. Stone stairs led up to a closed wooden hatch in the floor; an open door to the left led downward into the cellar. The element of surprise was lost and Bolan was severely outnumbered. He had to make a decision. It was a grand old barn, and it pained him, but he jacked a white phosphorus round into his M-203 and nuked the stairs heading up. Men above roared and screamed in alarm as burning white smoke and particulate funneled upward into the wooden barn above.

Bullets cracked and spalled against the stone at Bolan's feet as gunners above began firing down through the floorboards. The soldier hugged the wall and jacked a fresh grenade into the breech of his M-203 and didn't deploy the standoff probe. He aimed where the main floor support beams met overhead, and fired. With a direct hit the High Explosive Dual Purpose—HEDP—round was designed to penetrate two inches of steel vehicle armor. The ancient and brittle oak of the beams stood no chance. The upper floor of the barn dropped like a falling bridge. Men screamed as the floor fell out from beneath them, and they tumbled to the stone floor or their bodies broke on the stall divides. Bolan ran for the cellar door as the floor continued its collapse and a black Lincoln Town Car, a Jeep and two pickups joined the landslide. Orange light expanded and fire whooshed as the collapse of the floor sucked heat and flame from the stairwell into the upper story and the barn began to burn in earnest.

Bolan spoke into his phone. "Police and Fire, Bear. Report multiple shots fired. Multiple suspects. I'll be in the basement."

"Copy that, Striker."

The Executioner turned to the stairs leading down as hell erupted behind him.

A big man with slicked-back hair, wearing a suit, erupted out of the cellar stairs at the run. He carried a Glock in each hand and goggled at the sight of Bolan and raised his pistols. "Motherfucker!"

Bolan's silenced Colt whispered five rounds into the gunner's chest and sent him tumbling back down the steps. The soldier loaded a fresh grenade into the smoking breech of M-203. He tossed a flash-stun grenade down the stairs and turned his head as it detonated. Bolan locked the steel door behind him and descended to the cellar as the blast echoes reverberated around him. He stepped over the thug's corpse on the landing and entered the cellar. Two hanging bulbs lit the bare, stone enclosure, and the shock of the stun grenade had shattered a third. Another suited thug reeled from the sensory overload of the flash-stun grenade, drunkenly waving an Uzi pistol. Bolan cracked the man across the jaw with the butt of the Colt and dropped him. The cellar was a double space and Bolan went through the door between them, his weapon leveled.

The soldier caught sight of a snarling, bald, middle-aged man in an expensive suit just as the steel door of the safe room started to slide shut. The soldier made another decision. The door breaker wouldn't crack this door, and the full HEDP might kill the person behind it.

Either way, he wasn't going to let it close.

Bolan fired. The armor-piercing round breached the door inches before it locked, and expended its jet of molten metal and superheated gas into whatever lay behind. The soldier strode to the entry. The twisted and blackened door had stopped on its track. Bolan shoved and it slid back. Black smoke filled the enclosure as the phosphorus burned. The most fascinating aspect of the safe room was the second door opening onto a darkened tunnel. The soldier stepped over the blackened, blistered and moaning man on the floor and moved toward the computer at the burning workstation. He snatched the flash drive from the USB port as it started to melt. The desktop had taken a jet of molten metal. The screen was shattered glass and crumpled plastics, with sparks coming out of it. Bolan hit Eject on the keyboard and the tray miraculously opened, delivering a pitted and smoke-damaged disk. Bolan pocketed the data and turned on his suspect.

"Hi."

The burned man glared up at Bolan with pure, unadulterated hatred. "Fuck you."

"You have significant burns. You want medical help?"

The burned man opened his hand. He was holding a smartphone. An application on the screen was counting down from five. Bolan lunged for the second door and slammed the big red Close button with his palm as he dived through. The steel door slid shut with a hiss, and the soldier's world plunged to pitch-black.

The tunnel smelled of fresh earth, and it rained down on him as the ground shook with a significant detonation. The door didn't fly open, and heat and a shockwave didn't tear out Bolan's lungs. Dirt sprinkled down, but the tunnel didn't collapse. The soldier clicked on his tactical light. The fresh tunnel was about thirty yards long and ended in what looked like the belly of a brick barbecue. The soldier did a little mental math and smiled.

The tunnel ended directly beneath the well he had passed.

Bolan came to the brick and looked at the hatch above. He swung the latch lever and stepped back as the hatch door fell open with a clang and the foot of dirt that had covered it rained down.

Bolan grabbed rungs and started climbing.

The rungs disappeared and turned into what seemed like random holes and stone protrusions that would take more than a cursory glance to detect as a ladder. Bolan grabbed the lip of the well and pulled himself back onto the surface. The barn was hurling flames into the sky. Bolan watched the structure burn. He couldn't tell how many Lincoln County Regulators or guests had escaped while he had gone spelunking, and he wasn't going to step into the inferno to try to find out. Heat washed against him as he moved close to the fire.

Tucker was gone. The tracks in the dirt indicated he had headed toward the road rather than going back for Dale. Police and Fire would find Dale and the dogs. Sirens began wailing in the distance on cue. The mission wasn't FUBAR, but it could have gone one whole hell of a lot better. Bolan had never known rural, northeast white supremacists that were willing to blow themselves up for their cause. The soldier began his extraction.

Something very odd and very ugly was going on in Lancaster.

2

Stony Man Farm, Virginia

"This is some sophisticated code," Aaron Kurtzman admitted.

Bolan sat at the conference table with Kurtzman and Akira Tokaido. Each man had a laptop before him, and they were connected. The confiscated flash drive was connected to Kurtzman's computer and code scrolled down each man's screen. Bolan didn't know much about writing or breaking code, but if Kurtzman was impressed then so was he. "How sophisticated?"

Kurtzman made a noise. "Unless the Lincoln County Regulators happen to have an idiot savant cousin who sits in his overalls all day picking a banjo and dreaming in code?"

Tokaido laughed.

Bolan considered his brief relationship with Tucker and Dale. "It is difficult to imagine."

"Then this is outsider work. I'm talking top of the line."

"How top of the line?"

The computer wizard sighed in grudging admiration at the code scrolling down his laptop's screen. "This is so good there are only a handful of humans who have this kind of talent."

Bolan waggled his eyebrows. "And two of them work for Stony Man."

Kurtzman stopped short of blushing. Mack Bolan didn't hand out praise often, and when he did he meant every word of it. Tokaido did blush.

"Yeah, well, that's the problem, Mack. You guys yanked me out of nowhere before I became famous, and gave me a dream job. People like me are writing the new generation of computer code. A younger mind can do, accept and conceptualize things that an older one can no longer intuit, much less—"

"Watch it…." Kurtzman intoned.

"So like I'm saying. We can't just assume this is Russian, PRC or Iranian. In fact given who's using it, I think that makes it unlikely as hell."

Kurtzman frowned.

Bolan sipped coffee as the old school and new school of cybernetic warfare butted heads. "What is it, Bear?"

Tokaido interjected. "Bear says his gut says it smells military. And it does have an old-school, military vibe to it, I'll give it that. And it's kinda funny what Bear said about idiot savant. It's like someone with talent stepped out of a time machine from the past and started playing with the new toys. It's like he's brilliant but he's still learning."

"That's an interesting hunch."

Kurtzman nodded. "I agree."

Bolan turned to Kurtzman. "Anything off the disk?"

"Well, fire and blast damage don't exactly play well with CDs."

"Anything?"

"It was written by someone different, and with less talent. That was easy to determine. As a matter of fact, we can tell that the disk was written over with the new code."

"Any chance it's a Trojan horse?"

"I can't be a hundred percent yet, but I'd say no. The problem is the writer of the original code seems to know his stuff could be broken, so he relied a lot on simple word replacement, and it's smelling like the word replacement is personal recognition."

Bolan had run into it before. "So it's gobbledygook unless you get the reference."

"Exactly. The simplest example was the Japanese High Command's order to the Imperial Fleet to bomb Pearl Harbor. We had broken their code, but the order was simply 'climb Mount Fuji.' That could mean anything, except to the person who knew what it meant, and the only person who did happened to be Admiral Yamamoto. It certainly didn't mean anything to us until afterward."

"What words have we gotten?"

"Not enough. Due to the damage on the disk we have less than fifty percent decoded, and our certainty of accuracy is varying from forty-five to eighty-five percent."

"What are your strongest words?"

"I swear, Mack. It's like we're playing newspaper word puzzle codes, but we don't even have half the vowels yet. And that's on the crappy damaged code, much less the shiny new one."

"Anything."

"We have *Pennsylvania*," Kurtzman snorted. "That was a no-brainer. We threw down *Regulators* and think we have multiple hits. But the problem with word replacement is you can take it into infinite incarnations."

"Anything else?"

"Well, we're looking for a national security threat. We squeezed *president* out of it."

"The Lincoln County Regulators are going to assassinate the President of the United States?"

"Could be president of anything," Kurtzman admitted. "It could be the president of the Pennsylvania Hell's Angels chapter. They don't get along. If we assume our current replacements are correct, we also have the words *devil* and *town*, but I'm assuming those are code words for something else."

Bolan slowly straightened. "Why would you do that?"

"What do you mean?"

"You're strong on the word *Pennsylvania?*"

"It's our best, it's our first keystone to both codes and it keeps building words from the damaged disk."

"And that gave you *devil* and *town?*"

"Yeah."

Bolan took a long breath and let it out. He'd been raised in Pittsfield, Massachusetts. In his youth his mother had told him that hell lay across the Pennsylvania border if he didn't keep his nose out of trouble. "Duivelstad."

Tokaido blinked. "What?"

Kurtzman's eyes flared. "Well, now, that is an interesting leap of logic, Striker."

Tokaido looked back and forth between his boss and Bolan. "What?"

"Duivelstad," Kurtzman confirmed. "Devil Town, from the Dutch."

Tokaido blinked. "Yeah? And?"

Bolan sighed as he saw a personal worst-case scenario rolling out before him. "Duivelstad Penitentiary is the worst prison in the United States, and it's in Pennsylvania."

Duivelstad Maximum Security Prison

"HERE WE GO...." "Oh boy, this one is going to be trouble." Correctional Officer Frederic "Fatty" Barnes watched the new prisoner being processed, then approach the gate to general population.

"Oh, shit!" Officer Pablo Zavala straightened in alarm. "That's the special transfer!"

Barnes sighed. "What's special about his transfer?"

Zavala looked and acted like a matador who happened to be wearing a correctional officer's uniform. He gave Barnes a sad sigh in return.

Officer Fatty Barnes lived up to his name. He bore a disturbing resemblance to Porky Pig in a guard's uniform. Everything about him was round, pink and hairless. He lived with his mother and had failed the physical the last three times, but felt certain that his union wouldn't let him be fired. He mostly opened and closed doors, and despite being a poor student in high school he found he excelled at paperwork. His fellow employees at the prison were mostly fond of him. The cons called him Fatty to his face, but most were grudgingly aware that he went out of his way to treat everyone fairly. Despite his appearance, Barnes was very handy with the old-fashioned side-handled PR-24 baton he clung to rather than the collapsible clubs everyone else carried. And he was somewhat famous in the yard for talking people out of altercations rather than settling them.

Barnes also refused to accept favors, bribes, or take a taste of anything going on, which often left him out of the loop when it came to what took place beyond the yard.

Zavala glanced both ways and lowered his voice. "Listen, *gordo*."

Barnes had always like that Zavala called him *Gordo*. It still meant fatso in Spanish, but Barnes liked the sound of it much better. "What?"

"Word is they transferred him in from Gitmo."

"Guantanamo Bay? To here?" Barnes goggled. "Really?"

"Really, like from the secret wing, for political reasons. Check out this motherfucker."

Barnes checked out the motherfucker.

There was something about the prisoner that made Barnes nervous. The newb was big, but not that big. Duivelstad had plenty of those, men built like bodybuilders, circus strongmen and sumo wrestlers. In Barnes's experience the big prisoners were usually the least problem. His greatest unexplored passion was dog breeding, and like the giant breeds, Barnes found the big cons were usually the least active. They mostly lifted weights and stood around like nightclub bouncers for their respective gangs, intimidating people. It was the little, hatchet-faced guys built like whippets who started trouble and tried to shank everyone around them.

This newb was a new breed entirely.

Barnes took in the dishevelled black hair and the unshaved, strong jaw. His jacket read no tattoos, neither jail, gang nor military. He was an ongoing concern at six feet plus, but on top of that he projected like he was seven feet tall. Barnes had seen every type of prisoner walk through the gate: some shaking and crying and prime meat for the rape train; some mad-dogging everyone they laid eyes on; others acting like they didn't care at all. Some came in acting as if they owned the place, others came in believing they actually did. Barnes frowned as he tried to put his finger on what disturbed him now. It was something in the eyes. They were arctic-blue in the sun-darkened face, and they seemed to take in everything. The man moved in a state of absolute awareness. It wasn't like the con was acting as if he owned the place, it was more like he was going from point A to point B, point B might well be conquering Scotland, and woe unto anyone who stepped in his path.

The prisoner stopped before Barnes and Zavala. Duivelstad was a privately owned prison, and old-fashioned. It issued dungarees and denim shirts rather than brightly colored "jungle" jumpsuits favored by state and federal penitentiaries. The prisoner held his two issue standard-blankets, a pillow, his spare change of clothing and a paper bag containing whatever few permissible personal items he had been allowed to bring in.

Barnes sighed as Zavala immediately went in hard with his new-prisoner spiel. "No fighting, no fucking, no drugs or alcohol. You have been stripped and photographed. If you are found with any new tattoos at your next health inspection, you will face a loss of privileges. Needle marks or signs of drug use will be punished with the loss of privileges. As a newb you *have* no privileges, so fuck up early and you'll never see them. The rules have already been explained to you in processing. I do not expect to have to explain them to you again." Zavala's voice dropped low. "And I don't care how many special friends you make in the showers, gray-meat. You'll never know what a real ass-reaming is until the day you cross me."

The prisoner turned eyes like tombstones on Zavala. The guard stopped just short of taking a step backward and putting his hand on his pepper spray, but it was clear that had been his first instinct. Barnes sighed again. He launched into his own spiel, which he knew from long experience, his appearance and his somewhat high-pitched, slightly lisping voice was about as useful as talking into a wind tunnel.

"Listen, you're here for a reason, but while you're here, I'd like your stretch to be as easy as possible. I know the code, but if you are in trouble, and I mean really in trouble, ask. If you ask, I'll do whatever I can to help you. Understand?"

The prisoner turned his arctic-blue gaze on Barnes.

Barnes started as the prisoner flashed a disarmingly friendly smile. "Thank you, Officer Barnes. That's very kind of you, and I'll keep that in mind."

Barnes felt a strange, anomalous ray of hope and blushed against his will.

Zavala spit in disgust.

Barnes recovered himself and punched the button for the gate. "Man walking!"

Zavala stepped through to lead the prisoner to his cell. Barnes hit the button and the bars clanged shut behind them. Hoots and catcalls erupted from the tiers. Horrific offers and suggestions rang out. Bets were laid. All eyes turned on the new prisoner as, like Barnes, the inmates all tried to determine what breed of animal had just walked in. Duivelstad was a maximum-security facility, and it was overcrowded with murderers, rapists, arsonists, drug dealers, hit men and more than a few very high ranking organized crime members. The crimes committed within its walls rivaled the ones that had sent men here.

For the first time in Duivelstad's history, an Executioner walked into the general population.

The Computer Room, Stony Man Farm, Virginia

"DUIVELSTAD?" BARBARA PRICE was the Farm's mission controller, and she was incensed. "It's the worst prison in the United States!

Countries we've had extraordinary rendition treaties with have petitioned through the United Nations to have it closed!"

"It's pretty bad," Kurtzman agreed.

"And you knew that!"

Akira Tokaido actually looked a little green. "I've been studying up on prison slang and prison life. I've learned things in the last forty-eight hours I could have spent the rest of my life not knowing."

"I'm sure you have." Price had no sympathy for the young hacker. "But Mack isn't reading about it on Wikipedia, he's learning it the hard way."

"So anyway, yeah, Duivelstad is bad."

Price drove home the obvious, and that obvious was hanging over the entire team's head. "And Mack is in there with no communications, no intel and no weapons."

Tokaido grinned. "Mack Bolan is a weapon."

No one laughed. Price gave Tokaido a very cold glance. "Yeah, and I've signed up to be his pen pal. He can start receiving personal letters a week after processing. You got anything else on your end?"

Tokaido cringed.

"Barbara," Kurtzman said, "this was his idea."

"I know that." Price kept her wrath focused on Tokaido. "Tell me we have intel."

"Oh, we have plenty."

"Give me all of it."

"Where do you want me to start?" Tokaido said.

"The beginning would be good."

Kurtzman took the lead. "Duivelstad started out as a Dutch colonial town. The town had a fort, and the fort is the base of the Duivelstad prison we have today. During the Civil War, Southern prisoners were shipped there, and that's when the English translation Devil Town really came into use. It never got the press that Andersonville did, but it was a hellhole. After the war the fort was rebuilt to function as a prison, and at the time it was considered state-of-the-art. However, the builder, who was also the first warden, believed in redemption rather than rehabilitation. The prisoners were kept in nearly perpetual states of privation and isolation in their cells, relieved only by relentless religious instruction and severe methods of discipline. The warden also believed the same curriculum would be of benefit to the mentally ill. Many well-to-do families in the state shipped off their mentally ill or embarrassing family members to Duivelstad, never to see them again."

Price just stared. "So the inmates went mental and the mental patients went insane?"

"For over twenty years that was about the size of it. When the warden died it was reorganized. It went from being Bedlam to a landlocked version of Alcatraz. Religious redemption was abandoned, and except for a thin facade, rehabilitation was considered a foregone conclusion. Duivelstad became a repository for the Northeast's worst of the worst. One newspaper at the time wrote of it, 'Duivelstad no longer tries to save sinners, it has become a place where sinners go to get a taste of the hell that awaits them.'

"In the last century the Duivelstad facility was expanded, but in a very ramshackle fashion and without any sort of central plan. Parts of it are 114 years old. Literally, there are parts of the prison that don't have existing blueprints."

Kurtzman brought up a satellite photo on the screen. What looked like a medieval fortress with semimodern buildings attached squatted in the middle of a little valley. Two rings of twelve-foot high, razor-wire-topped fences encircled the entire facility. Several fenced-in enclosures of prefab buildings dotted the landscape. He zoomed in on the main facility. "You might notice they actually have a fence inside the walls. It's called the 'deadline'. Until 1962 any prisoner caught outside it was summarily shot by the tower guards."

Price had spent the greater portion of her life fighting evil around the world. It never failed to horrify her when she found it right here at home. "And this place is still standing because…?"

Akira Tokaido picked up the ball. "They've tried to close the place five times since the seventies. Twice in the past ten years. It went from a private facility to public, to private again. They almost closed it in the 1990s, but when the War on Drugs really kicked into gear, inmate populations across the U.S. skyrocketed. Duivelstad dodged the bullet because the entire correctional system was and still is short on beds."

"Now it's all political," Kurtzman said. "The prison guard unions in the state have a lot of pull, and they don't want it closed. They want it to go public again and they want to control it, so it's been tied up in litigation for years. And let's face it. U.S. prisons today are all overcrowded, Duivelstad is a straight-up animal factory, and no sane warden wants the D-Town boys transferred into their general population. Duivelstad is the inoperable cancer in United States corrections. There's nothing wrong with it that money and political infighting can't prolong."

"And we contact Mack how?"

"Until he is allowed to receive letters or conjugal visits, we can't. He's going to have to contact us."

Price was startled. "And just how is he supposed to do that?"

Kurtzman nodded at Tokaido. "Akira has already broken into Duivelstad's mainframe. As you might imagine it's not exactly state of the art. The facility has a computer area in the library with six desktops for inmate use. Internet access is strictly controlled, and computer time is a privilege that has to be earned. But if Mack can manage to log on, we can communicate directly with him and they'll never know, unless a guard is standing directly behind him looking over his shoulder. On top of that, we can fake an order from the governor or the Board of Corrections giving the warden instructions. But that's a last atomic option. If we do that and the warden figures it out, Mack's cover is blown and he's probably dead."

"Is there any good news?"

Kurtzman heaved a small sigh. "Like Akira mentioned. There's Mack himself. We agreed on several codes and passwords to be used in alternative media."

"What's an alternative media?"

"As in Mack figures out his own way to communicate with us that we haven't foreseen yet."

"That's it?"

"That's it. For now all we can do is keep crunching on the code Mack found, and make something out of it."

"And in the meantime Mack just sits in a cell and rots until he earns internet privileges?"

The computer wizard gave Price a leery look. "Actually, I think he's going to be really busy."

"Doing what?"

"We think something bad is going down. We don't have time for Mack to be a model prisoner and become a trustee."

"And?"

"You ever read *Will* by G. Gordon Liddy?"

"The Nixon operative during Watergate. No, why?"

"He went to jail for his part in the break-in. He was a middle-aged white man with no connections, and the U.S. government wanted his hard time to be hard. So he did what no one expected. He went on the offensive inside. A charm offensive, a fighting offensive and an intelligence offensive. Neither the prison administration, the guards nor the cons were ready."

Price didn't look convinced.

"Barbara? Try to think of it this way. Mack's not stuck in there with them. They're trapped in there with him. From the lowest sex-offending rent-boy to the warden himself, no one in Duivelstad is ready for Mack Bolan."

Duivelstad, Cell Block C

"HOME SWEET HOME, hard-ass." Officer Zavala lifted his chin at Bolan's new roommate and smiled. "Good luck."

Bolan walked into his cell. According to psychologists and feng shui experts, shades of blue and green were soothing colors. In a completely misguided effort in the 1980s all the steel in Cell Bock C had been painted an electric, *Miami Vice* blue. It wasn't soothing. It was a pastel house of horror. The first thing a man noticed when walking inside was the pervasive smell of human excretions and every orifice they had come from. The pervasive odor was nothing compared to what was coming out of Unit 2. Within the cell a man who could have been Officer Barnes's albino big brother in overalls, suffering from a dual case of acromegaly and morbid obesity, lolled on the bottom bunk and gazed at Bolan like a sumo wrestler Frankenstein in pin-eyed cupidity. His teeth were yellow turning to green. The man smelled like a dead wildebeest rotting under the African sun. He spoke in a thick, childlike Southern drawl. "The Todd says you're on the top bunk."

Bolan and his colleagues at Stony Man had done their homework. Duivelstad was a unique situation by United States correctional facility standards even on the best of days. Nonetheless, according to the regs, as a high-interest inmate transferred from military custody, Bolan should have been put in isolation for at least a week. Any facility, public or private, that had a prisoner with Bolan's cover story would have done so just to give themselves time to figure out what to do with him. The fact that he had been dumped immediately into the general population with a rape-walrus for a cellmate told Bolan the plan had already gone FUBAR.

It seemed the powers that be had decided that trial by fire was their best investigative venue on the new fish.

Bolan nodded and tossed his belongings on the top of the steel dissection tables Duivelstad called bunks. When a night attack came from whomever, he would prefer to be fighting down rather than trying to rise up, especially if it was three-hundred-plus pounds of corpulent hillbilly. "Cool."

Bolan could sense the prisoners in the adjoining cells and out in the immediate tier hanging on every word. Todd spent uncomfortable moments processing the soldier's response. "The Todd doesn't like your attitude," he finally declared.

Bolan had vainly hoped "the Todd" was someone not in the cell at the moment, rather than the hillbilly referring to himself in third person. But hope had run out in Unit 2, Cell Block C. The soldier's arctic-blue eyes stared implacably into the black holes in paper that were the windows to his cellmate's soul. "The Todd can go fuck himself."

Prisoners outside whistled and made approving noises. Bolan heard new bets pass down the tier. It appeared his bravado was appreciated, but not favored in the wagering. The Todd didn't seem to care at all for this new development in cellmate congeniality. He rolled up into a sitting position from his supine, Roman splendor with surprising alacrity for his bulk, and started to rise. "The Todd is angry." He didn't sound angry. Indeed, he licked his blubbery lips and smiled to reveal his rotting teeth.

A voice in the immediate cell to the right spoke in sympathy. "Aw shit! New fish gonna get laid and filleted!"

Catcalls rang out. Bolan didn't hear any guards calling for order or in inquiry. The new fish had been thrown to Moby Dick and a lot of people on both sides of the bars seemed to have some skin in the game.

The sexecution was on.

Bolan frowned. Todd's huge, sagging belly didn't hide his tumescence. Despite the vast avalanches of muscle and fat cascading down Todd's rib cage, they went in two different directions under his bib overalls like breasts. To a discerning eye, like Bolan's, between the chest waterfalls Todd's xiphoid process was covered only by skin and a millimeter of denim.

Bolan stepped forward to meet the rising Todd and thrust-kicked his heel into bone and cartilage. The lower tip of Todd's sternum snapped with a wet click. The man had already been fish belly pale when Bolan had entered the cell. Now his face went as white as chalk as his diaphragm perforated. Bolan snapped up his leg again and chopped his heel in a short ax kick to the solar plexus as Todd fell back.

Every bone in the man's body seemed to dissolve, and he toppled from the bottom bunk to the floor in a gelatinous cascade. Bolan estimated Todd had about five minutes to live without medical attention. Bolan raised his voice. "Guard!"

The Executioner stepped out of the cell. The cons in the tiers cheered wildly. Bolan rounded left into the adjoining cell. A black man with short, cinnamon-brown dreads looked up from a book he was reading. His surprise seemed split between the fact that Bolan was still alive, much less rectally intact, and that Bolan had the gall to walk in without an invitation.

The convict put down his book, rose, lowered his chin and turned slightly sideways. Bolan read the man before him. He was powerful, and if Bolan had to bet, the man's sentence was all-day. He was old-school, a longtime man, and he wasn't going to back down no matter what Bolan had done to the great white whale next door. The fact that the man before him lived next to the Todd and didn't take shit from anyone spoke volumes. Bolan smiled and shoved out his hand. "Cooper. Nice to meet you, neighbor."

The man stared at Bolan's hand as if it were dead vermin on the end of an arm. "You are one dead white devil."

"Yeah." Bolan shrugged. "But hopefully not by your hand."

"You have to earn that. You want to earn that?"

"No way. I want to be a good neighbor, like State Farm."

"Then you have five seconds to turn your white ass around and get out of my cell."

"Give me twenty."

Bolan's neighbor stared at him long and hard. People had been sizing up the soldier since he had walked through the gate. This man stared at Bolan with the wisdom of decades of being institutionalized. He came to a weighted decision. "This is the first time I have ever asked this of another man in this place, much less a white man I don't know, but why are you here?"

Bolan gave an incomplete answer, but an honest one. "I'm in trouble."

Boots rang on the catwalk as the guards hit the tier. "That you are," the convict agreed.

"I'm Cooper. I'll probably be dead soon." Bolan shoved his hand out again. "Nice to meet you…?"

The con eyed Bolan's hand with mild disinterest. "Kal. Nice knowing you."

Both Bolan and Kal recognized the sound of collapsible batons snapping open next door. Kal gave Bolan a sympathetic look. Profanity, and shock and awe spewed forth from the guards at the sight of the Todd's quivering, blood bubbling body.

"Cooper! Don't make me come and find your narrow ass!" Zavala roared.

Bolan shrugged. "Gotta go."

Kal sighed in mock resignation at Bolan's fate. "*As salaam alaikum.*"

Bolan smiled in sincere gratitude. "*Wa alaikum as-salaam.*"

Kal rolled his eyes. "I don't know you, but I think I'm going to miss you."

Bolan nodded. "I miss me already."

Zavala bawled out in rage. "Last chance, Cooper!"

Bolan strode out of Kal's cell onto the catwalk. "Yo!"

The Warden's Office

"Not an auspicious first day, Mr. Cooper," the warden remarked. Warden Ulysses S. Linder was known as "The Big U" in Duivelstad. He looked like the NFL noseguard from the 1970s that he was. He had a big square head, big square hands, and looked as if powerful machinery had forced his body into the gray suit that only his red suspenders held together. "Mr. Solomon is in critical condition."

"Who?" Bolan asked.

Linder gave him a very weary look. "Your cellmate, Mr. Cooper. Todworth Elias Solomon."

"Oh, you mean the Todd."

"Yes," Warden Linder conceded. "The Todd."

"That guy was bug fucking nuts, Warden. The first time he threw himself tits first against the shitter, I took a walk and struck up an acquaintance with the neighbor."

Linder gave Bolan a long look. That was another matter of interest. "Kal."

"Yeah, seems like a real interesting guy."

"You have no idea." Linder opened a thin file and let the few pages fall out of it. Well over eighty-five percent of the document was redacted. "Who are you?"

"I'm Matthew Cooper."

"Why are you here?"

Bolan looked confused. "I was under the impression you inducted me."

"Yes, I was paid a very large sum of money to take you on. Now, who are you and why are you here?"

"Legal counsel and the United States government have informed me not to discuss my case with anyone. If I do, I was informed I go back to Gitmo, and from there I get extraordinarily renditioned to Tajikistan or the Black Hole of Calcutta or someplace that owes Uncle Sam a favor."

The warden peered at Bolan from the bone shelves he called brows. "Again, who are you and why are you here?"

"It's not in my best interest to tell you."

"Someone paid a lot to have you buried here. It's not the first time. Your problem is whether buried and forgotten about or buried in the boneyard is up to me."

"I just want to do my time until I get transferred."

"Good luck with that."

"I don't want any trouble, I just—"

"Since you have struck up a friendship with Kal, you'll share a cell with him while the crime scene is investigated." Linder nodded at Zavala. "We're through here. Take Mr. Cooper and put him in Kal's cell."

Aryan Acres, the Yard

CLELLAND WILBERFORCE "THE FORCE" Scott sat in state in his fiefdom. His fief consisted of a set of ancient, graying wooden bleachers in one corner of the yard that had looked out on what over half a century ago had been a baseball field. The bleachers abutted one of Duivelstad's exterior walls, and a section of the deadline had been cut away to accommodate it. No one could sneak up on the Aryans in the yard when they assembled there, and for over a half a century unnameable shenanigans had gone on underneath them. Scott was a large, sleepy-eyed man with a mustache and goatee. Both they and his short number 2 haircut were shot through with gray. Compared to the muscle-heads surrounding him, he was built like a man who had done hard labor all his life.

Scott was surrounded by half a platoon of men. Some with shaved heads, some with mullets and others with Vikinglike long hair and beards. Nearly all of them were covered with Nazi, Nordic and White Supremacy tattoos. Scott didn't have a single tattoo on his body. He bore only one mark, which was the Circle of Iron. A branding iron, of which only four were currently known to exist, had been heated red-hot. The average human heart was the size of a clenched fist. Scott's fist had been measured, a branding iron forged, and the circle had been burned into the left side of his chest directly encompassing his heart. The heat had seared through his chest. Two men who had earned the Circle of Iron had died from the application. Another had died of natural causes and the rest of far-from-natural ones. Each time a Circle of Iron man died, a trusted messenger had been given his branding iron, gotten on his bike, driven east and not stopped until he had hurled the iron into the sea.

Scott lowered his well-thumbed copy of Niccolò Machiavelli's *The Prince*. He was reading chapter 3, "New Conquests Added to Older States," for perhaps the thousandth time. He stared down at his lieutenant. "So let me get this straight, Rollin. The fresh meat, on his first day deflates the Todd like a balloon, walks into Kal's cell unannounced and walks out alive?"

Rick "Rolling Thunder" Rollin met his leader's eyes. He was as big as Scott, and his hair had turned an odd shade of green from his affectation of dyeing it prison bottle blond. Tattoos covered every inch of his skin from the chin down, and he had Florida's swamps and ways stamped all over him. "Yeah, that's about it, Force."

Scott considered this strange and wonderful turn of events. The Todd was a force unto himself in D-Town. He wasn't aligned with anyone. The Todd never messed with anyone in the yard or the block and no one had any desire to mess with him. He hardly left his cell at all except to eat. He was a stone-cold psychopath, and he was happy to eat the treats his mother sent him and wait for his next cellmate. Whoever got assigned to be the man's bunky ended up his bitch, and his bitches quickly ended up in the psych ward.

"Rumor is this newb came all the way from Gitmo," Rollin added. "High-priority prisoner."

Scott had heard that rumor as well, and had stretched forth his hand outside Duivelstad's walls to find out more.

Kal was the flip side of a positively anomalous coin. "So he just walked into Kal's cell and said hi?"

"That seems to be the gist of it. For whatever reason, the new fish got a one-time pass. Maybe taking out the Todd had something to do with it. Can't imagine Kal and the Todd ever approved of each other."

"There is that."

Rollin's hand went to the shiv he carried at the small of his back in a sheath of flattened newspaper. "Brother, give me the green light and we dance the newb on the blacktop."

"Not just yet. We got big things on the horizon. I don't want any ripples until it's time for the tsunami.".

Rollin loved Scott's way with words. "No ripples."

"What else can you tell me?"

"Chatted up Fatty."

Scott smiled. One of these days he was going to have to kill Barnes, but he admired the fact that the fat man kept on trying. Fatty was determined to save at least one con before retirement. "What did Officer Barnes have to say?"

"Said this Cooper is one bad medicine motherfucker. Said he saw the Todd in the infirmary. He's, like, damaged beyond repair. Never gonna leave a bed."

"They're putting Cooper in solitary?"

"No. Word is the warden is putting him in Kal's cell. Said Kal's had his private shit for too long and it's time he got himself adjusted to reality."

"Situation solved. Kal hasn't kept a white celly alive in ten years." Scott smiled. "Cooper's dead by dawn."

"Hey, Bunky," Bolan walked into Kal's cell and tossed his meager belongings on the top bunk. Kal was so appalled he stopped in midstrike. The con stood shirtless in a deep horse stance with one fist extended. Every muscle of his body stood forth across his bones in isometric tension. Kal shot Zavala a withering look and then returned to staring into the middle distance and dismembering nonexistent people in slow motion.

Bolan rolled out his blanket and tucked his paper bag of belongings into the empty cubby. The two dominating features in the cell were a black velvet poster of Jim Kelly in a fighting stance from the movie *Enter The Dragon,* and a fairly extensive collection of books on homemade shelves. Bolan nodded at the top shelf. "*Zen in the Martial Arts.* A buddy of mine told me I always needed to read that. Do you mind?"

"No."

"No, you don't mind? Or—"

"No you may not," Kal growled.

"But I'm bored."

Kal scowled ferociously as he slowly shoved out both hands in dragon formations. "Try the Holy Koran."

"Ah." Bolan got one step forward before Kal's voice hissed as he extended a tiger claw at an opponent only he could see.

"There's a copy of it in the library."

"Oh, well, I already read it, anyway."

"You could try the Bible." Kal's hands twisted into something positively mystical. "A trustee brought a copy of the Gideons' and put it on your bunk for you."

Bolan looked at the Bible on his bunk. "I already read that, too."

Kal's spoke through clenched teeth. "They bear rereading."

"Man, don't you got nothing for a white guy about to die?"

Kal rose out of his stance. Bolan smiled at him like an idiot and mentally prepared himself to at least try to keep Kal from ripping a vein out of his neck and showing it to him. Instead, Kal marched to his book collection, ripped forth Walt Whitman's *Leaves of Grass* and flung it at Bolan, who caught it. Kal resumed his stance. "Try that. Try to read it without moving your lips or reading aloud."

"Cool, thanks." Bolan hopped onto his bunk, stretched out and cracked the book. "Poetry, huh?"

Kal vibrated with the incredible effort it took him not to kill Bolan until lights out, and moved from his horse stance. He stayed low and kept his dynamic tension, but now moved as if he was fighting within the confines of an invisible phone booth. Bolan peered at him over the preface page. "What style is that, anyway?"

Kal's brow furrowed mightily as he sweated.

"It looks like some kind of karate had bad sex with Shaolin Kung Fu."

Kal almost smiled against his will. His forearms twisted around each other like pythons and performed first a high and then a low X-block. Bolan thought he detected a neck breaker within the movement. Kal deigned to answer as he moved. "The karate was Shorin-ryu."

Bolan nodded at the poster. "Jim Kelly."

"Correct, and it had bad sex with Wing Chun."

"Bruce Lee."

"I was a seeker, back in the day. However, may Allah forgive me…"

"All praises unto him," Bolan agreed.

"But circumstances, both internal and external, over the years—" Kal shuddered with the effort of lifting his straight leg to vertical so that his knee was in line with his ear "—have forced me to adapt and change the teachings of my masters so much, that in my hubris I now think of it as my style."

"Which is what Bruce would have wanted in the first place. Nice."

Kal shot Bolan a bemused look. "So one hopes." He made some sort of kung fu by way of the Black Panther movement salute to the empty air or the gods, and straightened. He slowly dropped his hands open to his sides and lowered his chin to his chest. Kal's breathing slowed and he went deep into his meditations. Bolan went back to his book. He'd read the first fifty pages of a poem when Kal spoke again. "Is it to your liking?"

"Read it before." Bolan closed the book and smiled. "But it bears rereading."

"It does." Kal took a hand towel and began washing at the sink. "You may be the most fascinating cellmate I have ever had."

"Thank you."

"It is a shame you'll be dead soon."

"That is a shame," Bolan agreed.

"First they threw you to the Todd. Then they threw you in with me."

"Like a Christian to the lions."

Kal gave Bolan a frank look. "I've decided not to kill you unless you give me further reason."

"Thanks." Bolan nodded respectfully. "I won't."

Kal shook his head. "I won't protect you."

Bolan cracked his book open again. "I won't ask you to."

The Warden's Office

"THIS LITTLE SHIT, Cooper," Warden Linder said. "What do you make of him?"

"First off, he ain't so little." Captain of the Guards Roger Schoenaur flipped through the redacted file. He had just come back from vacation with his wife and family from Florida, and had missed the new fish induction fun. Schoenaur was running six foot one and looked like a man who could crank out a hundred push-ups, a hundred pull-ups or a hundred sit-ups on a bet, which he could. He had repeatedly won the Pennsylvania state arm wrestling championship in the 1990s, and had reached finals in the nationals several times. His lower body workouts consisted of stomping mud holes into cons that gave him offense. That was everyone in the joint. If an inmate gave Schoenaur genuine offense, he usually reached out, grabbed some part of the con's anatomy and squeezed. The three who had actually attacked him in the past ten years had enjoyed the unique privilege of having parts torn from their bodies.

Schoenaur had never worked any facility but Duivelstad, and didn't care to. But through the stories of transfers, he had become one of the most hated and feared individuals in United States corrections. He was the boogeyman, and he knew it, liked it and cultivated it. Throughout the U.S. prison system the phrase, "Well, at least you're not in D-Town shaking hands with Schoenaur," let inmates feel better about their stretch. His blow-dried, longer than regulation hair and golden-age-of-porn mustache showed a man who had never left the 1970s.

"He stinks," Schoenaur decided. "I don't like him."

"Neither does Zavala."

"For a spic, the Z has some instincts," Schoenaur conceded. "I don't like him, either."

Schoenaur frowned. "Have we been paid to like him?"

"Been paid to take him, but like I told him to his face, I'm not sure if it was to keep him buried or to bury him."

"Prison is an uncertain place," Schoenaur opined. "You got a preference, Chief?"

"Haven't made up my mind yet."

"You say you got him shacked up with Kal?"

"Yup."

"How's that love affair going?"

"According to rumor, Kal loaned him a book."

"Really." Schoenaur scowled. He didn't care for African-Americans and he didn't care for Kal at all. Kal was the one con who when he took him down he took him down in force, usually leading with pepper spray and crowding with ballistic shields followed by a bludgeoning. Kal was the one man in Duivelstad Schoenaur wasn't sure he could take in hand-to-hand combat, and that galled him. Warden Linder considered guards murdering prisoners an absolute last resort, and although decades old, Kal's quadruple murder conviction had a minor but devoted "truther" following in the media and on the internet. On top of that Duivelstad's black population respected Kal, and when consulted, Kal almost always advocated peace and personal improvement. Schoenaur had been plotting Kal's accidental and not so accidental death by proxy for years. All attempts so far had failed.

"So Kal's finally gone queer for this blue-eyed Cooper son of a bitch?"

Warden Linder guffawed. "Unless Kal and Cooper make sweet love in tender silence, I'm guessing no."

Facilitywise, Duivelstad was an architectural abortion of nature. But the main tiers were now bugged. "They talked?"

"They have. But this Cooper is one cryptic asshole. He's all smart remarks and Zen koans, and Kal's been a deep file from the moment he walked through the gate."

"So I'm thinking Cooper pulled an 'all the king's horses and all the king's men couldn't put the Todd back together again,' and Kal gave him a pass for his public service."

"That seems to be the way of it. They've had a meeting of the minds, for the moment. I'm thinking Kal is in nice-meeting-you and *vaya con Dios* motherfucker mode."

"He knows you put Cooper in with him to jack him up, and is being noncooperative."

"The man survived the Todd and Kal, and came out of Gitmo. He's a problem that needs to be solved."

Captain Schoenaur cracked his knuckles. "I'll solve all his problems. Or give him new ones. You just say the word, Warden."

Linder leaned back in his chair. "I knew I could count on you, Rog. Let's start fucking with him. Start with the playground stuff and work up to graduating class."

4

Mess Hall

"Hey, celly." All eyes in the hall watched as the man who had dismantled the Todd sat down at the otherwise empty mess table across from Kal. The con gazed heavenward for strength.

"Don't ever call me that again."

"Sorry. Mind if I sit here?" Bolan asked.

"You're pushing your luck."

Bolan craned his head around and looked at the Aryan Circle table. "Well, there's a seat over there, I suppose."

"I may come to regret not killing you."

"You wouldn't be the first."

"I don't doubt it." Kal ate a forkful of beans and rice and gazed sympathetically at Bolan's tray. "I haven't seen nutraloaf in a long time."

Bolan sighed at his breakfast. What sat in his tray couldn't be described as a loaf, a wad or even a brick. It was a vague fist shape of food. Some prisons had nutraloaf specially made for them. Others simply took all the ingredients of one of the daily meals, ground it up and baked it without benefit of seasoning. The only thing that could be said about nutraloaf was that two servings contained the minimum amount of calories to keep a grown man alive and functioning, and violent prisoners could eat it without utensils. U.S. prison authorities optimistically called it a "special management meal." In reality it was dietary discipline. It had been banned in several states as cruel and unusual punishment. Bolan shrugged. "Nutraloaf's not so bad."

Kal regarded him through the jaded eyes of long, hard time. "Oh?"

"Yeah, take two slices, bread them in seasoned flour, salt, pepper, paprika from the kitchen if you can get it."

Kal raised an eyebrow. "And?"

"Then you fry them golden-brown, pull them, butter them and put them on a warmed plate."

As an all-day, unwilling aficionado of prison food, Kal found himself interested against his will. "Really?"

"Yeah, then you fry a slice of Spam. Deglaze the pan with some water, or better yet juice from the canned pineapples if you can get it."

Kal leaned forward. "Yeah?"

"Yeah, then you scrape the brown bits from the pan onto the Spam before you put it all together. Oh, and man—" Bolan nodded knowingly "—if you can get your hands on some mustard?"

Kal was clearly painting the picture in his mind. "So it's good?"

"Yeah," Bolan acknowledged. "Dogs love it."

The Duivelstad mess hall went quiet as for the first time in living memory Kal threw back his head and laughed. Bolan picked up his chunk of tasteless horror and poured some of his carton of milk into one of the many, sadly empty hollows in his tray. In his War Everlasting, Bolan had partaken of that which crawled under rocks, that which flew in the blue vault of heaven, and just about everything else that a man could digest in between besides human flesh. Bolan held a thousand calories in his hand; he had work to do and no time to be picky. He broke his nutraloaf in two, dunked a chunk into his milk and tucked in.

He'd eaten worse.

Kal squeezed honey from a foil packet onto his cornbread. He had a packet of salt, pepper and ketchup for his meal, as well. The two men both knew discipline would fall like rain if Kal offered any of it to Bolan. "Have I mentioned you are one dead white boy?"

Bolan stopped munching prison loaf and smiled. "That's white man to you."

Kal snorted in derision, but his eyes narrowed. "Tell you what. I'll just call you Cooper and you just call me Kal."

Bolan resumed eating. "I'd be honored."

Kal stared ruefully into the middle distance. "Honor is all a man has in here."

"Honor is a temple of light. A man builds it brick by brick in his heart, and he lays his soul on its altar every day he wakes up above ground."

"Man—" Kal's eyes tried to bore holes into Bolan "—who the hell are you?"

"I'm Cooper, and I'm in trouble."

"I told you. I won't protect you."

"I know, but will you help me?"

Kal's voice dropped dangerously low. "Help you what?"

"Don't know yet." Bolan felt the beat down coming.

Kal squeezed ketchup onto his beans and rice, more honey onto his cornbread, and shoved both into his mouth. "Check my shit, white man."

The soldier shook his head. "That's cold."

Bolan and Kal both looked up as another con walked up holding his tray. He was white and Bolan noted he had no visible tattoos. The soldier read him as an upper echelon criminal, most likely an organized crime lawyer or an accountant. The man nodded at Kal, but he kept his eyes on Bolan. "Kal."

"Rudy."

"Mind if I sit down?"

Kal shook his head at a man who should know better. "We play chess in the library once a week, Rudy. We don't eat together, and that's in your best interest, not mine."

Rudy nodded at Bolan. "Actually, Kal, I want to talk to him."

Bolan nodded at Kal. "It's Kal's world. I'm just a squirrel, trying to get a nut. You want to park your butt, it's his table."

Kal stared at Bolan incredulously. He jerked his head at Rudy. "Your funeral."

Rudy sat down. "Cooper, is it?"

"That's me."

"I have it on good authority that you and I are going to be cellmates tomorrow. In the Todd's cell."

"Nice to meet you. Hope they fumigated it. The Todd was seriously cultivating his own signature odor."

"Listen, you took down the Todd."

Bolan gazed at Rudy innocently. "The Todd took a suicidal swan dive against the toilet, twice."

Rudy looked back and forth between the two most arguably dangerous individuals in Duivelstad. "Cooper, you're having breakfast with Kal."

"I'm having breakfast in Kal's vicinity," Bolan corrected him. "Kal just hasn't killed me yet. There is a difference."

Kal nodded over a bite of beans. "Truth."

Bolan dunked his other nutra-chunk and took a tasteless, sodden bite. "What do you want, Rudy?"

"I need help. I know Kal won't."

"You got that right," Kal confirmed.

"Kal doesn't take sides, but Cooper, I can pay you."

"Help with what?"

"My son is being processed into Duivelstad in forty-eight hours."

Bolan stirred the crumbled bits from his nutraloaf into his remaining milk to form a thin gruel. "If you can afford to pay me, you can afford to pay off whoever wants a piece of your boy."

"It's not a question of money, or him. It's a question of leverage."

Bolan tilted back his tray and finished off his breakfast. "Leverage on you."

"Correct."

"Someone wants to put you to work for them," Bolan surmised.

"Correct."

"Lawyer or accountant?"

Rudy raised a challenging eyebrow. "QA engineer."

Bolan regarded the con before him with renewed interest. "Quality Assurance?"

"I used to work for a computer company."

Bolan gazed upon a software engineer who had gone rogue. It was a new class of criminal that was popping up more and more in U.S. prison populations. Unfortunately, they almost never had any gang affiliations or pull, and unlike a lawyer or accountant on the inside, they didn't have prison yard saleable skill. They paid for protection, and if they couldn't they swiftly became the new woman of mystery on the block.

Bolan had found some very suspicious computer code in Lancaster. "You don't have any affiliations?"

"I do, but they're not what they used to be."

"Mafia," Bolan ascertained.

Rudy weighed Bolan heavily before answering. "I was christened Territizio Rudolpho."

Bolan kept his poker face and weighed the Mafia hacker before him. "That's not enough."

"I know you're new." Rudy took in the mess hall meaningfully with his gaze. "But what have you noticed about Duivelstad?"

The soldier ran his eyes across tables of disturbingly prevalent skinheads, mullets and wannabe Vikings. "It's the most white as rice prison I've ever seen."

Kal nodded. "You begin to see."

Rudy gazed toward the doors. The tables closest to them, the kitchen and the guards were clustered with men with more skin pigment. "The blacks and the Puerto Ricans are like forward fire bases in Nam. Constantly probed. Constantly under attack, covertly and more and more overtly. The Italians?" Rudy sighed heavily. "When the Big U came in, he wanted nothing to do with us. When he couldn't transfer us out fast enough, it came down to outright assassinations. We were ruthlessly weeded out. We have almost no pull now."

"But your services are required?" Bolan probed.

"I was never supposed to be here. Hell, I wasn't even convicted in Pennsylvania."

Bolan smiled. "You were drafted."

"The Big U wanted his computer system upgraded. He wanted the prison wired for sound, and he wanted it to be done on the q.t. and pass under the nose of state and federal inspection."

"And you did it."

"I did," Rudy admitted. "It was an honest trade for an easy stretch."

Bolan had already seen it a mile away. "But now the Big U wants you to be an earner."

"I refused. When his intimidation shit failed, well, my son, he's something of a loose cannon. He messed up. For the third time. Warden Linder called in markers. My boy was tried as an adult and sentenced to hard time, here."

Bolan nodded. "Okay."

Rudy blinked. "Okay what?"

"I'll do it."

"Do what?"

"I'll defend you and your son to the best of my ability. I'll put your lives before my own."

Both Rudy and Kal stared at Bolan, incredulous. Rudy looked at Bolan as if he beheld an escaped maniac or a Bengal tiger that happened to be sitting in a prison mess hall. "How much?"

"Someday, and that day may never come, I'll call upon you to do a service for me."

Rudy's jaw dropped. "You sick fuck."

"Bank on it, and I'm most likely going to be a dead fuck real quick, so the favor is going to come fast. I guarantee you it won't involve any hole in your son's body, or yours. I won't ask you or him to kill anyone or hold contraband for me. Everything else is on the table. Deal?"

Rudy looked like a dog that had chased a car and caught it. "Kal isn't backing your play?"

Bolan turned to Kal. "You backing my play?"

"Oh, hell no."

The soldier shook his head. "Nope. Kal pretty much temporarily tolerates me, and that's about it. We have a deal?"

"We have a deal." Rudy shook his head as if he had gotten the short end of the stick in a deal with the devil. "You want to give me a hint about what you want?"

Bolan rolled the dice. "I may need to get a message out to my people."

"Oh, shit! Listen. Internet access is strictly controlled in the library. And for that matter, you can be caught with drugs, guns or shemale strippers in this place, but they catch you with a cell phone, that's a peeing-blood-for-a-week-from-a-Schoenaur-beat-down and a hell stretch in solitary."

"And why do you think that would be?" Bolan asked.

"How the hell should I know?"

Bolan rolled his eyes.

Rudy sighed. "Because the warden has plans?"

"Seems likely. We just need to figure out what those are."

Rudy's jaw fell. "Tell me you're not a cop."

Bolan grinned. "Do I look like one? Smell like one?"

"No…"

"Then I just figured out my favor."

"What's that?"

"Earn for the warden," Bolan said.

Rudy visibly controlled his temper. "I just told you I didn't want to."

"Earn for the warden and tell me anything you can about what he is up to and what is going on in this prison."

The hacker balked. "I tell you I need a favor. I tell you I don't want to earn for the warden and I want you to protect my son, and you tell me to earn for warden and inform on him for you?"

"Yeah."

"And why the fuck would I do that?" Rudy asked.

"Because then I'll owe you a favor."

"What favor are you going to do for me?"

"I don't know yet. But I'll make you a promise, Rudy. As of

now, no matter what choice you make, anyone who wants a piece of you or your son has to go through me. If they get you in a place I can't follow, you will be avenged. If they kill me, then by others."

Bolan felt Kal's eyes burning into him from the side. Prisons were a great deal like glacially paced open warfare. Life here consisted of vast stretches of worry and boredom punctuated by short, sharp upheavals of horror. The latest upheaval had come, and Bolan was the fifth Horseman of the Apocalypse. Kal wasn't pleased.

Bolan kept his eyes on Rudy, but he spoke to both men. "Shit's coming down."

Rudy stared at Kal helplessly. Kal stabbed his fork into his rice and beans. "Fuck you, Rudy. Dig your own grave. Your chess lessons are over."

Rudy looked at Bolan like a drowning man grabbing at a rope. "I accept."

Kal rose. "As for you, Cooper, your breakfast privileges are revoked. I won't kill you tonight. But after roll call tomorrow, after you and Rudy are all puppied up? If you step into my cell again without permission, I'll put you on a gurney next to the Todd."

"Duly noted," Bolan acknowledged. "And thank you for your patience."

"Fuck you."

Kal took his tray and stalked back to the return counter.

Bolan nodded at Rudy. "I'm growing on him."

BOLAN SETTLED IN. The Todd had done some significant bleeding and disgorged serious amounts of internal bodily fluids under Bolan's ministrations. Maintenance had given the unit a thorough decontamination and the cell smelled of bleach and cleanser; and that was a huge step up from the all-pervasive Todd funk Bolan had first walked into. The soldier unrolled his blankets and hit the top bunk. He cracked *Leaves of Grass* and paused. "Yo! Kal!" he shouted. "You want your book back?"

"My parting gift to you, Cooper!" Kal snarled.

"Cool." Bolan went back to reading. He weighed the risk of trying to stop Kal from breaking his thumbs, and wrote on the inside cover with the stubby pencil he'd bought from the commissary. The soldier flashed the word at Rudy with supreme casualness.

Cameras?

Rudy absorbed the query like the pro he was, and yawned and shook his head.

Bolan wrote "Sound?" And flashed it.

Rudy nodded.

The soldier rolled off his bunk and stepped out onto the tier. Rudy followed a few minutes later. The soldier and the hacker leaned on the railing and gazed down at the common area.

"People are talking about you," Rudy said.

"I'm worth remarking upon."

Rudy sighed in disgust. "Oh, for God's sake…"

He wasn't talking to Bolan.

A young man approached timidly across the tier. He had to be at least eighteen to be in Duivelstad, but he had the face of a younger teen. He walked with the hunched, haunted demeanor of a man made ancient by a thousand subjective years in hell. Bolan had seen a great deal of human evil, and he recognized the scooped crescent scars of human bites on his arms and the right side of his neck.

Rudy glared. "Bobbie? What the fuck?"

The broken young man ignored Rudy and continued to try but continued to fail to meet Bolan's eyes. "I'm Bobbie-John."

"Cooper."

"I'm—"

Bolan nodded. "I know."

Bobbie-John shook.

"What can I do for you, Robert?"

"When I came here, I knew what would happen. As a new fish I was Force's. But then he told me I was going to earn for him. I told him he and his friends could take what they wanted, I couldn't stop them, but they'd have to kill me before I'd be a whore."

"So Force threw you to the Todd."

Bobbie-John clutched at golf divot scars on his arms and shuddered. "You took him down."

A cold wind blew through Bolan. Duivelstad was piling horror upon horror, but he had a mission. "What do you want?"

Bobbie-John looked both ways. It didn't matter. Half the block was pretending not to watch. The other half was watching in open interest. Bobbie-John reached down the front of his pants.

Rudy recoiled. "Oh, for…"

The young man came up with a king-size candy bar from the

commissary and held it out. "I heard you're on nutraloaf. I bought you this."

Bolan took the candy bar. "Thanks."

"You d-don't owe m-me nothing," Bobbie-John stuttered and looked at his shoes. "I mean, I just want to thank you, and you know, if you want, I'll…"

Bolan kept his face neutral and nodded. "I know."

"I just wanted to thank you. A lot of cons want to thank you."

"You're welcome."

Bobbie-John turned and walked away, holding the horrible scars on his arms.

Rudy made a noise. "You're making friends and winning influence."

"We try."

"Yeah," Rudy scoffed. "With the house catamites."

"*Catamite.* That's a word you don't hear in conversation every day," Bolan whirled on Rudy, who started and backed up until he met iron bars. The soldier loomed over him. "You want your son to join Duivelstad Team Catamite?"

Rudy's teeth clenched.

Bolan smiled without an ounce of warmth. "Team Catamite just professed their undying love and gave me a candy bar. What the fuck have you done for me in here, Rudy?"

To his credit, Rudy met Bolan's burning gaze. "I'm working on it."

Bolan turned back to the tier railing. "Good to know." He unwrapped his candy bar and had to admit the chocolate, caramel and nougat were a blessing after the nutraloaf. The tier door slammed open almost on cue and a three-man wedge of guards advanced with their boots clanging on the metal floor like storm troopers. The point of the spear was Captain Schoenaur. Zavala and a guard Bolan hadn't seen before flanked their captain. Schoenaur had rolled up his uniform sleeves to reveal the veined, bowling pins of horror he called forearms. Bolan had read the file Kurtzman had compiled on the captain. None of it was good. Schoenaur managed to glower and grin at the same time at the half-eaten candy bar in Bolan's hand.

"What the hell is that, Cooper?"

"Chocolate bar. Packed with peanuts." Bolan took another bite. "You want some?"

Schoenaur's smile was a travesty on his face. "That, Cooper, is a dietary infraction."

Bolan popped the remaining bite into his mouth, chewed and swallowed it. "What? You're going to put me on nutraloaf?"

"Oh, Cooper." Schoenaur cracked his knuckles. "First you tap at my window, and now you're knocking at my door."

"I'm sorry, Captain." Bolan held out his hand. "Could we shake and let bygones be bygones?"

"You really are new here."

"I'm new to this whole thing. I apologize for disrespecting you, Captain. I don't want any trouble."

Schoenaur smiled like butter wouldn't melt in his mouth, and held out his hand. "I give every newbie one free pass."

The entire tier held its collective breath as Bolan and Schoenaur shook hands. Schoenaur really did have forearms the size of Popeye the Sailor's. However, they really did taper at the wrist like bowling pins. Bolan bypassed the traditional bone crusher and curled his hand around Schoenaur's wrist in the Roman handshake. For a split second Schoenaur blinked at this unexpected development. Bolan took that heartbeat to choke up on Schoenaur's wrist so that both men literally held each other's wrist joints. Schoenaur instinctively started to squeeze.

Bolan was a heartbeat ahead of him.

The soldier was no arm wrestling champion, but he had spent his adult life digging fighting positions, rappelling down ropes, climbing sheer rock faces and buildings, and all too often hanging by his hands. Decades of battle on every continent had given Bolan a grip like a clam and fingers like cold chisels. He was no martial arts expert, but he often lived, trained and fought beside men who were. He had worked very hard at perfecting a number of techniques in what he considered his candy store of useful flavors. This technique had many names, but in Chinese kung fu it was called eagle's claw. It could be used on various parts of the human body, but Bolan had put in the hours to master it mostly so that he could make opponents drop a weapon without crippling or killing them. Bolan's thumb ground between Schoenaur's wrist bones to bore into his radial nerve. The soldier's second finger parted muscle and tendon to grind into the captain's inner wrist to find the ulnar nerve. Bolan squeezed and tried to make his finger and thumb meet in the middle.

Schoenaur went white.

The soldier's eyes burned into Schoenaur's as they shook hands. "Nice to meet you."

The guard captain tried to squeeze back. There was no doubt Schoenaur's grip strength was inhuman, but Bolan had not only short circuited two of the three major nerves that would get Schoenaur's fingers firing, but he had turned the captain's neurons into an electrical fire burning out of control from his fingertips to his shoulder. Sweat broke out on Schoenaur's brow. He was no longer trying to break Bolan's bones. The captain was using every last ounce of will not to scream.

Bolan suddenly released his grip and spoke loudly enough for everyone on the tier to hear. "Thank you for being so understanding, Captain. I won't break dietary restriction again. Thank you for not reporting this."

It was profoundly disturbing that Schoenaur hadn't screamed, much less dropped to his knees. However, scores of eyes on the tiers saw Schoenaur's fingers twitching and convulsing as he withdrew his hand. It was another bad sign that he let his hand fall to his side rather than cradling it. He smiled at Bolan and spoke so that only the two of them could hear. "You're dead."

Bolan nodded. "I get that a lot."

Schoenaur spoke aloud. "Just once, Cooper. Because you're a fucking terrorist from Gitmo, I have to let you slide. Don't let it happen again." The captain and his retinue stormed down the catwalk and the door slammed shut behind them. In the population, terrorists were in the same league with child molesters and arsonists. They weren't popular. Schoenaur hadn't done him any favors, but it beat having every bone in his gun hand broken.

A voice spoke aloud from three cells down the tier. "Motherfucker shook hands with Schoenaur."

Murmuring and close conversations began breaking out around Cell Block C top to bottom and stem to stern.

5

"YOU'RE A GOD," Rudy opined. "A dead god. Like dead as a door-nail, but still a god."

"You know people keep saying that." Bolan shrugged. "I feel healthy as a horse."

Rudy took a bite of his spaghetti and eyed Bolan's tray. "Not for long."

Bolan considered his fourth meal of nutraloaf. Bobbie-John's candy bar loomed large in his memory and was sorely missed. The soldier's milk ration had been replaced by a bottle of water. The seal had already been cracked. Bolan held the bottle up to the glare of the sodium lights above. There were no visible signs anyone had done anything unmentionable in it. Then again, there was a laundry list of things you could put in a bottle of water that were clear, tasteless, odorless and could mess with every part of a human's body fatally or otherwise. Bolan had taken out the Todd, had not been taken out by Kal, and had faced down Schoenaur. The soldier had taken the first three rounds. The enemy had just won its first round of psychological warfare.

Minor though it was, Bolan was eating dry nutraloaf tonight.

Rudy was right. Everywhere he went, which wasn't far, given his current restrictions, he got nods and murmurs of respect. The Aryan Circle by contrast had been remarkably reticent about the whole Schoenaur situation, and that spoke volumes to Bolan.

The soldier steeled himself to the task at hand.

He broke his loaf in two and looked for obvious signs of tamper-ing. The fact that the food looked like a browned hunk of housing insulation and was stale left most lines of inquiry beyond ground glass up to the imagination.

"My son gets processed in tomorrow," Rudy stated.

Bolan bit into what might as well have been baked sawdust, and struggled to chew and swallow it. "I look forward to meeting him."

A voice belted out from one of the Puerto Rican tables. "What'ch you lookin' at, pink person!"

All eyes went toward the doors. A welterweight Puerto Rican with bronze skin and a skull-tight bronze-orange afro stood up from the PR table. What could only be described as a steroid infested Caucasian monstrosity with a shaved head wearing overalls half rose to his six and a half foot height at the Aryan Circle table. The pink person swiftly turned purple. "You want a piece of me? That's a Puerto-ri-can't situation, Tavo!"

Tavo unleashed a stream of Spanish invectives.

Guards burst through the commons doors. The catwalk above rang with boots.

Bolan ran his eyes quickly over the Aryan Circle table as shouting broke out. All eyes were on Tavo. The soldier scanned the Puerto Rican table and met the gaze of a stocky, well-built man with a high, tight haircut and positively satanic looking mustache and beard. Satan opened his right hand to stretch a rubber band between his thumb and forefinger like a slingshot. A foil packet appeared in his left, and the man sent a condiment flying with unerring accuracy across the space between their tables onto Bolan's tray. The soldier swiftly palmed the packet. It was honey butter. Someone had written "Schoenaur? Nice" with a marker over the cartoon honeybee and cow.

Bolan nodded his thanks.

The "pink person" had already turned his attention elsewhere. "Not today, Tavo! Sit down! I'm eating!"

The dining denizens muttered their disappointment for the loss of some grand entertainment.

Bolan glanced down as a carton of milk slid across the linoleum floor from a table of African-American gentlemen and came to a halt by his foot. None of the Muslims looked his way. All appeared to be intent on the ruckus. Bolan hooked the carton with the toe of his issued shoe and pulled it in beneath the table.

Across the hall Tavo sat down angrily.

The Aryan goon glared in victory and went back to his spaghetti and meatballs.

Bolan swiftly spurted honey butter onto both halves of his meal. He tore the pack in two and licked the foil before gnawing into the product-improved nutraloaf. "Who's Tavo?"

"Tavo is the closest thing to a star we have around here. He was headed for the Summer Olympics in London. They said he stood a good chance of taking the Gold, but he got mixed up in drugs and a shootout in a club, and wound up here."

Bolan eyed the skinhead monstrosity. "Who's Frankenroid?"

"That's the Mad Dog, Sawyer Love. About five years ago Love was the hot thing for about an eye-blink in mixed martial arts. Then he got a dealer level steroid beef, possession of cocaine, resisting arrest, and multiple charges of assaulting a police officer and assault with the intent to commit grave bodily harm. Everyone knows it's only a matter of time before Tavo and Love are going to meet in the Hunger Games. Love's the current champion and has been since he was transferred a year ago. He's jacked up some people. Word is Tavo has hands of stone, but the Pennsylvania boxing commission won't be officiating this one. I think Tavo is in for a world of hurt."

Bolan raised one eyebrow. "The Hunger Games?"

"That's what they started calling it in here two years ago, you know, since the movie."

"There're fights."

"Closed circuit. I was the one who upgraded the computer feed and the cameras. You wouldn't believe how big the Asian market is. Who needs MMA when you can watch American convicts tear each other apart for real with no rules?"

Bolan could well believe. In his War Everlasting he had seen a price put on every aspect of human life. "And the winners get food privileges."

"That they do, among other things. You might have noticed that Love's spaghetti has meatballs."

"What other kind of privileges?"

"Internet, credit in the commissary." Rudy made a face. "And like, you know."

"Like Bobbie-John."

"Yeah, he was going to be one of those privileges until he grew a spine and said no." Rudy's face twisted in memory. "Then the Todd bit it out of him. We all heard the screams. The guards on duty didn't do shit."

Bolan palmed the empty foil honey butter packet and slid it up his sleeve. "Who's my Secret Santa?"

"That's Billy Cachon, known as Billy the C. The Puerto Rican king. He runs La Neta in here."

Bolan had worked with members of La Neta in Puerto Rico as

allies, and dealt with others harshly as foes. They were the most powerful Puerto Rican gang in the continental U.S., both in prison and outside. Bolan turned his gaze back to the Aryan table and watched Sawyer Love chew spaghetti with his mouth open. The soldier turned his gaze to the head of the table and found the man known as the Force watching him. Force had deceptively sleepy eyes, but as the two men locked gazes, the force behind those eyes was palpable.

Force tried to read Bolan and failed, save that he confirmed what he already knew: Bolan was the most dangerous single individual in Duivelstad.

The soldier confirmed what he had already suspected: the Force was the master of his domain and a stone-cold killer of men.

Force broke eye contact and said something to a brutal-looking, greenish-haired man beside him. Bolan returned his attention to Rudy. "The Hunger Games. You said a man can earn library privileges, or a conjugal?"

"Give the fans a good fight and—oh, shit! Are you serious?"

"Don't tell the warden I asked. Suggest to him I might be a good candidate, like you want something out of it, and he'll need to convince me."

"So I'm carrying your water now, too?"

Bolan took the carton on the floor between his feet and deposited it beside Rudy's hip on the bench. "No, you're carrying my milk to my cell for me for later. Then you're going to talk to the warden."

Rudy shook his head as he untucked his shirt to facilitate the milk smuggling. "Asshole."

PATRICK RUDOLPHO ENTERED the cell block carrying his meager belongings. Catcalls, whistles and innuendo greeted him. He had long hair, was whippet lean and held his chin up as he walked into the storm of hazing and sexual harassment. Zavala and Barnes followed him up onto the tiers. Rudy stepped out and gazed on his son. The reunion was nothing to celebrate. The hacker simply held out his hand. His son shook it. The hazing faded significantly. Every inmate inside knew the story, and every inmate inside was a man of woman born. Father and son cons stood on the third tier shaking hands in Duivelstad. Even the most jaded lifer found the scene emotionally challenging on some level. Bolan leaned against the bars with his arms folded across his chest, and had to admit he was a little moved.

Zavala and Barnes turned and left Patrick to his fate. Barnes paused. "Cooper."

"Yes, Officer Barnes?"

"As of this afternoon you have yard privileges."

"Thank you, Officer Barnes."

"Try not to screw up."

"I'll try," Bolan replied.

Barnes shot Bolan a look and followed Zavala down the stairs.

"Dad," Patrick said.

"Son," Rudy replied.

"I'm sorry I did this to you."

"I can live with it. So can you. We have to. It's your mother I worry about."

Patrick bit his lip.

Bolan pushed away from the bars. "You have no idea the position you've put your father in. You have given his enemies leverage. You have put yourself within the grasp of rapists and torturers of every stripe, and that has put him within the grasp of evil men."

Patrick regarded Bolan warily. "You know, I have a custom, first-person shooter character who looks almost exactly like you."

"I'm not surprised."

"Jesus, Dad. Who is this guy?"

Rudy shook his head. "Has he mentioned the position you've put me in?"

"I didn't know you could buy mercs in prison, Dad."

Bolan smiled. "You can buy anything in prison, Patrick. Including you."

The young man flinched.

"As of now," Bolan stated, "I have your back. And your dad's."

"Jesus, Dad, you hired this psycho? Why don't you just make a deal with the warden?"

"I did. Then the warden broke the deal. He stopped dealing and starting giving orders and making threats. When that failed he pulled you in. None of that matters. Rudolphos don't earn for anyone except our Family. We don't take orders from anyone outside the Family. The warden is going to learn that, the easy way or the hard way."

Patrick stared at his father with newfound awe, then warily at Bolan. "So?"

Bolan shrugged. "So keep you head up, your ass down and your nose clean. If you know what's good for you, do what your father tells you. If you want to live, do whatever I tell you whenever I tell you. I won't tell you twice. I'll just walk."

Patrick stiffened.

The Rudolpho patriarch spoke. "Son, we're in debt to this man."

Patrick was a new-school, young gun criminal, but he had grown up surrounded by wise guys. His father's words rang through him. "Right. Got it. On it. So what's the plan?"

"Your father is going to pretend to capitulate to save your narrow ass and gather intel. I am going to continue to act like a wild card."

"What you want me to do?" Patrick asked.

"Behave."

The young man bristled.

"Stay close to your dad at all times. Some guys may call you Daddy's boy, but most of the cons will respect the fact that you're blood and do what your father tells you. If someone drops a punk card at your feet, don't pick it up. Look to me. If someone drops the soap in the showers—" Bolan shook his head "—don't pick that up, either."

The Rudolphos laughed. It was an unusual sound in Duivelstad, and the rare times it was heard it was mostly ugly. It was a sound that was becoming identified with the dangerous, blue-eyed newb. Bolan dropped his voice so that only Patrick and his father could hear it. "If everything goes to hell? There's a book on my bunk. *Leaves of Grass*. You go next door and hand it to Kal. You say 'Cooper is giving you your book back,' and say *'A Promise of California.'* You got that? Rudy, that goes for you, too."

"What the hell does that mean?"

"It means you have a fifty-fifty chance of Kal helping you or putting you in a wheelchair shitting out a plastic bag. It's the nuclear option. I don't recommend it unless all is lost."

Rudy just stared. Patrick didn't understand what was going on, but he knew something big was. "Right."

"So now what happens?" Rudy asked.

"You two have your family reunion." Bolan stretched his arms and yawned. "Me? I'm going to take a nap. I have yard privileges after lunch, and I think it's going to be a hoot."

Stony Man Farm, Virginia

AARON KURTZMAN HUNCHED under the evil eye Price gave him. She watched him squirm for several long seconds. "What's the word?"

"No word. Mack hasn't logged on any of D-Town's computers, and he hasn't established an alternative line of communication yet."

"Nothing about his status on any of the penitentiary computers?"

"If they've reclassified him or put him in for any kind of restrictions or punishment, it's all off the record. His jacket going in was sparse in the extreme, and nothing has been added to it since."

"So he could be dead already, and we'll never know until someone decides to input it the prison computer and file a report with State Corrections?"

"Um, yes." If looks could have killed, Kurtzman would have been splattered all over the walls.

Price folded her arms. "Why don't you just get Able Team and Phoenix Force transferred in, get what you need, burn the goddamn place to the ground, extract Mack and be done with it already?"

"We don't have permission to do that."

Price's expression spoke volumes about all the times both Mack and Farm personnel had acted without official sanction.

Kurtzman had been expecting this conversation and pulled his ace. "Though you're right, we should send someone in to check on the lad."

"Oh, yeah?" Price's eyes narrowed. "Who?"

"You."

A very cold, almost imperceptible look of bemusement ghosted across the willowy blonde's face. "He can't have a conjugal for at least three more days, and last I heard that was a privilege they can grant or deny."

"No, I don't have you in mind for that."

Price blinked and her face slowly turned to stone. She and Mack had enjoyed an on-again, off-again relationship in the past. "And why not?"

Kurtzman sought for a diplomatic answer. "We all agree that

whatever is going to happen is going to go down soon. When and if Mack gets a conjugal, it's going to be our one golden opportunity. We can't mess it up."

Price arched an eyebrow.

"It may be our only opportunity to improve Mack's TO and E."

"Table of Organization and Equipment."

"We're going to try and sneak some things in."

Price's face went flat as she did the math. "Oh."

"Yeah, we're going to put Carmen on that one."

Carmen Delahunt was the polar opposite of Barbara Price. Price had once been a model. Delahunt was a middle-aged red-headed handful of curves, and a divorced mother of three. "She might be better for that," Price conceded. "So what is your plan for me then?"

Kurtzman held up a Department of Justice ID badge that Hal Brognola had sent to the Farm via courier. The badge had Price's face on it and denoted a very high pay grade and seniority. "Mack is supposedly a transfer from Gitmo. Maybe he can't have visitors or see his lawyer for three more days, but is Warden Linder going to tell the Feds no when they demand to look in on their prisoner?" Kurtzman took a plane ticket out of a drawer and slid it and the DOJ badge across the table. "You've got a plane to Pennsylvania tomorrow at 10:00 in the a.m. Tonight we'll work up your script. Tomorrow you go check on our boy."

6

BOLAN TILTED BACK his head and enjoyed the first rays of the sun to strike his face in days. The soldier breathed deeply. The smell of grass and dirt and wind from beyond the perimeter was a benediction after the overwhelming smell of hundreds of men locked in cages, day after day performing bodily functions natural and less so. A century of men eating somewhat less than optimally digestible meals had left a facility whose stone walls literally sweated flatulence in summer.

Bolan let out his breath and took in the yard.

It consisted of a patchwork of dirt, weeds and a few scruffy strips of green lawn intersected by concrete walkways running between the buildings. There were none of the usual basketball courts, weight-lifting pits or other sports facilities. The interior fence of the deadline cast a pall on all the outdoor activities. Exercise in the yard in Duivelstad seemed to consist mainly of spending a few precious moments outside the molded, mildewed and orificially odored confines of the cell blocks, and smoking cigarettes. Bolan glanced over and checked out Aryan Acres. Most of the inhabitants checked out Bolan in return.

The soldier smiled at his admirers. Milk and honey butter had improved his mood. Sawyer started to stand up, but Rollin put a hand on the giant's shoulder and sat him back down. Longer ago than Bolan cared to think about, he had declared his War Everlasting. Ending up in prison had been the worst case of all scenarios. Now he languished in the worst prison in America, by choice. All in all he was doing okay. The prison bitches liked him, the Puerto Ricans admired his style, the Muslims had given him a carton of milk and he had the Rudolphos by the short hairs as intelligence assets.

Hard won instincts told Bolan time was swiftly running out.

Team Rudolpho walked up. Patrick appeared to have had a

scared-straight moment sometime around five minutes inside general population, and followed his father like a shadow. Rudy spoke low. "I did what you wanted, Cooper. I was installing new software on the U's computer and told him you were perfect for the Hunger Games."

"And?"

"And I stuck to the script. I told him the only thing I can get out of you is that you miss your wife. Like, really miss her, and that she and her situation is the biggest leverage the Feds have on you. I told him to dangle a conjugal and supervised library internet privileges, and you just might fight. I told him you'd probably put on a better show than Tavo."

A voice shouted out from Aryan Acres. "Hey, girl!"

The con Rollin had stepped down from the bleachers and now leered at Patrick from twenty yards away. "Yeah, I'm talking to you, Patti-cakes! You had a shower yet?"

Bolan noted with approval that Patrick clenched his hands into fists rather than flinch. The soldier narrowed his eyes as the young man took a step forward and bellowed in defiance, "Yo! Rollin! Why don't you put on your little bitch sundress, get on your bike, roll your way back to bitch acres and get your shamrock-shake green head bobbing pretty beneath the bleachers! I got a dime to do and no time for you, fool!"

The yard erupted in catcalls, whistles and cheers from corner to corner.

"Patrick, I told you to look to me," Bolan muttered.

Patrick snarled in mixed fear and fury. "I'm right next to you!"

Rudy sighed, but there was some pride in his son in it. "The boy has a mouth on him."

Patrick kept his eyes on target and his attention on Bolan. "Any advice?"

"Yeah, you have to stand up for yourself against Rollin, no doubt, but you just insulted the entire home team. Don't do that again."

"Sorry."

"It's too late for sorry." Bolan stepped forward. War with the Aryan Circle had always been inevitable. They had just made their first move, and as far as the soldier was concerned it was about time. If the war was joined, then having the first battle under a blue sky with half the population watching was just about as good as it was going to get. "You want a piece of the kid? You have to come through me."

Rollin stepped forward, but leered at Patrick. "Wow, inside only one day and already you're a two-daddy Patti!" Aryan Acres roared at this new height in big house humor. The rest of the yard was silent as it watched. The guards on the wall were suspiciously uninvolved. Bolan heard a radio crackle behind him. He suspected they were probably laying bets, and that told the soldier all he needed to know.

This fight was sanctioned. How he had taken out the Todd and survived as Kal's Caucasian celly were mysteries that were about to be solved, and his fitness for the Hunger Games tested. If Rollin whipped him it would be stopped before Bolan was crippled, or at least before he was killed.

Rollin's voice dropped low just for Bolan. "Now as for you…"

Bolan suddenly strode fast to his right toward the gate to the yard. Rollin moved to cut him off, as the soldier knew he would. Bolan had found the sun in his face mighty fine after four days inside. Now Rollin got to enjoy it. The con blinked and squinted as the slanting afternoon rays shone straight in his eyes. The enforcer moved to get out of the sun and Bolan countercircled. The soldier's shadow followed Rollin like a compass needle. Rollin roared as he suddenly realized what was happening.

Then he charged.

The con was big, as tall as Bolan and about twenty pounds heavier, but a good bit of that was fat around the middle. His left hand extended in a claw as his right drew back in a hamlike fist. That told Bolan that Rollin was the kind of con who liked to grab men smaller than him and start pounding on them.

Bolan didn't feel like being grabbed, much less pounded.

The soldier strode into spitting distance. He dropped to one knee and threw a right hand lead aimed two inches below the top button of the enforcer's fly. Bolan buried his fist into Rollin's bladder. The Aryan Circle enforcer made a hissing noise like a lizard being stepped on. Only his momentum kept the con moving forward. Bolan didn't retract his arm. Instead, he stood up underneath Rollin and sent him teeter-tottering over his shoulder in a fireman's carry.

The blow and the throw had been a two heartbeat blur of action. Bolan walked two steps away before Rollin hit the ground behind him like a sack of potatoes. The soldier turned.

A carbine cracked from the wall and a bullet dug a divot in the crabgrass three feet to Bolan's right. Schoenaur's voice bellowed over a bullhorn. "Freeze!"

Bolan stood unmoving over his adversary.

Shouts, curses, threats and invectives rose into the air over Aryan Acres as if from an enraged troop of baboons. Aryans spilled forward like a bench clearing at a hockey game. Schoenaur called out like God on High over his public address system. "Tear gas!" Bolan glanced up at the tower and saw two guards with six-shot, revolving, 37 mm grenade launchers shouldered. Schoenaur held up his hand like the captain of a firing squad. "In five…four…three…"

Every con in the yard, including the hostile Aryans, dropped to their knees and put their hands behind their heads with the oiled alacrity of practice. Bolan followed suit. He scanned the walls as carbines and grenade launchers tracked the kneeling populace. Bolan gazed at Schoenaur's mirrored sunglasses. The distance between them was too great for Bolan to read the guard captain's face or body language. "Exercise period is over! Return to your units, by cell block! Starting with C!"

The inhabitants of C Block rose from wherever they were in the yard and began streaming toward the gate. Bolan looked behind him before he joined his block mates. Rollin lay curled up on the ground. The Aryan enforcer's jeans were soaked from crotch to thigh. The wetting of the faded denim was taking on an ugly pinkish-red hue from the con's ruptured bladder. Rollin cried as he clutched himself.

"Tell the Force from me to go fuck himself," Bolan ordered.

The soldier joined the Rudolphos in the file moving toward the gate. "Rudy, tell the warden I'm in."

"So you think he's a soldier?" Linder asked.

Scott nodded at the warden. "He doesn't walk like a jarhead or act like some guy just returned from Afghanistan, but you should have seen him take down Rollin. One shot, surgical, and now my boy is peeing pink through a catheter in the infirmary in a rack next to the Todd."

"We've dealt with soldier boys and their attitude problems in here before."

"That we have," Scott agreed. "But if this asshole was at Gitmo, he's a soldier who fucked up really bad, or he was into some kind of spooky shit and did something or saw something extra special to end up here."

"You think he's Special Forces?"

"That, or he's got to be some kind of martial arts master like Kal, but he doesn't give off the bullshit Zen seeker vibe."

"And what kind of vibe does inmate Cooper give off?"

"He gives off serious asshole, and he proves it by ripping people new ones. Right after he burst Rollin's bladder, he specifically told Rollin to tell me to go fuck myself. Personally, I admired the style, but something is going to have to be done about that on my end."

Linder's chair creaked as he leaned his bulk back. "I had a talk with Rudy this morning."

"Italian Mafia," Scott scoffed. "Jesus, do they even exist anymore besides on HBO?"

"He's useful."

"Bringing in his boy was smart, but now he's got Cooper for a guard dog. I don't see too many cons of any stripe stepping up to do anything about that now."

Linder gave Scott a sly look. "You don't think Cooper can be taken?"

"Icing Cooper is easy. Shackle him up, put him in isolation and have your man Schoenaur pop his head like a cyst. You don't want the blood on you or your men's hands? Get him in the laundry room alone, and me and ten of my boys will take him. I don't care what Spec Op bullshit he knows, he'll get a few of us, but once he's taken a few shanks to the nuts and the guts? Like death and taxes, it's inevitable." Scott leaned back, as well. "But you don't want that."

"Not just yet," Linder admitted.

"So what did your boy Rudy have to say?"

"He says that Cooper misses his wife, and that Cooper is willing to fight in the Hunger Games for a conjugal and maybe some library time."

Scott steepled his fingers as he considered this piece of information. "Well, now, that does present some interesting possibilities."

"So I was thinking."

"You going to let him fight?"

Linder nodded. "I'm thinking yes."

"You going to agree to his terms?"

"He wants the conjugal up front." Linder gave Scott an ugly

smile. "It seems he's worried he might not be able to enjoy it afterward, depending on his opponent."

"Well, now, a man who's been beaten senseless can still enjoy a blow job, but what the hell is going to do in the library? Look at the picture books and eat paste? I think our boy Cooper has his priorities reversed."

Linder threw back his head and laughed.

"You going to go along with it?" Scott asked.

"Oh, I think so. My distributors have been clamoring for the next fight."

"You got an opponent in mind?"

Linder locked eyes with Scott. "As a matter of fact, I do."

"IT'S ON," RUDY stated.

Bolan looked up from his book. "When?"

"It's the Hunger Games, Friday night lights and Friday night fights."

"My conjugal?"

"He said sure." Rudy was clearly concerned. "I think he agreed to it a little too easily."

Bolan rolled off his bunk and stepped out onto the tier. Rudy followed him. The soldier had two days. Not enough time to get in any meaningful training. The best thing he could do was rest and eat as much food as he could scrounge. "You going to be in attendance?"

"A couple of trustees will be doing the filming, but I'll be coordinating the feed for the internet. So yeah, I'll be in the room, but I'll be busy. Don't look to me when Love gouges out your eyes and skull-fucks you." Rudy didn't like anything about the plan. "I'll light a candle for you at Sunday service."

Bolan smiled. "You'd do that for me?"

Rudy blinked. "Sure. I give you my word."

"Thanks."

"You know you're supposed to be guarding me and my son, not going *War of the Gargantuas* with the most gargantuan son of a bitch in this house for pussy privileges."

"Better I deal with Love sooner rather than later, and I'd prefer a controlled environment rather than receiving the Love after a sewing machine shanking in the showers. As for pussy privileges—" Bolan suddenly loomed close and Rudy leaned back "—you're just jealous."

"I get one every three months. My next one is two months out. That's the problem with conjugals. If you're lucky enough to get them, it's all you think about, and time between them drags even harder than time normally drags in this place. Sometimes I almost wish my wife had divorced me. Waiting for her, knowing she's a weapon they can use against me, and scared shitless the warden will use it? Sometimes I think the lifers with nothing are the happiest here."

"You could always willingly decline your conjugals."

Rudy laughed. "Fuck that!"

"That's what I thought you'd say."

"All right, it won't be much yet, but what can I do on my end?" Rudy asked.

"Honestly, I could use some fuel between now and the fight."

"You're on dietary restriction and I'm watched pretty close."

"You have money?"

Rudy gave Bolan a wary look. "I have money."

"Get some to Bobbie-John. Does the commissary have energy bars?"

"Yeah, really bad ones."

"I'll need six, a Snickers, and an energy drink come Friday."

"That can be arranged."

"Tell him he can buy anything he wants for himself as long as it's not so much it arouses suspicion."

"Bobbie-J will get the word."

Things quieted as Zavala came marching down the tier, boots ringing like those of a storm trooper. "Cooper!"

"Yo!" Bolan shouted out.

"Some bitch wants to see you!"

Rudy gazed at Bolan in mild awe. "That was fast."

7

BOLAN WALKED INTO the warden's office flanked by Zavala and Barnes. Schoenaur stood behind Warden Linder giving Bolan the hard stare. The soldier allowed his eyes to flare at the sight of Barbara Price in an immaculate charcoal suit, wearing a DOJ badge around her neck.

"Oh shit!" A man who accompanied Price wore a marshal's badge that proclaimed him to be Marshal Avery Roy, but Bolan suspected that he was one of the Farm's blacksuits.

Price instantly took Bolan's cue and gazed on the soldier as if he was something she'd scraped off her shoe. "Oh shit is right, Cooper. Do you think we forgot about you?"

Bolan backed up a step and felt the tip of Zavala's baton in his back. "Have a seat, Cooper."

The soldier made a show of very reluctantly taking a seat across the desk from Warden Linder. Price ran her eyes up and down Bolan to take in his physical state and look for any body language cues. "You've lost weight."

At the same time she blinked in Morse code: U-OK?

"Food's not as good as Gitmo," Bolan replied.

He blinked back. OK

"You look a little pekid."

OUT? Price asked with her eyes.

"Ain't no palm trees or white sand beaches around here, neither."

NO.

"You need to talk to me, Cooper."

"We have a deal."

Price blinked STOP to indicate she was no longer blinking in code. She had ascertained that Bolan was alive and well and didn't want extraction. "We had a deal," she continued. "You aren't dead, nor have you been extraordinarily renditioned to a black site dungeon in Bucharest. But you still haven't told us everything we want to know."

"I told you exactly what you wanted to know."

"Yes, but now we want to know everything you know."

Bolan lifted his chin. "Not a chance."

"You know I could whisper in Warden Linder's ear what you did and why you're here. Some of your fellow inmates might not like it."

Bolan grimaced.

Price sighed and made a show of throwing the curve ball. "Heard the warden is considering giving you a conjugal."

Bolan made a show of stiffening.

"You know, I'm not going to raise any objection. I suggest you and your lovely wife have a lovely time, and then I suggest you have a long hard talk about how you want the rest of your lives to go down."

She nodded at Linder. "We're done here for the moment. I thank you for your patience and the Justice Department thanks you for your cooperation."

Linder just shrugged.

Bolan kept the smile off his face. Price had a career in undercover work if she wanted it.

Schoenaur led her out. Bolan looked at Linder. He knew the warden would want to have a sit down about this little meeting in the very near future, and it wasn't likely to be a pleasant conversation. The only good news was that Bolan was willing to bet the interrogation was most likely going to wait until after the fight.

The warden jerked his head at the door. "Get the fuck out of my office, Cooper."

PATRICK LIFTED HIS pants cuff, pulled down his sock, and a train of energy bars clattered to the cell floor. He lifted up his other cuff and pulled out a Snickers and a Mars bar, then stepped out onto the tier. Bolan and Rudy followed. Patrick rolled his eyes. "The Mars bar was from Bobbie, personally. I think he likes you."

Bolan scooped up his loot and slid all of it save one under his mattress. Bobbie-John was a young gay man in prison with a long stretch ahead of him. After the initial assaults he would have most likely found a lover or even a prison husband. After having been thrown to the Todd he was damaged goods. Prison had its own very hard, cold set of rules. The only way to ever stop being a man's bitch was to become another man's, or to kill the man who had made you one. However, with the Todd out of sight and out of mind on permanent medical disability, some of the stigma, like some of Bobbie-John's scars, would fade with time.

Bolan nodded. "I have redeeming characteristics."

Patrick raised his hands beseechingly. "Yeah? Well, dude, you know people saw me talking to him, and now they're all whistling and shit. What's that going to do to my rep in here?"

"If I live long enough, that won't matter," Bolan replied.

"And what the hell does that mean?"

"It means don't pick up the soap, and keep your nose clean. You already screwed up in the yard."

"Yeah." Patrick grinned. "But that was awesome!"

"It was. Where's my energy drink?"

"I couldn't walk away from Bobbie-J with that down the front of my pants. It would have been the icing on the cake."

Bolan had to give it to him. "I can see that."

"You'll have it Friday afternoon."

"Thanks."

"No, thank *you*."

Bolan peeled his energy bar and bit into it. It tasted like nutraloaf with a wispy swathe of peanut butter running down the middle, and a few forlorn chocolate chips acting as outriders. "Good work." Bolan looked to Rudy. "How's the library looking?"

"The librarian is an old lifer, Lincoln Whitmore. He was a little afraid when I showed up and upgraded the computers. He thought I was out to steal his job, but now we're tight. I haven't approached him yet, but I think he'll help when the time comes."

Bolan choked down the last of his energy bar. "You Rudys do good work."

"If we were that good we wouldn't be here, but you're welcome. What now?"

"I need a nap. I got a conjugal tomorrow and a fight Friday."

"You know they say that weakens a fighter's legs."

The younger Rudolpho smirked. "Of course, if you're a cup half-full kind of guy, you could think of it as the condemned's last meal."

Rudy shook his head at his son. They were Mafia and they believed in fate and jinxing things.

Bolan waggled his eyebrows at the lad. "Son, you've never eaten better."

"CHRIST COOP…" OFFICER Fatty Barnes stared at Bolan's wife in awe as she emerged out of Duivelstad's west gate into the outer fenced areas. You could hear the whistles still following her from within the walls.

A female corrections officer led her out. Bolan had never seen Renzo before, but of the three women who worked at Duivelstad she had the reputation as the hottest, and she would have been hot anywhere. She was short, dark and Italian, with bright green eyes. The word was that Renzos had been guards at Duivelstad for a hundred years. She was the first female corrections officer of the family and apparently the last of her line. Officer Renzo led Bolan's beloved spouse toward the conjugal area known in D-Town as Jungle Park.

Barnes sighed in unrequited admiration. "You are one lucky SOB."

"If I was lucky, I wouldn't be in here, Officer."

"Man, if I had had that coming to visit me for conjugal, I'd knock over a bank tomorrow."

Bolan nodded. Carmen Delahunt was something to see. She was former FBI and one of the hottest things to ever come through Quantico. The bloom was slightly off the rose, but Delahunt could still hold her own against women ten years younger. She had dressed down to the white-trash max in tight jeans, a tube top she was just about falling out of, and a jeans jacket. If there wasn't a hole in the ozone layer over Pennsylvania it wasn't through the lack of hair spray Delahunt had used to pile her scarlet hair up high. She popped her gum and squealed at the sight of Bolan. "Hey, baby!"

Delahunt broke into a tottering, jiggling run in her four-inch, cork-heeled sandals, and flung herself into Bolan's arms. She shoved her tongue down his throat and spent long moments trying to suck out his lungs. Barnes and Renzo shot each other amused looks. Delahunt leaned back and began poking Bolan's ribs and pinching him. "Oh, baby! You've lost so much weight!"

Bolan grinned. "Did you miss me?"

Delahunt reattached herself to Bolan's face like a limpet.

Barnes cleared his throat. "You have until five o'clock, Cooper. You haven't earned an overnight yet."

Delahunt turned goo-goo eyes on Barnes. "Who's he, baby?"

"That's Officer Barnes," Bolan replied. "He's one of the good ones."

Barnes's cheeks colored against his will.

"He's cute as a button!" Delahunt planted a big wet one on Barnes's cheek before he could react. The guard flushed beet-red. Delahunt had painted a perfect Kewpie doll kiss on Barnes's face in red lipstick. Bolan didn't want to imagine what his own face looked like right now. Barnes tried to regain some composure as he unlocked the gate to the conjugal area. Jungle Park consisted of six dilapidated, beige, 1970s-vintage Winnebago camper trailers mounted on blocks and surrounded by their own ring of fencing topped with razor wire.

Barnes gave his memorized spiel. "You're in Unit 2. First trailer on the right. Once you're inside you will not come out for any reason. If you have a problem or either one of you want to leave before five, just pick up the white phone by the door. It's connected directly to the guard station."

Bolan nodded. "Got it."

Barnes unlocked the door to Unit 2 and stepped back to allow the happy couple to enter. Bolan followed Delahunt inside. Unit 2 smelled of disinfectant and pine-scented air freshener. A small stack of clean sheets and towels lay folded on top of the foldaway table.

"You two have a good'n," Barnes said. The door clicked shut behind him.

Bolan pulled back a curtain. Barnes and Renzo were walking to the main facility. Renzo had neither wiped Barnes's face nor made him aware of that fact that Delahunt had branded him. Bolan smiled. Renzo had decided to let Barnes have a little street cred.

The soldier gave the unit a quick once-over. The shower worked. So did the lights. The sink worked, but the gas stove had been ripped out and covered with a sagging plywood counter. The microwave worked. The mini-fridge worked, and it contained two frozen dinners and a six-pack of bottled water.

Delahunt scratched behind her right ear and under her right eye in question about prying sound and vision devices.

Bolan shook his head and held up a finger. He conducted a thorough search. "I had it on good authority we are currently off the radar, and my guy was right."

Delahunt draped herself across the little square dining booth and waggled her eyebrows. "So, how's it hanging, bright eyes? Inquiring minds want to know."

"To the left. As always."

Delahunt laughed. She ran her eyes over the bridal suite. "Well, now, I'll admit this is a first. But I've been in worse. Just a sec. I have to go powder my nose." She rose and closed the door to the tiny bathroom behind her. A moment later the sound of a wolverine gargling bleach in the snow shook the camper. Bolan listened as the toilet flushed and the sink ran for a few moments. Delahunt came out looking a little pale and shaky, yet proud. "Here you go, sunshine!"

Delahunt tossed a small, snake-shaped plastic package onto the table.

Bolan looked at his present with admiration. Delahunt had disgorged eight inches of high-explosive flexible charge with a detonator pin in each end. "You rule."

"I'll deny that I said it, but I've swallowed bigger."

Bolan laughed aloud.

"Laugh all you want." Delahunt gave the package a rueful look. "Those pins hurt, and I've had more practice than you."

Bolan had swallowed evidence before. This would be his first length of explosive. "I can't imagine."

Delahunt tossed a ballpoint pen onto the table. "That's for you, too. Compliments of the Cowboy."

"Where did you hide that?"

"Where do you think?"

"I can think of two possibilities...."

"Get your mind out of the gutter. The Cowboy drove it into my shoe and sealed it. We'll pound it into the sole of your shoe to get it out of the trailer."

"What's it do?"

Delahunt took up the pen. "Cowboy special." She snapped her wrist as if the pen body was a collapsible baton. Three inches of a surgical steel, ice-pick spike clicked out.

Bolan felt some relief. He would have had to expend a great deal of the little cred he had to get a shank. "Inner city defense pencil."

"With a twist," Delahunt cautioned. She screwed the pen apart and the inner barrel and a very small bullet fell out. "The Cowboy couldn't figure out a way to put a .22 Long Rifle or a .25 into it, so he put in a .22 short. You have one shot out of the back end. You twist the pocket clip to cock it, and depress it to fire. You will have almost no velocity. Kissinger says stick your arm out straight if you have the time, and aim over your thumb knuckle. Go straight for the face."

"You tell him I said thanks."

Delahunt hawked and spit a .22 short onto the table. "You have one reload."

"I think I'm in love."

Delahunt winked.

Bolan gazed back toward the trailer's over-cab bunk. "So… nothing?"

Delahunt held up her right thumb, simulated an act of oral outrage and then popped her cheek with it. "Dream about it."

"That's all I get?"

"You get a TV dinner and my charming company." Delahunt cracked her knuckles. "Plus I give excellent back rubs."

Delahunt watched with appreciation as Bolan stripped off his shirt. He kicked off his shoes, eased himself up into the bunk and sprawled out on his stomach. "I've been in lockup for eighty-six hours, and I am a little tense."

Delahunt snorted and rose. "That's the best you can do?"

Bolan turned his eye toward the mini-fridge. "You can have the Salisbury steak dinner, plus the mini-tacos from my tray."

Delahunt clambered into the bunk and threw a leg over Bolan. "You romantic schemer you."

The soldier groaned as Delahunt's fingers stopped short of actually piercing his flesh. For a data analyst she had very strong hands.

"Five o'clock in the p.m., Cooper!" Barnes knocked on the door. "Back to population!"

Bolan awoke from the best sleep he'd had in four days. Prison had messed with him more than he wanted to admit. Delahunt had crushed every knot of tension out of his back, and spooning with her and dropping into dreamless sleep for six hours was neck and neck with the pen weapon and the flexible charge as the best thing that had happened to him in Duivelstad. They had driven the pen into the sole of his shoe with the heel of hers, and Bolan gave it fifty-fifty he'd make it past inspection. Delahunt had demanded he eat both dinners, and after one mild protest Bolan had licked the aluminum clean on both trays.

He had briefed her on every aspect of the goings-on at Duivelstad. Delahunt was appalled at the idea of the Hunger Games, and Bolan didn't want to think about Kurtzman's and Price's reactions.

The soldier unspooned himself from Delahunt. He rolled off the bunk and landed lightly on the floor. Officer Barnes stepped back slightly at the sight of Bolan's bullet, blade and shrapnel scarred frame in prison-issue boxer shorts. Renzo took it in with appreciation.

Bolan stretched, yawned and grinned at Barnes. "How are you this fine afternoon, Officer?"

"You're an asshole."

"No, I'm a dick. I have it on good authority."

"I'm sure you do." Barnes raised his voice. "Mrs. Cooper?"

"Coming!" Delahunt called.

"You probably already know this, Cooper. But you both have to be searched."

Bolan looked back at Delahunt as she showed up at the door in her jeans and her bra. "You okay with that, baby?"

Delahunt gave Barnes the goo-goo eyes again. "I want Barnesy to do it."

Barnes went scarlet.

Renzo shook her head at her fellow officer and gave Delahunt a pointed look. "When you're ready, Mrs. Cooper. And please, we need to speed this up."

Delahunt spun and made a horrified noise. "My hair!"

Bolan left the door open as he turned. "Let me get some pants on."

8

BOLAN AWOKE TO the sound of a baton rattling across the bars of his cell. "Wakey, wakey, eggs and bakey, Cooper!" Zavala called. "It's fight night!"

The cell block broke out in a storm of cheering and jeering.

Bolan arose. He took the energy drink from under his pillow and popped the top. Zavala scoffed at the infraction. "You're going to need it."

Bolan drank the flavored soda water in long slow gulps. He crushed the can and tossed it in the corner. Patrick gave him a thumbs-up. Patrick's father had already left hours ago to set up the audiovisuals for the fight. Bolan stepped out on the tier, stripped off his shirt to catcalls, and tossed it back into his cell. He stood in his prison-issue wife-beater and nodded at Zavala. "Let's do this."

The soldier followed Zavala through the steel door and into the corridor that only guards used. They went downstairs and exited into a small yard Bolan had never seen save in satellite photos, and walked across it to a back door the soldier knew led into the gymnasium. They stopped in a small vestibule with rusted lockers that had been used when Duivelstad had a boxing team in the seventies. Zavala glanced at him. "You want to wear your shoes or not?"

Bolan kicked them off.

They walked down a short hallway, and Zavala kicked open the gymnasium door.

Bolan entered the Hunger Games.

Hoots, screams, whistles, cheers and catcalls met his arrival as he came through the door. The first thing of note was the boxing ring. It was gone. Four steel posts set in the floor marked the dimensions of a standard ring, but the surface they demarcated was sweating, grimy concrete. Suspicious stains streaked the concrete in swathes and blotches. Storm fencing stretched between the posts at a five-foot height. The coils of razor wire topping it would discourage anyone from trying to vault it. As Bolan took in the unforgiving iron and concrete, he regretted losing his shirt and shoes.

The second thing he noticed was the crowd. It was small, and made up exclusively of lifers sitting in folding chairs. None of them would ever make parole and talk about what had happened this night. The following day the lifers would be courted, bribed and brown-nosed by the rest of the population for each one's version of how the fight had gone down, and the stories would be endlessly debated.

Scott nodded out of a phalanx of hard-core Aryan Circle cons.

Of note were Duivelstad's two current transgender inmates, Marilyn and Black Widow. Marilyn was, indeed, a striking facsimile of Marilyn Monroe from her last film, *The Misfits,* right down to the little cotton sundress. Black Widow bore a strikingly horrific resemblance to the boxing champion "Iron Mike" Tyson dressed and coifed like Pippi Longstocking. Bolan surmised both were part of the reward for winning.

Marilyn gave Bolan a winsome wink as he approached the ring. Black Widow grinned and showed Bolan her missing front teeth as she gave him the middle finger. "Sorry, baby! But your pink ass is going down tonight!"

Hoots and hollers met her judgment.

Bolan stripped off his wife-beater and winked as he tossed it to Marilyn, who clapped her hands and caught it. The crowd went berserk.

A trustee Bolan didn't recognize opened the gate, and the soldier stepped onto the filthy concrete. Two trustees with steady cams took close-ups of Bolan. Schoenaur and four guards from other blocks stood out of camera range. Two held grenade launchers. The other two held stun guns. Schoenaur held a drawn, K-Frame .357 Magnum revolver with a bobbed hammer and custom grips. It was the weapon of a fast-draw artist.

Bolan focused on the task at hand. No one had explained the rules because there were none. He was pretty sure that at this point, involving an inmate the Feds had an interest in, the proceedings would stop short of a killing; but Bolan was very sure that Warden Linder wanted a bloody mess made for the fans, and made of his least favorite inmate.

Bolan gave a show of cracking his knuckles for the crowd, and waited on Sawyer "Mad Dog" Love.

The soldier's spirits sank and the crowd erupted as Tavo Salcido burst through the door throwing Puerto Rican gang signs, pounding his fist over his heart in solidarity and roaring boasts and invectives in Spanish to the rafters. Bolan examined his unexpected opponent. The powers that be had groomed Tavo for the Hunger Games, and he had been given extra food and time to train. He wore no shirt and his chiseled physique radiated strength, speed and health. He was an athlete who, despite his circumstances, was at the peak of condition. He held up taped fists to the adulation of the crowd.

Bolan had made a plan for dealing with the Mad Dog. His plan had gone right out the window.

Zavala gloated. "Win or lose, hard-ass? You lose."

The guard was right. Warden Linder had thrown Bolan a curve ball. Salcido was one of Duivelstad's few genuine celebrities, and despite being a cocky bastard he was also friendly, handsome, always joking and popular. Crippling or killing him wouldn't win Bolan any friends. Letting Salcido pound his skull in wouldn't help Bolan with his mission. Things had just gone FUBAR.

Black Widow jumped up and down, shrieking like a banshee and clapping for Salcido. Most of the crowd joined her. Despite Bolan's showing against the Todd and Schoenaur, Tavo Salcido was clearly the crowd favorite.

He entered the ring strutting like a rooster, and Zavala closed the cage behind him. The Puerto Rican shook his head happily. "You heard my girl, *ese*! Tonight, your pink ass goes down!"

The crowd cheered.

"This is going to hurt you more than it hurts me," Bolan replied.

The crowd jeered and whistled.

Salcido looked at Bolan and sighed. "I like you, Cooper. I really do, but you're going down tonight, and for the thousands of fans watching at home, I gotta take you down hard."

The soldier gave the boxer credit for seeming to be genuinely sympathetic to his plight. And Bolan knew Salcido was right. The fans who were paying to watch this wanted a hard fight, or failing that, something so drastic they would leap out of their seats at the horror and rewind it a hundred times to catch every nuance of the human destruction.

Bolan smiled and spoke low just for Salcido. "Out of respect for Billy the C and the kindness he showed me, I'm going to take it easy on you, *hermano*."

Salcido's eyes flared.

The crowd went quiet as Schoenaur raised his revolver. The skylights rang as he pulled the trigger. Bolan recognized the sound of a blank. Salcido had been here before. According to Rudy, the man had won three fights to win the right to face Love.

Bolan had been tossed into the caldron and thrown in Salcido's way.

The Puerto Rican came straight in with his left hand jab working like a piston and his right hand ready. He was a welterweight, but he had hands the size of a superheavy and had earned his way up as a knockout artist. Bolan wanted none of it and backpedaled. The crowd booed. Salcido cut off the ring like the expert he was, and Bolan felt storm fencing yielding against his back and razor wire cutting into his shoulders all too soon.

Salcido went to work.

Bolan wasn't a boxer. He knew how to cover up, but Salcido had dissected pros. His taped fist slammed into Bolan's biceps to crush the power out of his arms. A left hand slipped past the soldier's guard and the crowd screamed as Bolan's head jerked with the impact. The soldier couldn't help but raise his hands. Salcido's fists instantly flew beneath Bolan's elbows and dug into his ribs as if he were digging a grave. More than one ally and adversary had remarked that if you blinked when you fought Bolan, you died in the dark. But Salcido was younger and faster. He had what they called in the blood sports "heavy hands." He was blindingly fast and his blows fell like it was raining hammers. Salcido's right hand skidded off Bolan's forearm and nonetheless skewed the soldier's vision as it connected. The crowd roared. Razor wire sliced into Bolan's skin as he leaned back and jinked right to stay out of range of the Puerto Rican's fist.

Bolan had exactly two heartbeats to admire the artistry as Salcido did the Ali shuffle and switched to southpaw. It turned out that the man was left-handed. The soldier's vision narrowed down to a dark tunnel lit by purple sparks as his adversary's left-hand lead shot through his guard like a cannonball and crashed into his jaw. The crowd screamed when Bolan buckled and fell to hands and knees.

Salcido threw his fists up in victory. "They said he took out the Todd! They said Kal respects his shit! They said he was the shit!" Salcido grinned triumphantly at the Black Widow. "You and me and Marilyn makes three, baby!"

Black Widow pantomimed a sexual act, to the delight of the

fight fans. Salcido turned back to Bolan. "Now, get up, motherfucker! Get up and—"

The soldier rose, spit blood and raised his hands.

Salcido took in Bolan, the look in his eyes and his current condition. The boxer lowered his chin and raised his fists. "Well, all
right then. Let's finish this."

Bolan's bell had been rung more times than he liked to think
about. It was a credit card that was going to have to be paid off
sooner rather than later. That didn't matter. This night there was
a battle that had to be won. Bolan stepped forward, put up his
hands and whipped his right shin into Salcido's thigh just above the
knee. He took a hard jab to the chin for his effort, gritted his teeth
and slammed his shinbone into the back of his adversary's knee.

Salcido staggered backward.

Bolan bore in.

He faked a right-hand lead and the Puerto Rican couldn't help
his instinct to raise his hands.

Bolan put every ounce of strength into his round kick into Salcido's quadriceps. The man groaned as he took the mother of all
Charlie horses and fell back into the fencing and wire, hopping on
one leg. Bolan stepped in and threw a right-hand lead that crashed
into Salcido's mouth like a train wreck.

Salcido rubbernecked with the blow and buckled back into the
fencing. He lay back and made a pretense of rope-a-doping.

Bolan slammed his shin again into Salcido's blackening thigh.

The man sagged into the links. Bolan charged and threw his
shoulder into Salcido's torso like a fullback breaking a tackle.
Fence links rattled as the boxer bounced off the barrier and flew
forward against his will.

Bolan used his opponent's momentum, slamming a hand into
Salcido's throat and the other into the boxer's crotch as he came
off the fence. Bolan roared with effort as he pressed Salcido over
his head. The soldier lost the momentum and toppled forward to
dump his load. The Puerto Rican went through wire and fell at the
feet of Marilyn and Black Widow, wreathed in bloodied, sprung
coils of razor-sharp steel.

For one pregnant second the crowd was stunned into silence.

"Send me a bigger one!" Bolan roared. He spun and pointed
his finger at Scott. "Send me the biggest you've got!"

The crowd went mad. Bolan shot his fists skyward in victory.

The chant of "Coo-per! Coo-per! Coo-per!" coalesced and began to shake the gymnasium.

The Aryans began chanting "Love! Love! Love!" in response, but Bolan's new fans were handily winning the team-spirit war.

Bolan spit more blood and held up his bloodstained hands for the cameras.

He hoped the show had earned him some library privileges.

The Computer Room, Stony Man Farm, Virginia

THE FEED ENDED.

Kurtzman was stunned. Price was outraged at the gladiatorial combat she had just witnessed. "Did you see that? It's like an arena in ancient Rome!"

Once Delahunt had briefed Kurtzman's team, locating the Hunger Games feed had presented no problem. The computer team leader had been recording the fight, and he clicked back to the start. This time he kept his eyes off Bolan and his opponent and watched the periphery to see what he could pick up of the crowd, the surroundings and any other clues. He and Akira Tokaido would parse it frame by frame until the wee hours—Hunt Wethers was at a conference—but Kurtzman wanted another viewing to let his second impressions sink in.

"Oh!" Tokaido gasped as the soldier's first kick thudded home in the rerun. "That's going to leave a mark!"

Price scowled at the hacker ferociously.

"That's our Mack!" Delahunt's eyes glittered with cupidity as Bolan pressed Salcido over his head and threw him through the razor wire.

The four of them watched with the same awe they had the first time as Bolan whirled to the camera, bared his teeth in a bloodstained leer of triumph and called for a bigger one.

"He's like some hero out of myth," Tokaido enthused. "Defying the gods."

"Don't you mean someone out of one of your first-person shooter games?" Price muttered. "Tell me we have enough now to take down Linder and close Duivelstad for good."

"Oh yeah." Tokaido nodded without taking his eyes off the screen. "We can easily prove the feed came from D-Town."

"We have him on trafficking in blood sports, conspiracy, cruel and unusual." Kurtzman restarted the clip. "I can think off the top of my head of a hundred laws he's broken."

"So?"

"So Mack didn't go in there to break up the Hunger Games and close Duivelstad. There's something bigger going on. Mack thinks it's going down soon. If we have the Feds raid the place, and Linder lawyers up, the guards all say talk to my union rep, and the inmates all get transferred and scattered to the four corners of the United States while it turns into a giant jurisdictional fight. The fact is we don't know what we're looking for, and that means there is a very real possibility that we won't recognize it when it slips through our fingers. The other thing is that Mack hasn't asked for us to come in, or for extraction." The feed stopped on Mack Bolan with his fists raised in brutal dominance. "And if he wanted that, he would have figured out a way to tell us right there."

Price was far from pleased. "So we just sit and wait."

"No," Kurtzman replied. "We let the man work."

Warden's Office

"DID YOU SEE that?" Warden Linder asked.

"I was right there at ringside," Scott replied. "What did the fight fans have to say about it?"

"Same as always, the fight was too short. A few aficionados thought it was a little too boxy and kickboxy. They went berserk when Cooper gorilla-slammed Tavo through the wire."

"So they want to see more of Cooper."

"They're clamoring for it. We'll make a killing on Cooper versus Love."

"Undoubtedly."

"You saw what he did to Tavo," Linder said. "You're not worried about it?"

"No," Scott scoffed. "Tavo's a boxer, good one, but a boxer, and not a bare knuckle one. To be honest, he never stood a chance. The only reason Cooper has a mark on him at all is because he tried to take our Olympic contender down easy. He ate a few fists for the camera, and so that he could take Tavo down without crippling or killing him."

"You think Sawyer can take him?"

"You know, I've been wondering about that after Cooper shanked Rollin with his fingers in the yard. Normally, I'd said yes."

"But?"

"But Cooper took out the Todd."

Warden Linder was surprised. "You don't think Love could've taken the Todd?"

"Love could've take the Todd apart, but it would have cost him about a pound of flesh to do it, and he'd be in the infirmary getting rabies shots. Cooper walked out of the House of Todd without out a mark on him."

"So what are you saying?"

"My lad Love is U.S., Grade A, number-one brute. But Cooper, that man is brutal. Love knows enough to protect his eyes and his nuts in the Hunger Games while he's breaking his man down. We've seen him do it half a dozen times. He's owned that pit since the first day he stepped inside it. But this Cooper knows shit, nasty shit, like the kind of shit where he pulls a vein out of your neck and shows it to you while you lose control of all your bodily functions."

"Well, your man Love is taking on Cooper next Friday. I've got backers in Tokyo and Singapore putting up seven figure numbers for the fight."

"And what are you going to do if Cooper wins, Warden?"

"I don't know, try to coerce Kal into being his next opponent? What are you going to do, Force?"

Scott frowned. "I believe a best-case scenario for both of us is that Cooper loses, and loses bad. Like to the tune of Love putting him in a wheelchair, but letting Cooper keeps his eyes, his tongue and enough brains left in his head for the Feds if they still have any use for him."

"I agree, but how do we make that happen?"

"Love will do his part."

"What about Cooper? You think he's going to lay down for that? The only leverage anyone has over him is his wife, and according to the Fed lady she's in protective custody. I don't know if I have the juice to find her, much less before the fight, and the paying public wants this weekend's Friday night fight at the Hunger Games to be the best ever."

"There's one way I can think of to make Cooper take his trip to the woodshed, and it won't be willingly."

"How's that?"

"The new meat in the Hunger Games needs tenderizing before you throw him in the fire."

Linder smiled as he saw it perfectly in his mind. "I'll put Schoenaur on it."

9

"YOU GOT LIBRARY privileges," Rudy confirmed.

Bolan lay on Rudy's bunk because climbing up into his own was too painful. In the meantime he reaped the rewards of winning the Hunger Games. He laid his face in ice packs while Marilyn massaged his back. Before she had murdered her boyfriend with a meat cleaver, she had paid for her surgeries as a celebrity look-alike masseuse who specialized in happy endings. Bolan was grateful for hands even more powerful than Delahunt's, and that nothing untoward was pressing into the small of his back. Black Widow apparently brewed the best coffee in D-Town and the smell that came from the pot on the hot plate she had brought with her sent Bolan's salivary glands into overdrive.

She kept up a steady patter. "Oh, sugar! When you said bring me a bigger one, you won me over!"

The name Hunger Games wasn't just window dressing. Two pizzas and two buckets of chicken with biscuits, coleslaw, and macaroni and cheese had come with the winning. Bolan was spreading the wealth. Patrick and Black Widow were stuffing themselves, and Rudy beelined for the chicken bucket. Bolan lifted his head. "Hey, Blondie?"

"Hmm?" Marilyn responded.

"Hold that thought."

Marilyn slid off and joined Rudy at the trough. Bolan went over to the cornucopia with a disposable plate and took out a few morsels and a spork. "Be right back." He went to the neighboring cell and stepped inside.

Kal lowered a dog-eared book and shook his head sadly. "I told you not to enter my cell without permission, Cooper." He put his book aside and rose.

"But I have a Wonka Golden Ticket," Bolan protested. He brandished the spoils he had held behind his back.

Kal stared very long and hard at an original recipe chicken breast and a biscuit sitting on top of a half pint of mac and cheese.

"You were cool to me when you didn't have to be, Kal." Bolan held out the food. "This is a one-time thank-you and propers. You don't owe me nothing."

Kal sighed once again, as if he was doing something against his better judgment. "This is becoming a habit, and a bad one." He took the food and nodded at his bunk. "Have a seat. I allow myself some sweet tea from the commissary on Saturdays. You want some?"

"I have coffee."

"I know, I smelled it."

Bolan raised his voice. "Widow, baby? Would you bring Kal some coffee?"

Black Widow squealed.

Kal looked as if he was starting to have a headache. He tore into the mac and cheese with determination. Black Widow came in oohing and ahhing and gasping at everything she saw. Her unheard-of trip into Kalville would be all over D-Town within hours. She stopped short of curtsying before Duivelstad's resident tower of Black Power. "Here, Kal. I didn't know how you take it. Do you—"

Kal visibly struggled to be polite. "Black is fine. You're very kind, thank you."

Black Widow giggled and handed Bolan his. "Here you go, Coopy."

Bolan winked.

Black Widow blushed and turned to leave. "You boys have a nice little sit-down."

Kal's knuckles creaked around his spork.

Bolan sipped coffee and watched Kal. The longtime man wasn't forcing himself to eat, he was deliberating forcing himself to ignore every other factor and enjoy it. Kal scraped the foam plate clean, dropped the whitened bones on it and licked his fingers.

"Thank you, Cooper."

"You're welcome."

Kal sipped his coffee. His eyebrows rose.

Bolan nodded. "They say she brews the best in the joint."

"No one says 'joint' anymore, Cooper."

"Sorry, the overwhelming majority of lockups I've known have been in foreign countries."

"Why do I have no trouble believing that?"

"No idea."

"You know what your problem is?"

Bolan spread his hands. "I'm riddled with them. Which one do you have in mind?"

Kal's eyes narrowed. "I believe you can dig this, I am going to explain it to you. Once. Remember that fortress of light you mentioned?"

"I do."

"Well, I found myself in an unacceptable situation. I found myself in Satan's fortress. So I built my own." Kal pressed his finger to his temple and then over his heart. "Here, and here. It ain't very bright, it ain't very comfortable and it sure as shit ain't pretty. But I can live here." Kal glanced around his cell at his books, his posters and his few belongings. "They can take all this away, but they'll have to use jumper cables, blowtorches and pliers to break down my fortress. You understand."

"And I keep asking you to step outside your zone."

Kal nodded. "Something like that."

"So can I ask you a favor?"

Kal's face went blank.

"Will you hold something for me?"

Kal's face went far from blank. Bolan wouldn't have been surprised if storm clouds had gathered in the cell and lightning had flashed out on the tier. The soldier reached behind his back again and took out his two most prized possessions. "This is a seven-ounce link of flexible charge. Those are push and press detonators stuck in each one." Bolan snapped his wrist on his camouflaged pen and deployed the surgical needle. "This is an inner city defense pencil."

Kal stared at Bolan as if he were a flying monkey from *The Wizard of Oz* who had just flown into his cell and perched on his bed. "How did you sneak these in here?"

Bolan grinned. "My wife is awesome!"

Kal wasn't laughing. "Can I ask you an honest question?"

"Shoot."

"What's about to happen?"

"Everything," Bolan answered. "Or nothing. If I don't live to retrieve those, they're yours. You'll notice the charge is pinched into seven sections. Just twist one off, push it into the lock of any door in your way and press the pin. Each one will open any door in this place, cell, security or otherwise. The shiv? Give it to any Aryan of your choosing through his eardrum, with my compliments."

Kal chewed his bottom lip as he stared at the implements of war on the bunk. Bolan knew Kal was once again considering killing him.

The soldier played his last card. He took the folded title page from *Leaves of Grass* from his pocket and tossed it on top. "No matter what happens, I have people looking into your case. I won't embarrass us both by asking whether you did it or not."

Kal's fists clenched against his will.

"But memorize that phone number and then eat it. I know your lawyer hasn't done shit for you in years. But contact him and give that number to him. You'll get new evidence sweeps. New witness interviews, and the best DNA tests science can provide. All from the top level of the DOJ."

"Who are you?"

"I'm Cooper, and I'm in trouble."

"You keep saying that."

Bolan locked eyes with the most dangerous lifer in D-Town. "Because it's half-true."

Kal had spent half his life in hell. He had spent that time forging an image of himself that he could look at in the mirror every morning, an image that would withstand living out the rest of his life inside the walls of Duivelstad. Now, twenty-five years in, Mack Bolan had careened into Kal's iron regimen with nothing but bullshit, bravado and the inexplicable, blowing his horn inside the walls of Jericho and dangling the horrible, willfully forgotten concept of hope.

Kal shook. "You sick motherfucker."

Bolan finished his coffee and left the cell.

Kal didn't tell the soldier to take his shit with him.

BOLAN LIMPED INTO the library with Rudy. Rows of bookshelves filled the sweating stone vault. Intermittent fluorescent lighting left the establishment in a patchwork of glare and shadow. It was turn-of-the-twentieth-century Duivelstad architecture and truly was the library for lost souls. A few inmates sat at tables reading books or working on their cases. The most prominent feature of the establishment was a dinner-size table in the middle of the library with eight computer monitors of varying description. Bolan smelled Renzo's perfume, but didn't immediately see her. Rudy nodded at the circulation desk. It consisted of a folding table with a beige monitor the size of an old-fashioned television. Rudy nodded at the man behind it. "That's the man."

Bolan took in Lincoln "Link" Whitmore. He could have passed for Abraham Lincoln's frail, fraternal twin brother in prison garb. Whitmore looked old enough to have been in the box during the assassination. He was pushing seventy, but Rudy had informed Bolan it was his heroin addiction that had mummified him. Whitmore sat typing away, peering over his reading glasses.

Rudy tapped the edge of the desk. "Hey, Link."

Whitmore looked up and smiled. "Oh, hello, Rudy!"

"This is my friend Cooper."

Whitmore removed his reading glasses. "Well, behold the conquering hero."

Bolan held forth a wedge-shaped package wrapped in paper towels. "Pleased to meet you."

The old man took the package and began opening it. "What is this?"

"Meat lovers special."

The old man sighed when he saw the two slices of cold pizza. "Ah, the spoils of the Hunger Games. And to what do I owe this generosity?"

"Common sense."

Whitmore raised a bushy white eyebrow. "Oh?"

"Librarians are like dentists and car mechanics, Mr. Whitmore. You want to stay in their good books."

"I see." Whitmore smiled to reveal a set of startlingly huge white teeth. "Shameless bribery, then."

"Flattery is next."

He bit into the pizza and closed his eyes as long forgotten flavors of real bacon, real cheese and nonmystery meats filled his palate. "That will not be required. You may consider my kingdom conquered, Mr. Cooper, and thank you."

"I'm supposed to have internet privileges."

"I was informed you do, Mr. Cooper."

"Cooper will do."

"As will Link. Where would you like to go? I fear the web security here is somewhat severe."

"I want to go onto the NASDAQ and check my stocks."

Whitmore shook his head. "The software will be blocked from any buying or selling. You have to understand, any financial transaction in Duivelstad outside barter is very often made under duress."

"I understand. I just want to check on it. It's what my wife is living on at the moment."

"I see. However, you should I know I will report everything you do to the warden. Despite the pizza, I won't jeopardize my position as librarian, and a trustee, for you."

"I wouldn't ask it of you."

"Then by all means, let us go check on the Bulls and the Bears." Whitmore raised his voice. "Officer Renzo?"

Renzo came out of the stacks with her thumb in the middle of Volume II of *The Decline and Fall of the Roman Empire*. "What's up, Link?"

"Mr. Cooper would like to check the stock market," Whitmore announced.

"So let him."

Whitmore went to the inmate computer table and unlocked a monitor. "There you go."

Bolan glanced at Renzo's reading choice. "Studying for a course?"

"Nope, just reading up on the folks."

"You seem more Sicilian than Roman."

"You are a man of discernment and taste." Renzo perked an eyebrow. "And you have fifteen minutes, convict."

Bolan took a seat, brought up nasdaq.com and typed in his user name and password. Whitmore perched his glasses back on his nose and peered at the scrolling financial data. "You have a very interesting portfolio."

"I have very good adviser." The NASDAQ site Bolan scanned was a Trojan horse set up by the Farm. The stocks he clicked on, or didn't click on, told the Farm that he was all right. He didn't need extraction, and that his recon at Duivelstad was ongoing. This session was also the opening handshake with Kurtzman. From now on Bolan could go onto any computer in D-Town and, if he could get a minute without someone looking over his shoulder, could open a chat window with the Farm. Another interesting fact was that Bolan's War Everlasting had given him access to secrets that the worst of Wall Street's insider traders could only dream about.

Renzo's jaw dropped. "Dude!"

Bolan noted he had gone from convict to dude. "Take notes. I'm at eleven minutes and counting."

Renzo's lovely face went third generation Sicilian prison guard. "And just what kind of debt do you think that will engender?"

"One promise."

Renzo looked at the screen with longing and at Bolan with open disgust. "Try me. Try me and watch what happens."

"Just one thing."

Renzo's hand went to her baton. "What?"

"Just don't step on my feet when you finally club me," Bolan asked. "I'll break my ankles when I fall."

"You are a charming motherfucker, I'll give you that."

"Deal?"

"I will not step on your feet when I beat you down."

"Awesome!"

Bolan clicked a key and looked at his portfolio summary. The graph showed a black line spiking highest. That told Bolan that according to every factor Kurtzman had been able to put into his equation, it was most likely Duivelstad's Puerto Rican population that was digging a tunnel.

Bolan clicked off the dummy NASDAQ. "Can I check sports?"

Renzo leaned in again. "I wish you would."

"Where else can I go?"

Whitmore smiled wanly. "Anywhere within reason, but reason is a very harsh mistress in here."

"Lithuanian lactating lesbian teens dot com?"

Whitmore's face went blank. "God, I wish."

"This session is over!" Renzo declared, but she seemed more bemused than outraged.

Bolan clicked off. "Thanks, Link, Officer Renzo."

"Come anytime, Cooper," Whitmore said.

Bolan rose. He was going to have to have a sit down with Billy the C, and he had just gotten through beating the C Man's best man like a rug.

10

Stony Man Farm, Virginia

"WHO'S THE MAN?" Tokaido whooped.

Price and Kurtzman looked up from a huge stack of files and data crunching respectively. Price narrowed her eyes at Tokaido. "That would be Mack."

Tokaido cringed slightly. "Well, yeah, most definitely, but…" Tokaido suddenly swelled with pride again and pumped his fists. "I rule!"

Kurtzman clicked a key and brought up what Tokaido had been working on. A smile slowly worked its way across his weary face. "You have been busy."

Price leaned over Kurtzman's shoulder and eyed the monitor. "Akira?"

"Yes, Barbara?"

Price sighed. "You do rule."

"They were blind, but now they see…." Tokaido hit a key and every screen in the Computer Room filled with what appeared to be a very strange satellite-image schematic of Duivelstad. "We all know D-Town is the funkiest prison in the U.S. But the Bear figured out if anyone had a tunnel there it was the PR's."

Price frowned in distaste.

"I mean the Puerto Ricans. I mean La Neta. Anyhoo, rather than trying some kind of high imaging route, I got ahold of a Department of the Interior geographical mapping satellite."

Kurtzman nodded happily. "With ground-penetrating radar."

"Between the ancient sulfur mines, the old fortress sewers, the old and new construction, D-Town's underground is a mess. You can see that in the imaging. Just about all of it seems to be sealed off. But if you assume La Netas want a tunnel, and the warden has dispersed them, and they own a corner of Cell Block C…"

Price saw it. A thin line that left C Block and moved across the dead earth space of the yard. It branched into a lower case "y." One branch hit Block A, and the other stopped short of the ancient drainage system. "Billy the C is trying to reach the old sewers."

"He already has, if you ask me. You can see where they screwed up and ran into Block A. The Aryans own that lock stock and barrel, and the C and his people don't want to pop underneath them. I'm chalking that up to Billy the C and his peeps not being master masons. The line to Block A is a straight shot. They screwed up and tunneled along a wrong line. The secondary branch goes straight to the sewers. They figured their shit out."

Price frowned again.

"Sorry. Anyhoo, I think they're just waiting for the right moment to break into the sewers and crawl out."

"So Mack could have an escape route," Price mused.

Kurtzman looked at the image long and hard. "If the C is willing to let him use it, or Mack has the juice or the moxy to take it from him. We need to have a chat with Mack ASAP."

"He hasn't opened one up yet. My best bet is we tweak his Puerto Rican stock portfolio. I know the rule about assuming, but I'm betting Mack gets it."

Price nodded. "I am too. Do it."

Tokaido made the adjustments to the dummy NASDAQ.

Bolan already knew La Neta was the most likely tunneler in Duivelstad. Tokaido had spiked their symbolic stock through the roof with the coded instruction to buy, buy, buy.

RENZO WATCHED THE stock symbolizing the PR tunnel shoot through the roof. "Should I buy?"

Bolan read the tea leaves. "I'd be careful. I'd be very careful." He knew he needed to be very careful, as well. He had pounded Tavo Salcido like a nail, but since then the PRs he passed in the yard gave him distant but respectful nods. Bolan had beaten their champion, but it seemed most of Tavo's fans had managed to switch gears, and wanted to see the soldier take Sawyer Love to the toolshed. Bolan wasn't sure that would be enough to make Billy the C hand over God knew how many months and years of burrowing through the earth with plastic sporks or whatever hand tools they could fashion or steal.

The soldier knew he was going to need some kind of leverage.

Schoenaur swaggered into the library with Zavala at his heels.

The captain almost seemed to be in a good mood. "I want a word with you, Cooper."

Renzo frowned. Bolan was getting the impression the guard captain wasn't much loved by most of the troops.

Schoenaur jerked his head, and Renzo went over to the circulation desk. Bolan clicked off the NASDAQ. The captain spoke low. "Hunger Games. You want it?"

"Do I have a choice?"

"Strangely enough, we try to keep this voluntary, but I wouldn't recommend saying no."

"When?"

"Monday."

Bolan didn't blink. "I still have bruises from Friday."

"It's a command performance. You and Love. The fans want it. The warden wants it."

"I'm in."

"Good."

"What about what I want?"

Schoenaur shrugged. "What do you want?"

"I want to talk to the warden."

"You know, we all figured you'd say that. He's waiting, and he don't like waiting."

Bolan rose and followed Zavala out of the library. Schoenaur fell into step behind him. They took a left turn and went down an empty corridor Bolan had never been in before.

The soldier knew everything had just gone FUBAR.

Bolan spun and ripped a palm heel uppercut Kal would have been proud of. Killing a man by breaking his nose and driving his septum into his brain was a myth. No matter how hard you hit it, the septum just broke into pieces rather than flying into any higher functions like shrapnel. Bolan tried to drive Schoenaur's septum into his brain, anyway. The captain of the guards rubbernecked as the bridge of his nose shattered. Bolan spun on Zavala.

Pennsylvania karma came around as two stun gun probes hit Bolan square in the chest and Zavala held his trigger down. Voltage rocketed along the soldier's every nerve ending. He had been hit with electricity before and had withstood it. He took the voltage now. Zavala gasped in horror as Bolan shuddered like a palsy victim and spoke in tongues as he ripped the probes out of his chest by the wires.

Zavala clawed for his baton. "Oh, God! Oh, God!" Bolan took a step forward and regretted not having killed Schoenaur. He heard the guard captain drawing behind him, but the juicing had turned Bolan's muscles to jelly and his bones to clay. He turned as if he was twisting in quicksand.

Bolan's body locked like tetanus as Schoenaur's stun gun probes hit his lower back. His legs failed him with the second hit, and he collapsed to the floor. He writhed in a human electrical circuit of hell as Schoenaur held the trigger down and drained the battery into him.

The soldier convulsed in the fetal position as if he was having a seizure.

Schoenaur held his blood-streaming, broken beak as he clicked his radio. "Cleanup on aisle four." Blood poured down the front of the guard captain's khaki uniform blouse as he clicked in a fresh cassette of probes. "That is going to cost you, Cooper."

Bolan's world went white as Schoenaur hit him with electricity again. The soldier barely heard Zavala's voice rise in concern. "Captain, you're going to fry his brain, or give him a heart attack."

"Naw, Cooper's a genuine hard-ass. Aren't you, Cooper?"

Two corrections officers burst out of a door and came running down the corridor. One was black, huge and had a shaved head. The other was white, just as tall, with a shaved head as well, but as lanky as a scarecrow. Both men looked leerily at Schoenaur's mutilated face, but reserved comment.

"RayRay, Stu, escort Cooper into the lounge."

Bolan felt himself being seized and dragged down the corridor to the door the new guards had come through. RayRay and Stu bum-rushed him through it. Bolan sprawled onto ancient tiles. There wasn't much loungy about the lounge. It was a bare stone cube of a room with a tile floor that had a suspicious drain in the middle of it. A coil of hose hung on a hook, connected to a spigot. An ancient, opened canvas tool sat in one corner. Bolan caught sight of the implements beside it and knew the hurt locker had just yawned open and swallowed him. He spied two lengths of rubber hose. They were stiff like sausages and both ends had been plugged. In Bolan's youth such weapons had been known euphemistically as "whompers," and the wrong sort of cops had used them to administer back-alley order among the local African-American youth.

Of far more concern was the Lancaster County telephone book with a square-headed metal-shaping hammer on top.

"Cooper, I would like you to meet Officers Johnson and Stewart. We call them the wrecking crew around here, and they are about to make a wreck out of you."

For one moment, Bolan considered rising.

Schoenaur and Zavala hadn't reloaded their stun guns and didn't have guns. If he was willing to maim and kill, the soldier knew he could take Zavala, and was pretty sure he could take Schoenaur. Other than the fact that they were very large men and trained corrections officers, Johnson and Stewart were unknown quantities, but they turned the odds to the tune of four to one, and Bolan had just been electrocuted three times. The rubber hoses and the phone book told him they weren't allowed to kill him.

He steeled himself.

What happened next was just going to have to be endured.

"RayRay, Stu? Take his legs. He went all jungle-boy and stripped down last time against Tavo, so no bruises up top and no head shots, but hurt him bad." Schoenaur turned to leave.

RayRay frowned. "You don't wanna watch?"

"Naw, I gotta go clean up." Schoenaur smiled at Bolan past bloody teeth and the flattened squid that had once been his nose. "I'll watch him fight Love."

Schoenaur left with Zavala in tow, and they closed the steel door behind them. There was no preamble or conversation. RayRay and Stu went to work.

The rubber hoses began falling like rain.

"UP AND AT 'em!" Fatty Barnes called. "And you have a visitor in half an hour, Coop!"

The bars in Cell Block C rattled on their tracks and clanged open. Inmates bitched, moaned and groaned and roused themselves for the morning count. Bolan gritted his teeth as he sat up and put his bare feet on the cold concrete. He hadn't slept more than five minutes at a stretch through the night. He'd spent the time trying to find any position that was comfortable. There had been none. When he shifted, burning fire shot through his body. Rudy had taken one look at Bolan after the beating and let him have the bottom bunk again. The soldier arose feeling as if the sky had opened and poured forth bowling balls. The rubber hoses had turned the muscles of his legs to rubber. His joints felt like hot sand. He limped toward the urinal like a fourteen-year-old dog with hip dysplasia and put a hand on the wall to steady himself.

The internal damage was worse.

The telephone book was to prevent overt surface blunt trauma bruising. RayRay had held it in place while Stu had used Bolan like an anvil, strategically striking over the soldier's right kidney and left lower abdomen.

Bolan kept his moan of agony behind his teeth as he painted the bowl red.

"Jesus." Rudy's face told Bolan all he needed to know about his condition. "You're all fucked up."

A number of responses came to mind. "Yeah…" was all Bolan managed.

"You're fighting Love Monday night. It's all over the blocks."

"Yeah."

"You're going to be even worse off tomorrow."

Bolan grunted in agreement.

Rudy's face twisted. Bolan duly noted the hacker's concern and put it in the man's plus column. Rudy shook his head. "What the hell are you going to do?"

"Win."

"You're going to beat Love? In your condition?"

"Do I have a choice?" Bolan asked.

"Not so much."

Bolan hobbled back to the bunk and sat down gingerly. "So how was your day, honey?"

"You know, you really shouldn't talk like that in here," Rudy warned.

"Sorry. What's happening on your end?"

"Oh, Link is being a pain, as usual."

"How so?"

"Well, I like him. Hell, everybody likes him. He's a genuinely nice guy, who has a kind word for everyone. He's taught a bunch of inmates to read over the years and doesn't ask anything in return. Everyone knows he's a junkie. He has some kind of stipend that comes in, and he mostly spends it on junk. Sometimes you can see him shaking, but he's never borrowed money or stolen from anyone."

"So what's the problem?" Bolan asked.

"The Big U wants all of D-Town's computers modernized, and with Link it's like pulling teeth. I swear the guy still uses floppy disks. I mean, I get it, the library and the computers are his place of power in here, and some part of him must resent that I'm here disassembling a system he spent years building up out of nothing. But Christ, every single file I need is a battle, and he insists on giving them to me one at a time, and only after he's cleaned them up himself. I've seen his hard drive—it's not like he has some secret stash of porn in there—but I swear, every single file is in the weirdest, trippiest code you ever saw. It's like he wrote it himself."

Bolan's kept his voice neutral as he rose. "Well, that sucks."

Rudy followed him out. "What?"

"Can you break it?"

The hacker blinked. "What?"

"Given that you know Link, you've seen his code and seen it translated, can you break his code?"

"Uh, that's not normally what I do. I usually Trojan horse my way into people's files rather than actively break code."

"Can you?"

"I can try," Rudy said.

"Do it."

Officer Barnes came back from his taking his count. "You ready, Cooper? The warden and your visitor are waiting. Word is that it's your blond lady friend."

Bolan steeled himself not to limp. "Let's do it."

BARBARA PRICE READ Bolan's body language and didn't like what she saw.

OK? she blinked.

Bolan blinked back.

HURT.

"So what the hell do you want now?" Bolan snarled.

"Same thing I wanted last time, and I'm running out of patience," Price said.

OUT? She asked with her eyes.

"Shove it," Bolan said.

NO, he blinked.

"Now that's just not polite."

This meeting had come completely out of the blue. The only reason Bolan could see for it was that something bad had happened, and Price was here to warn him. Bolan got his answer a second later.

TUCKER, Price blinked.

Bolan kept his feelings off his face. He had expected Tucker and Dale to get picked up, just not processed and dumped back into D-Town this fast. Bolan suspected priors and not being able to post bail had gotten the wannabe Regulators posthasted back into population while awaiting arraignment.

"Shove polite."

WHEN? Bolan asked.

TOMORROW, Price confirmed.

Bolan rubbed his temples and blinked rapidly.

FIGHT TOMORROW NIGHT.

WE KNOW.

Bolan sighed. "So what do you want?"

"Next week, you are going to have a visitor who really wants to talk to you. My advice is that you sing like a bird."

"And if I don't?" Bolan asked.

"Cooper, you've put me in an awkward spot. You won't be reasoned with, and it seems you can't be intimidated. This is your last shot, Cooper. You either start using the brains your momma gave you or someone is going to have to pound them out of your head."

Warden Linder smirked slightly at his desk.

"I'll sleep on it."

"You do that." Price gave Bolan a cold look and made a phone out of her hand with her thumb and little finger. "You have a change of heart, call me."

Barnes escorted Price out.

The warden heaved a sigh. "You know, Captain Schoenaur isn't pleased with you. He wants to be your opponent tomorrow, except I won't let him."

"He only says that because he knows you won't let him." Bolan's smile was like a wolf skinning its teeth. "Let him."

Linder's face went blank for a moment, and then he threw back his head and laughed. "Well, now, that might be true, Cooper. But you have humiliated the man twice, and I hear you made Zavala scream in fear like a little girl."

Zavala bristled.

"You're right, Cooper. Schoenaur doesn't want a piece of you in a fight, fair or otherwise. He wants your ass, and it's gnawing at him, and sooner or later he may just forget my orders, jump the reservation and have his way with you, the hard way, with you in restraints, while he paints his picture of revenge, mostly in red."

"Didn't know you were a poet, Warden."

"And do you think I'll be able to do anything about it? Do you know what the correctional unions are like in this state? They're pit bulls, Cooper. I'll be lucky if I can give him a written reprimand."

"Is there something I can do for you, Warden?"

"Yes. Sing, anything and everything you are or are not going to tell your DOJ visitor Wednesday."

"And if I don't?"

"Cooper, we both know you're going to get hurt very badly tomorrow. But if you satisfy me that you've told me everything of possible interest, I'll have Love take it as easy on you as he can."

"Some choice."

"We're talking the difference of a hope of you limping into that meeting, or driving a wheelchair to it with your tongue. I'm getting the idea your lady friend won't care which."

Bolan was silent.

"I bet your wife will."

The soldier put some rage into his face.

"You know, I hate to say this, but Mr. Love has been informed of your date with the wrecking crew." Bolan had suspected that. Linder leaned his elbows on his desk and his smile was sickening. "Tell me, Cooper. How do you feel?"

Bolan smiled back. "Right as rain."

Linder's face went flat and he leaned back. "You can have as much food as you want, if you can hold it down." The warden shook his head at Bolan as if the soldier was an idiot who couldn't be reached. "Get some sleep. You're going to need it."

11

TUCKER ENTERED THE cell block sweating with fear as he did the walk. The cons smelled it instantly, and their cacophony of intimidation rose to thunder. Toilet paper rolls sailed down like streamers at a very unpleasant parade. Word had gone out that the newbie was a Lancaster County Regulator, but Tucker wasn't making a good first impression. Even his erstwhile Aryan allies frowned. Barnes escorted the new prisoner into the population, whispering furiously for him to buck up.

Bolan stepped out from behind a column. "Hey."

Barnes blinked. "Cooper?"

Tucker started to turn his head to look Bolan's way.

The soldier swung. In kung fu it was known as an ox-hand blow. It was really a karate chop, but using just the pisiform carpal bone in the bottom of the heel of the hand. It was interesting how that knob of bone fit like a key into the hollow of the temples or the solar plexus. That knob of bone also dovetailed perfectly against the mandible where it met the skull. Bolan slammed his pisiform into the left side of Tucker's face an inch before his ear.

Tucker's eyes rolled as his mandible unhinged and he dropped broken-jawed and unconscious to the floor.

Barnes's baton rasped from its retaining ring as he took a step back. "Jesus Christ, Cooper! What the fuck!"

Bolan stood over his prey, but lowered his hands. "Regulators? That's just more Nazi fucking effluvium as far as I'm concerned."

Barnes pointed his baton at Bolan in warning. "Cooper! Stand down!"

"Do me a favor, would you, Officer Barnes?"

Barnes's left hand went to his belt and the sheathed canister there. "Would that be before or after I pepper spray you and beat you into oblivion?"

Bolan stood with his hands at his sides. "Either will do."

Barnes couldn't help his curiosity. "What?"

The entirety of C Block held its breath to hear the answer.

The soldier smiled. "Tell Love I'm fit as a fucking fiddle, and when the Hunger Games are done I'm going to shit biscuits and gravy on his grave."

C Block exploded into cheers.

Bolan watched Barnes do the math. Everyone knew Schoenaur and Zavala had escorted Bolan away from the library. Everyone had seen or heard about the state of Schoenaur's face. Everyone knew about the wrecking crew. The current state of health of the inmate named Cooper was a constant source of speculation, and had sent the betting on the Hunger Games in wild directions.

Bolan had dropped a punk card named Tucker on the ground for Scott and Love.

He had also put Tucker in the infirmary for a week, eating through a straw and incommunicado, and Bolan was a good ninety percent sure Tucker hadn't had time to process and recognize him before he had been knocked unconscious.

Barnes slowly lowered his club. "I'll tell him you said that."

"Thank you, Officer Barnes."

"Now, I want you to go to your cell, send out Rudy and Patrick, and sit on your bunk until I or any other guard say otherwise."

Bolan nodded. "Will do, Officer."

He received a standing ovation. It took every ounce of will to not show what the act of walking downstairs and taking out Tucker had done to him.

"WELL THAT WAS interesting," the warden commented. He sat in a small council of war with Schoenaur, Scott and Officer Johnson. "What's the story on this Tucker?"

Scott sighed. "He's Lancaster Regulators, and a probie. We're affiliated with the Regulators. From what little I know, Tucker seems to be about as baffled as Adam on Mother's Day, real yes-and-no kind of guy."

"And so Cooper took him out because?"

"Well, I suspect that was a message to me, Warden," Scott replied. "And you."

Linder looked to his guard captain. "Anything of interest on this Tucker?"

Schoenaur spoke nasally through the bandages taped to his

face. "Only thing of note is he was picked up near the Lancaster fire."

Both Linder and Scott stared for long moments. "And?" Linder prompted.

"He was smoky and sooty, with nothing much to say for himself. He was on probation and had a previous warrant out. His return ticket to D-Town while awaiting arraignment is a no-brainer."

Scott turned to the warden. "I think maybe Cooper shouldn't leave that ring alive."

"I don't like coincidences any more than you, Force, but I'm having a hard time putting Guantanamo Bay and Lancaster on the same page. On top of that the DOJ is riding Cooper like a government mule."

Scott shrugged. "So what are they going to do? I mean, really, what are they going to do about it? Raid D-Town? Close it down?"

"Scrutinize," the warden replied.

"There is that."

"Probably not enough or in time to do anything, but we just don't need the hassle right now. We can take out Cooper at any time."

Linder turned a cold eye on Officer Johnson. "Speaking of Cooper, I'm curious about the fact that he even had the gumption to go downstairs and take Tucker out in the first place. RayRay, I thought you and Stu had put some hurt on the man."

Johnson shifted uncomfortably. "Warden, we pounded him like a nail, and the captain gave strict orders to handicap Cooper for Love, not put him in the infirmary."

Schoenaur grunted. "Those were my orders, and in RayRay's defense, Fatty seems to have a good relationship with Cooper. He never saw it coming, and Cooper blindsided Tucker ugly, another one of those nasty-ass shots he seems to specialize in."

Linder kept his eye on his wrecker. "RayRay, tell me Cooper is not ready for Love."

"He'll be able to walk to the ring, put his hands up, maybe do some of that nasty-ass Special Forces shit if Love is dumb. But he won't be able to stick and move. When it goes to the ground, which it always does with Love, Cooper'll only have two limbs of any use. If Love gets in any kind of trouble, one leg sweep and Cooper goes down and doesn't get back up. One body shot, front or back, Cooper shits out his liver on live TV."

"Force," Linder asked, "you still want it?"

"Yeah, and Love definitely wants it. He knows everything Officer Johnson just said. He'll take his time, break Cooper down, and then administer some real pain, blues and agony."

"We want him alive, walking out alive or carried out, but alive."

"Nothing is certain in life, but I predict Cooper will remember what Love does to him for the rest of his days, when it rains. That is, if he lives long enough to see rain again." Scott looked around the room at Warden Linder, Schoenaur and Johnson. "And somehow I have the feeling that is just not happening."

KAL STRODE INTO the cell flanked by Marilyn and Black Widow. Rudy and Patrick looked up in shock. Bolan was in too much pain to care. Kal gazed down at Bolan critically. "How bad is it?"

"I'm awesome."

"Strip," Kal ordered. Bolan laboriously levered himself up on the edge of the bed and struggled to get his pants off. Kal shook his head. "Help him."

Marilyn and Black Widow peeled off Bolan's dungarees. Marilyn gasped. Black Widow started to cry. Bolan's legs were sheathed in vast swathes of black and purple welts from the rubber hoses. His bruises had bruises, and those bruises swam in their own nebulae of blues and yellows. There wasn't much recognizable Caucasian flesh left. Kal produced two small brown bottles with labels covered in Chinese characters. Bolan raised a hopeful eyebrow as Marilyn and Black Widow pulled off his socks. "Dit Da Jow?"

Kal nodded. Dit Da Jow was a Chinese bruise liniment favored by Asian martial artists. It was popularly known as hit medicine, and God only knew Bolan had taken some hits recently. "Where'd you get it?"

"The Asians in D-Town are housed as a unit in D Block. A guy named Gau runs them and runs the heroin traffic in here. Link introduced me years ago. Every six months when I renew my Iron Palm training I have them smuggle me in some." Kal held up the first bottle. This is 'cold' liniment. We're going to hit you with it now, before bed, and when you get up in the morning, to try to deal with the bruising and soft-tissue damage. This one is 'hot.' It's too soon for it, but we don't have any choice. We hit you with that midday and right before the fight, so you're at least some kind of limber."

"Thanks, Kal."

"Lay back." Kal tossed the first bottle to Marilyn. "Ladies."

Marilyn poured some liniment into her palm and rubbed her hands together. "Ooh!"

Black Widow did the same.

The ladies went to work on Bolan's legs. He gritted his teeth and stopped just short of writhing. The "cold" liniment wasn't. Tingling, burning and prickling sensations began fighting with the throbbing and the pain of bruised flesh being pushed around by feminine hands that were anything but.

Kal smiled in mixed sympathies. "No need to be gentle, ladies. Rub it in good and do it again. Front and back."

Rudy and Patrick watched the proceedings in fascinated horror. Bolan focused, took a deep breath and forced himself to relax.

"They give you the phone book and the hammer?" Kal asked.

Bolan sighed as he genuinely relaxed into his therapy. "Just below the rib cage on the right in back, and low to the left abdomen in front."

"Kidney and colon." Kal's face twisted with anger. "You peeing blood?"

"Like a racehorse."

"Motherfuckers. Here."

Kal produced one last bottle.

It was a standard water bottle from the commissary that appeared to have been used as a spittoon. Bolan eyed the brown backwash that filled about a fifth of the container. "This is a personal gift from Gau," Kal explained. "I have no clue, except that I figure it must be some kind of Chinese prison pruno internal medicine. He told me to tell you to take half now and half tomorrow, and to kill that motherfucker Love."

Bolan took the bottle and chugged down half of what tasted like yard clippings that had been simmered in a provocative broth of old gym shoes. "Awesome."

"Ladies, put some of the hot on his belly, and use the cold on his lower back and kidneys when you flip him over."

Bolan's back felt like rigor mortis and his guts like a broken furnace leaking coal embers. Whatever Gau had sent along blossomed in the soldier's stomach. He let out a long belch and some of his pain seemed not necessarily to ease, but to turn from agony into some sensation that could only be described as strange. Yet the change was welcome. Bolan sighed involuntarily and sagged into his bunk.

Kal nodded. "I'll be back later." He tipped his head at Rudy and Patrick, and they followed him out.

Marilyn winked and whispered as she began rubbing "hot" against Bolan's belly. "Happy ending?"

"I'm in training."

Marilyn tossed off a "your loss" kind of shrug.

"But if a happy ending is tomorrow night I win and you ladies get a chicken dinner—" Bolan let out another sigh "—then winner, winner chicken dinner and that happy ending is definitely on."

BOLAN SIGHED AND kicked the flush pedal.

It wasn't good, but the bowl was a pale pink rather than scarlet, and his morning ablution came with a dull ache rather than the sensation of urinating battery acid. It was better, and he could feel his legs beneath him as if they were actually a part of his body. Kal, Gau, Chinese medicine, a few hours of sleep and the strictly chaperoned fingers of the ladies of Cell Block C had done him a world of good. Bolan did a slow deep knee bend. His battered legs protested, but they obeyed. He twisted through a few slow-motion repetitions of kickboxing knee-to-elbow lifts and was pleased his insides didn't squirt fire. He could move. He could fight. But if Love managed to land one solid fist or, God help him, a knee or a kick to the gut, Bolan was fairly sure his insides would tear apart like old wet towels and slide out of him.

But the soldier felt he had at least a shot at staying out of a wheelchair, and failure wasn't an option.

Rudy leaned on the tier railing outside and flashed a flash drive. Bolan walked out onto the tier without a discernable limp. "Is that what I think it is?"

"I downloaded a bunch of Link's files. I'm pretty sure he won't know."

"How sure?"

"Like, fifty-fifty."

Bolan gazed around C Block. "In here those aren't bad odds."

"No, they're not."

"Did you break the code?" Bolan asked.

"Not yet, but would you like some more good news?"

"I could use some."

"You saw the movie *Shawshank Redemption?*" Rudy asked.

"Yeah, bits and pieces here and there."

"You remember how the hero was a banker and got a leg over on the inside by doing the guards' taxes for them?"

Bolan smiled at the good news. "The guards ask you for help with their laptops."

"And their phones, and their iPads, and downloading the latest patch on World of Warcraft, why they're having problems posting videos on YouTube, pirating first run movies. You name it." Rudy produced a pencil and a piece of paper without being asked.

Bolan wrote down an internet address and a password that would attract the Farm's attention. "Memorize that, then eat it."

Rudy glanced at the paper once and popped it in his mouth with a grin.

"You have any clients with an internet connection today?" Bolan asked. "I may not be around after tomorrow's Hunger Games."

"Yeah, Barnes."

Bolan's brow furrowed. He liked Barnes.

Rudy read Bolan's mind. "Yeah, I like him, too. He'd lose his job if it came back on him. Of course, if it comes back on me, a visit to the lounge with the wrecking crew is probably the best I can hope for. But by the same token, Barnes is technically illiterate. I can send the data to whoever you want while he's watching, and he'll thank me for it."

Patrick came out onto the tier bearing the last of the internal hemorrhage home brew. "Time to take your medicine, Coop."

Bolan reminded himself not to breath through his nose, and downed about half of it.

"So what does it taste like?" Patrick asked.

"It tastes like Chinese medicine." Bolan held out the bottle. "You want some?"

Patrick held up his hands. "No, man, it's for you. You need it." He nodded and polished off his medicine.

"So," Rudy asked. "Barnes, today?"

"Do it."

Bolan handed Patrick the empty bottle. "You get what I asked for?"

"Bobbie-John got it for me, but yeah." Patrick looked both ways and handed over a tube of wood repair epoxy stolen from the workshop. "I don't think Love is going to stand around while you try to glue his feet to the floor."

"I expect you're right."

"So what's it for?" Patrick asked.

"I'm going to sniff it before the fight."

The young man gaped. "You're kidding."

"Yeah, I am, but I need to ask you for one more favor."

"What's that?"

"Lend me your toothbrush."

Patrick stared at the glue. "You're kidding."

"No—" Bolan shook his head "—I'm not."

12

The Computer Room, Stony Man Farm, Virginia

"BEAR!" TOKAIDO SHOUTED. "You need to look at this!"

Aaron Kurtzman tapped a key and his screen filled with files. He heaved a huge sigh of relief. Bolan had found a way to communicate outside the library. Kurtzman chose a file with the provocative title Look Familiar?.doc. It opened simultaneously on Tokaido's screen and the young hacker made the appropriate response. "Holy shit!"

Kurtzman nodded. Holy shit was right. It was different, less advanced to the computer expert's eye, but it looked distinctly like the code Bolan had captured from the Lancaster farm before it had gone up in flames. He opened a file called Suggestions. doc. It was a short, bulleted list of someone's progress on breaking the code, and possible word matches. Kurtzman shook his head. "This is above Mack's pay grade when it comes to computers. Who sent this?"

"Tracking…" Tokaido rapidly clicked keys. "It came through a private server, but a service area that includes Duivelstad's county. Definitely came from within D-Town." His forefinger hovered. "If do this we're breaking U.S. privacy law and violating a state employee's—"

"Do it."

He clicked. "It came from the laptop of Officer Barnes." Tokaido pulled up Barnes's records from the hacked Duivelstad employee files and stared at the man smiling happily in his photo ID. "I can't imagine this guy being in cahoots on this."

"No, I think Mack got this Rudolpho guy he told Carmen about to take a big chance." Kurtzman began opening more files. The disk Bolan had retrieved from the Lancaster probe was damaged. This new information might just be enough to plug the gaps. That and the suggestions Rudolpho had sent along would— The computer expert stopped on a file and smiled. "Akira! Prisoner records! Look up everything D-Town has on file for one Whitmore, Lincoln Cornelius, aka 'Link,' and then I want his entire life story from cradle to conviction."

"Bear, it's fight night in fifteen minutes," Tokaido warned.

Kurtzman sighed. "I know."

Duivelstad Prison

"FIVE MINUTES!" ZAVALA'S voice echoed in the locker room as he shouted through the door. Marilyn rubbed Bolan's shoulders. Rudy was in the gym coordinating the AV feed, but the younger Rudolpho was in the locker room acting as Bolan's manager. The soldier self-assessed. He'd had his two "hot" Chinese hit medicine treatments this day, three rubdowns and two showers as hot as he could stand it.

Bolan figured he was operating at a pretty solid twenty-seven percent of optimal.

He had fought wounded many times before, wounded far worse than he was now. The only difference was that here the battle had rules. Bolan never fought by any rules other than his own, but this battle was a horrible, artificial construct. The rules of the Hunger Games were simple and there were only three of them: no eyes, no balls, and except for chokes and strangles, no throat attacks.

That took far too much for liking out of Bolan's arsenal, wounded and outweighed as he was.

"Coop?" Patrick asked.

"Yeah."

"Remember that joke you told about sniffing the glue?"

Bolan was pretty sure where this was going. "Yeah."

Patrick had a bad habit of looking both ways before he produced contraband in prison. He literally pulled a mixed bag of powder and pills out of his pants. "I figured if you wanted it, you would have asked for it, but I also figured maybe you're the kind of who wouldn't ask for it even if you did need it."

"Thanks." Bolan eyed the bag. "Meth?"

"I wouldn't dignify it with the name, but yeah, it's crank."

"No, thanks. The pills?"

"OxyContin."

Bolan thought about that long and hard. Banishing the pain was a terrible temptation in his condition, but by the same token his condition was the condition he was in. His guts were a mess, and the only food he'd been able to tolerate in the last twenty-four hours were flavored gelatin, butterscotch pudding and milk. In a battle with Love, Bolan couldn't afford the likely side effects of nausea or light-headedness. "No, but thanks."

"I figured, so I figure after we can—"

Bolan tilted his head toward the toilets. "Flush it."

"What!"

"You don't deal and you don't use, not in front of me and not while you live in my house, and your father wouldn't approve."

Patrick was appalled. "You know what this cost me?"

"I appreciate that, and I don't care."

Marilyn spoke quietly as she kneaded Bolan's traps. "I'll take the oxy, and Widow definitely wants the crank."

Bolan had voluntarily stepped into the worst maximum-security prison in the United States. He had known he would have to leave most of his scruples at the gate. By the same token his circumstances made paying his debts a samurai-like duty.

"You heard the lady."

"But—"

"I owe the ladies, Patrick, and that means you do, too."

Patrick manned up admirably. He grinned and handed over the bag to Marilyn. "Thank you, and thank Widow, for all your help."

Marilyn beamed in so similar a fashion as her namesake it was heartbreaking. "You're most certainly welcome."

"Showtime!" Zavala bawled. Marilyn made the baggie disappear and resumed shoulder rubbing as Zavala marched in. He scowled as Bolan laced up his prison issues. "Shoes?"

"I jammed my toes bad on Tavo." Bolan gave Zavala a bitter look. "And we both know I'm not throwing a lot of round kicks tonight."

Zavala grinned nastily. "No, no you're not. Now let's see if your girlfriend or your bitch slipped you anything. Weapons check."

Marilyn stepped back as Bolan rose. The soldier held out his arms as Zavala gave him a final pat down before the fight.

Zavala had already missed it.

"Let's go."

Patrick stuck out his hand. "Coop, cripple the dick."

Bolan shook his hand. "I will."

Marilyn took out a lipstick and painted her mouth red. She tilted her head coquettishly. "For luck?"

Bolan bent down and presented his right cheek.

Marilyn branded her favorite animal.

Bolan figured the fans would love it. He cracked his knuckles at Zavala. "Let's do it."

The permanent scowl Zavala had developed since Bolan's incarceration deepened. "Your funeral, fuck face."

Bolan followed him into the gym with Marilyn in tow.

The crowd erupted at his entrance.

The audience was bigger than last time. Bolan was pretty sure some of the cons had paid the warden for the privilege of ringside seats. He was shocked to see Kal in the audience, but kept it off his face. Kal nodded once and spoke a single word. It was lost among the cheering and whistling, but anyone could have read his lips.

"Win."

Black Widow smiled and blew Bolan kisses. Marilyn blew kisses into the crowd. Bolan's fans were slightly in the minority, but vocal. His detractors sat in conspicuous silence as he entered. The Aryans suddenly stood with Nazi-like precision, *sieg heiled* as a unit and began chanting, "Love! Love! Love!"

Bolan considered his opponent as he approached the ring. Sawyer Love usually radiated adrenaline. It wasn't good that he stood in the ring simply looking relaxed and ready. The Mad Dog was in his zone. He'd broken a sweat back in his locker room, and he lazily shifted his weight from foot to foot and rolled his head. He wore mixed marital arts trunks and fingerless gloves. His head was freshly shaved.

The new addition to the ring was a gate, but it was still topped with razor wire. Bolan didn't feel much like climbing tables, and welcomed it. The crowd hushed as he stepped into the ring and the gate was locked behind him. Bolan was six foot three and two hundred twenty pounds. He was an impressive figure of a man. Even without steroids, Sawyer Love was a freak of nature. It was a pure David versus Goliath matchup. Bolan was sure the fans on pay-per-view were going berserk. His problem was that David was peeing blood, there wasn't a sling in sight and the only stone was the floor beneath them.

Schoenaur raised his revolver off camera.

Love ran his eyes up and down Bolan, trying to read what kind of shape he was in. The Mad Dog didn't make any boasts or threats. This wasn't the mess hall or the yard. Sawyer Love was a genuine twenty-first century gladiator, and he let his actions speak for him. They were actions people in Tokyo, Hong Kong, Moscow and various points east and west were willing to pay five figures to watch. He nodded once. "Coop."

Bolan nodded back. "Love."

Cheers and jeers restarted.

Schoenaur's Magnum revolver echoed in the gym like a cannon shot.

Love just stood waiting.

Bolan looked right, looked left and spit on Love's chest.

The crowd howled.

The Mad Dog never took his eyes off Bolan. "Nice."

"What does it take to motivate you?" Bolan asked.

"Blood, your blood," Love answered. "And the more of it I see the more motivated I'm gonna get."

"Nice." Bolan stepped to his left.

Love instantly dropped into a crouch and brought up his hands. He kept his eyes on Bolan's crippled legs, watching to see how he moved. The soldier shook his head, curled his hands into claws and spit on the floor. He grimaced and put his toe in his spit and smeared it in a line across the concrete.

The audience started going crazy.

Love smiled. "Nice."

"Fuck you." Bolan beckoned him. "Come within reach of these hands and watch what happens, you son of a bitch."

Both men knew Bolan wanted Love to come in and take something terrible in exchange for taking the soldier down. Love started juking and jiving. It wasn't quite the Ali shuffle, but it cost Bolan to keep his opponent in front of him, and he lost sovereignty over his spit line.

The Aryans lost their professional mien and screamed for blood. "Fuck him up! Kill him! Kill him!"

Love raised his right foot for a leg kick. Bolan gritted his teeth and shuffled backward awkwardly, away from the threat.

For the first time pure venom dripped from Love's lips as he pictured Bolan's Waterloo perfectly in his mind. "Nice…"

Bolan took a big step forward and cocked his hands.

Love raised his own in defense.

The Executioner did his own Ali shuffle and switched from left to right foot forward. He cocked his hip and threw the hardest left round kick of his life. He hadn't been able to sleep more than an hour or two at a time for the past twenty-four. So he had spent it painting coats of clear epoxy across the toes of his shoes, and while they dried he had painted coats inside. The epoxy was guaranteed to dry within six hours. During World War II the OSS—the Office of Strategic Services, precursor to the CIA—had issued steel-toed dress shoes to its undercover agents with instructions on the worst places to apply them to a human body. Bolan had gotten four coats of epoxy in, both inside and out.

He drove the toe of his shoe into Love's outer right thigh just above his knee.

The problem with epoxy resin was that it was brittle. Bolan felt the epoxy fracture, but the damage was done. Love gasped and staggered back with the impact. Bolan cocked his right hand for the kill. Love raised his own hands in a predictable high guard, and tottered on his remaining leg.

Bolan shifted his stance and threw his right round kick high.

The soldier's homemade foot fortress dovetailed like a custom-made battering ram into Love's left armpit. Sawyer Love's face went white with shock and his jaw went slack.

There was a reason why, when humans had heart attacks, the first major sign was tingling down the left arm. The nerve bundles under the armpits were bad places to get hit. The human heart was on the left side of the body and the nerves there went straight to it. When martial arts had first become popular in the United States, in the fifties and sixties, most books published by the Asian masters incorporated a striking chart, and the effect of a hard strike deep into the left armpit was usually described as "possible death." In modern martial arts circles it was debated whether this was hyperbole or myth.

Sawyer Love dropped to the concrete.

The crowd in Duivelstad turned into the coliseum of ancient Rome.

Pieces of clothing, including a white dress, and food were flung into the ring as tribute. Bolan raised his fists in victory for the cameras.

"Bring me a bigger one!"

The Aryans recovered from their shock, and flying folding chairs followed screams of hatred and rage. Everyone in the audience had been weapon-checked, but fists and folding chairs sufficed as the Hunger Games devolved into a bench-clearing brawl.

Zavala shouted a well-known refrain over a megaphone. "Tear gas and sting balls! Five! Four! Three…"

Schoenaur pointed his .357 Magnum revolver at Bolan's head. "Stand down, Cooper!"

Bolan's gaze narrowed. "Love needs a defibrillator right now."

Schoenaur was clearly fighting his every instinct to shoot Bolan.

The soldier shouted above the noise like the sergeant he had once been. "Defib, Schoenaur! Now!"

Schoenaur was quite possibly the most corrupt correctional officer in the continental United States, but he was a trained professional and his training took over. "Zavala! AED ringside! Now!"

Bolan glanced over at Scott.

The Aryan Circle leader shook his head and cut his thumb across his throat, silently saying the soldier was dead.

Bolan forked his fingers at his eyes, shook his head and pointed back at Scott.

No, you.

Bolan buckled as he was hit with a Taser from behind.

The Computer Room, Stony Man Farm, Virginia

"OH…MY…GOD…" Barbara Price couldn't believe her eyes. She had seen Bolan operate on satellite imaging and gray security camera footage. She had seen him in desperate battle in person, but those few times had been in the fog of war. This was her second and most brutal Mack Bolan pay-per-view. A man lay at his feet. Bolan raised his hands in victory as fan debris rained into the ring. A revolver held by a man whose face was just off camera rose toward his head over the razor wire. The soldier dropped to the floor as silver wires spun into his back.

Then the camera cut out.

Tokaido couldn't contain himself. "Toe kick to the heart! I thought that was a myth!"

"What the hell is wrong with you!" Price shouted.

Tokaido searched for an answer that wouldn't put him in the doghouse. "Barbara, like we won. Mack won."

Kurtzman spoke quietly. "Barbara, he's right. Mack just bought himself breathing room, and by your own recon Mack's hurt badly. If he had lost, Love would have put him on a gurney and they would have had forty-eight hours to decide whether he lived or died, or done God knows what to him to extract information. Now, I don't think they'll dare mess with him until after your meeting on Wednesday. It's worth celebrating, and you need to start thinking about your strategy for the visit."

"You're right." Price slowly decompressed. "I just can't stand watching it."

"So don't."

"Last I heard we were helping Mack with this mission, and I'm the mission controller around here. I have to."

Price squashed her emotions and squared her shoulders. "Aaron?"

"Yes, ma'am?"

"Let's see it again. Frame by frame. There are definitely differences and new faces since the Tavo fight."

"On it," Kurtzman confirmed.

13

C Block, Unit 12

BOLAN ATE TAPIOCA pudding in Marilyn and Black Widow's cell and watched Team Cooper eat steak. Rudy, Patrick, Bobbie-John and the ladies gorged themselves. A half bottle of D Block, Chinese triad froth had appeared in Bolan's cell by magic, and he concentrated on slowly ingesting the internal medicine and eating soft foods. Bolan was the hero of the hour in D-Town. Love had literally died at Bolan's hands and required herculean efforts to resuscitate. The "toe of death" was already a thing of legend. The Mad Dog was currently on display in the infirmary next to the Todd, Rollin and Tucker.

Bolan had a nice little streak going.

He also felt like hell. The two kicks he had thrown had undone all the work the hit medicine had done for him. Everything had started swelling again, and his bruises once more throbbed down to the bone.

Still, victory was sweet.

The soldier's every instinct told him that Link Whitmore was code source. Bolan looked up to see Kal leaning in the cell doorway. "A genuine toe kick to the heart. Man, you only read about that in old karate books. Hell, you don't even read about it. That technique falls under the category of arcane reference."

"Saved you a steak."

Black Widow giggled, blushed and handed Kal a large foam container and a sweet tea. Kal opened the box and raised an eyebrow. "You saved me two steaks."

"No, it's a porterhouse," Bolan said. "They took out the T-bones so we couldn't shank anyone with them. According to rumor the salad isn't anything to write home about, but you probably won't see hearts of romaine and baby spinach again for a while. I hear the baked potato is awesome." He sighed and held up his pudding cup. "I can vouch for the tapioca."

Kal folded himself into the lotus position on the floor and cracked his sweet tea. "Thank you, Cooper."

"Thank you, Kal. Your help saved my life, and seeing you at ringside meant a lot. I owe you."

"You do, and do you know how I got a seat?"

"You told the warden that if I lost you'd be Love's next opponent."

"That's right."

"And he told you that if I won you'd be my next opponent."

"That's right." Kal looked at Rudy.

The hacker shook his head. "The cell isn't wired."

"God, I hope not!" Marilyn giggled.

Kal looked intently at Bolan. "Tell me it's not going to come down to me and you."

"It won't come to that," Bolan confirmed.

"And you know this because?"

"Because I'll be dead or D-Town will be closed for business before that ever happens."

The cell went silent.

Kal grunted suspiciously and began sporking into his steak.

Rudy's fork hovered over his baked potato. "You really mean that, don't you?"

Bolan ate pudding. "I do."

The Computer Room, Stony Man Farm, Virginia

KURTZMAN STARED AT a very thick, inconclusive and highly redacted file. Lincoln Whitmore was a mystery.

"The man's a total enigma," Tokaido opined.

The computer wizard reserved comment. The man had served as a forward observer pilot in Vietnam, reaching the rank of first lieutenant. Whitman had won the Distinguished Flying Cross and earned the Purple Heart in the same mission, being severely wounded when his aircraft took bad flak, but still managing to locate a downed pilot. He had then loitered, using his marking rockets, as he and his crew fired their personal weapons out the windows and doors to hold off the enemy.

After two tours Whitman had gone on to fly for Air America,

the only known intelligence agency owned and operated airline, where his record was highly redacted. Two years before the hostilities in Vietnam ceased he had apparently fallen off the planet.

"Air America." Tokaido was excited. "This guy is old-school cold warrior."

Kurtzman nodded. Air America had flown money, guns, drugs, commandos, informants, prisoners and anything else that needed to be moved under the radar everywhere from the capital cities to the darkest corners of Southeast Asia. Many of Air America's pilots and air crewmen had gotten involved in some very bad extracurricular activities. Some had been swallowed by the darkness and never come home. Others had brought some very bad business home with them.

Whitmore had come home, gone to college and gotten his degree from MIT in the fledgling industry of computer science, and then joined the CIA as a legitimate analyst with a desk, a necktie and an ID badge. He'd quit the Company in less than four years for undisclosed reasons, and gone into private work as a computer programmer.

That was when trouble began to find him.

Whitmore's rap sheet had had the holy hell redacted out of it, as well. The recurring theme was drug trafficking and possession beefs. Throughout the late 1980s he had beaten them all, and many of the cases had been mysteriously dropped. Then in 1992 he had gotten stung in a drug deal and done a nickel in Florida. This was followed by two possession counts and two more stretches. He'd moved to New England, and at the dawn of the new century Whitmore had fallen afoul of Pennsylvania's three-strikes law and had been sentenced to the stretch that would most likely see him die behind Duivelstad's walls.

"What do you think?" Tokaido asked.

"I think at some point in the seventies Whitmore was transporting the sweet stuff for Air America, or on his own time. I think he never quite recovered from his injuries and I think he got a taste for it, and it's a taste he never shook."

"Getting high on your own supply," Tokaido quipped. "It's the road to ruin."

"It's the road to D-Town, anyway," Kurtzman agreed. "If you're disciplined, heroin is probably the easiest addiction to hide from the outside world."

"Until you make a mistake," Tokaido commented. "And Whitmore was working for the CIA. They got some people over there with very sharp noses."

"That's how I see it. They let him leave quietly, and because of his past service—or things he knew, or both—they got some of his cases overturned or dropped. Then at a certain point they cut their losses and set Whitmore loose."

"So we have an ex-CIA agent-computer expert engaging in shenanigans in the library."

"Shenanigans is a mild way of putting writing code for the Aryan Circle behind the walls of Duivelstad. Most white supremacists are hardly worth the skin they inhabit, but the Aryan Circle count some very bad people with some very nasty habits among their ranks. Homeland Security has been eyeballing them awfully hard for the past few years. From what I've gleaned there have been rumors and chatter for months that they are up to something very big. I think what Mack has found confirms it."

"So what are we going to do about it?"

"Well, until we get another love letter from Mr. Rudolpho, I suggest we work on breaking Whitmore's code."

The Library, Duivelstad

BOLAN CHECKED HIS portfolio. The code informed him that the Farm's bottom line was that Lincoln Whitmore had a very high order of probability of being Duivelstad public enemy number one. There was also a very high probability that he was in cahoots with the Aryan Circle, and they were up to something very bad. These were things Bolan had already suspected. A consensus of opinion was nice, but the soldier had hoped for something a little more conclusive.

Rudy rounded the table and spoke low. "I might have something, but I'm not sure."

Bolan slid his eyes over to the circulation desk. Renzo was laughing at something Whitmore had said. He was a charming old son of a bitch, Bolan had to give him that. "What?"

"I was working on 'Jersey.' The President will be in New Jersey at the end of the week, and it was close in the code stream, real close, but it kept not working. And then I realized I was forcing it."

"And then what did you realize?"

"That if I took out the *h* the word *Jericho* worked perfectly."

"And the walls came tumbling down?"

"Yeah, and when I plugged that in it gave me more words."

"The symbolism seems a little obvious," Bolan remarked.

"And Link is an old man, institutionalized, a drug addict with an inconsistent supply stream. He never expected to have his code discovered, much less broken, and he likes the symbolism."

Bolan looked over at the ancient, incarcerated cold warrior behind the circulation desk flirting with a beautiful woman he could never have. "There is that."

"So you like it? 'And it came to pass at the seventh time, when the priests blew with the trumpets, Joshua said unto the people, Shout; for the Lord hath given you the city. So the people shouted when the priests blew with the trumpets, and it came to pass, when the people heard the sound of the trumpet, and the people shouted with a great shout, that the wall fell down flat.'"

"You're good," Bolan said.

"The Aryans will shout, but who's going to blow the horn and tumble the walls of D-Town down? You think the Aryans have a tunnel?"

Bolan decided to show a card. "The Puerto Ricans have the only tunnel in Duivelstad that goes anywhere."

Rudy was incredulous. "You whipped Tavo and Billy the C gave you his tunnel?"

"No, the C doesn't know I know, yet."

"So how do you know the PR's have a tunnel?"

Bolan raised an eyebrow.

Rudy sighed. If asked, he would have said nothing his cellmate did or said surprised him anymore. Save that it would be a lie. The man just kept topping himself. "Yeah, whatever. So if the Aryans don't have a tunnel, then how do they tumble down the walls of D-Town?"

Bolan gave Rudy the eyebrow again.

Rudy sighed when saw it. "They have a bomb."

"I'm thinking maybe more than one, if they want to get out of here and kill the President."

"Jesus. So what do we do?"

"I need you to directly contact my people ASAP and get me their full report, and tell them what we think and see if that generates any leads."

"I can't see how any of that will generate any proof on the bad guys."

"I don't need proof, I just need enough to point me in the right direction, or enough to start something and force their hand."

The Warden's Office

"HE KILLED LOVE," The veins of Schoenaur's huge wrist and right hand danced and crawled as he methodically squeezed a racquet ball. Since the infamous Cell Block C handshake, Schoenaur had gone back into training. Since having his nose broken he had re-doubled his fast-draw practice in the bathroom mirror every morning. "Killed him with his toe."

"How is Prisoner Love?" the warden asked.

Zavala answered. "According to the doc, Love suffered a massive heart failure induced by violent external trauma. Said he's never seen the like."

"And his ring career?"

Zavala shook his head. "Over."

Schoenaur scowled. "We gave you Cooper on a platter, Force. What the hell happened?"

"Cooper killed Love with his toe. I don't think anyone could have predicted that." Scott regarded Schoenaur drily. "And for that matter, I was under the impression Cooper was pissing fire, shitting ketchup and could barely walk, much less wield death with both feet."

Warden Linder had given Officers Johnson and Stewart long, hard and separate grillings about that. The problem was he knew both men well, knew their methods, had seen their results and had no reason to believe they had somehow shirked their dirty duty. The fact was the two men were confirmed sadists who enjoyed their work immensely. How Cooper had managed to go poison foot on Love was one more in a mounting series of enigmas that were all named Cooper. "I'm growing tired of Prisoner Cooper."

Schoenaur straightened in his seat with eagerness. "And it's about goddamn time."

Scott sighed. Always being the smartest man in the room was harder than most people knew. Since Rollin had been put in the hospital, Scott had been reading Machiavelli as well as the samurai Miyamoto Mushahi's *The Book of Five Rings* and Sun Tzu's *The Art of War.* He had pored over them morning and night like other men might pore over the Holy Bible, attempting to find hidden meaning spring up between the lines. Scott had done this inserting the name Cooper for the enemy as he had read the ancient Italian, Japanese and Chinese masters' stratagems for overcoming their foes. These studies had resulted in an unexpected epiphany, and one that brought a whole host of problems with it.

"Has it occurred to anyone that Cooper is not what he appears to be?"

Zavala frowned. "He's a cop?"

Scott snorted. "No, cops going undercover in prison is TV bullshit. We all know it's easier to just pay a snitch or make one your bitch, and no cop would ever enter the Hunger Games."

"So he's some merc hired by the FBI? CIA? DEA?" Schoenaur suggested.

"If he was, the Hunger Games would have brought D-Town down after the first match. He's not here to investigate that, prison abuse or corruption."

Warden Linder steepled his fingers. "He's here to investigate us."

"He may not be totally sure of that yet, and even then he's still not certain what he's trying to uncover. But something brought him here."

Schoenaur wasn't seeing it. "Like what?"

"The farm in Lancaster County was attacked by forces unknown, and burned to the ground. Maybe the data wasn't erased or completely destroyed, like we thought. Maybe someone left some clues. What I know is this—our operation suffered an anomalous setback in the Lancaster clubhouse, and then this Cooper appears at D-Town's door almost like magic and now almost owns the place."

"You're saying Cooper is some kind of nongovernment organization fixer, and he's here trying to figure out what we're up to?"

Scott relaxed his mass back into his chair. "It's a theory."

"So we kill him," Schoenaur asserted.

Linder weighed the possibilities. "Then that blond bitch shows up Wednesday and asks where lover boy is."

"But if Force is right, then she's part of the scam."

"Yes, and if we can't produce Cooper, she hits us with the Hunger Games."

Zavala frowned. "And she knows about that how?"

"We have to assume that wasn't his wife he spent the day with in Jungle Park. We have to assume they know about the Hunger

Games and were probably watching. They can shut us down anytime they want, but they still don't know what exactly is going on."

"So what the hell do we do?" Schoenaur asked.

Scott answered. "We move up the timetable. Once we blow the horn and the walls come down, neither Cooper nor any of his undercover bullshit will mean anything, and it will be an awfully convenient time for him and every other loose end to die tragically."

14

BOLAN RAN HIS eye across the tiers. Men smoked and talked, argued and socialized. Down below at the tables some played checkers, cards or chess. Others lazed about listening to their portable music players, or read. Some ground out endless push-ups in their cells. Work details in the laundry or the kitchen were privileges that had to be earned. Time in the shop was reserved for exemplary prisoners or those the warden favored. For most of the population now was another of the endless hours between meals where there was nothing to do but mark time and vainly try to fill it.

This was a new battlefield for Bolan. Prison was what it was, and it was a waiting game. Bolan was a trained sniper. He could outwait a rock if need be, but his every instinct was screaming that he had to make his move and soon.

"We're running out of time, and running out of options," he remarked.

Rudy leaned on the rail and took a long breath. "So you're going to force the issue?"

"Yeah."

"About goddamn time, if you ask me!" Patrick opined. "I say we kick this pig!" Patrick's elders and betters gave him matching looks. The young man cringed. "Sorry."

A part of Bolan did admire Rudolpho the Younger's enthusiasm. "It's going to happen soon enough."

Rudy gave Bolan a bold grin. "Cheer up, I bought you a present."

"Presents are good."

Rudy checked his watch and grinned again in satisfaction as Officer Barnes entered C Block carrying a laptop. The guard came up to the tier and gave Rudy a sheepish look. Rudy gazed skyward for strength. "What did you do this time?"

"I didn't do anything!" Barnes protested.

"No patches or software without telling me?"

"No!"

Rudy looked off to one side leerily. "Did you download something you wouldn't want me to see?"

Barnes blushed beet-red. "Oh, for the love of— No! Of course not!"

Rudy shook his head. "This is becoming a habit, Officer."

Barnes regained his composure. "You have something better to do, Rudolpho?"

"Well, I was watching Cooper stare grimly into the middle distance, and listening to my son give me a load of shit, but I can get that any day all day."

"You'll take a look at it?" Barnes asked hopefully. "The screen keeps freezing."

"Better to be busy than bored. Full disclosure, you got nothing private on here since the last time I looked at it?"

"Nope, but I do want to get online and play tonight after work."

Rudy nodded. "You will."

"Thanks, Rudy!" Barnes walked off happily, solid in the knowledge his world would be Warcrafting this evening.

"You set up his laptop to malfunction," Bolan surmised.

Rudy looked at his watch. "Johnny on the spot." He looked at his son. "Let's talk." They went into the cell, where the Rudolphos began a lengthy discussion of intimate computer programming details. Bolan sat on the bunk with the laptop and connected. He punched in the password he had given Rudy, and hit Send + Silent.

Kurtzman's chat window popped up instantly.

I have news, he typed.

And? Bolan typed in return.

Kurtzman gave Bolan a rapid rundown on what he had unearthed on the Force. Clelland Wilberforce Scott was a genuinely spooky dude. Most white supremacists in Bolan's experience had long ago jumped their charter, and besides sporting Nazi tattoos and shouting a few slogans, their main concern in life was running guns and drugs and controlling territory like any other criminal gang. Still, there had always been a shadowy upper echelon that still believed in the main mission. Bolan scanned Scott's jacket and the notes Kurtzman had compiled. He was serving life for first-degree murder, conspiracy for the killing of a federal judge, and being found in midplan to kill a second. Scott was a legend in the New England criminal circles, and since his incarceration was referred to in hushed tones as the "Fuehrer behind the Walls." He was widely known to reach out from behind the walls of Duivelstad as a king-maker, an adviser, and by proxy, an executioner. In New England's underworld Scott was what went bump in the night, and if something horrible was about to happen in D-Town, he had to be the man behind it.

Bolan scanned the file on Lincoln Whitmore and saw the perfect storm forming on the horizon.

The more the soldier read the more his suspicions were confirmed. Old-school CIA agents all had a mantra: *Die Someplace Warm.* Bolan was starting to get a very strong feeling that Lincoln Whitmore had no intention of dying behind the walls of Duivelstad.

Kurtzman typed, I went through as much Air America data as I could get my hands on. A lot is missing, even more is redacted. But I began trying to link data streams, and given where Whitmore is, and your current Jericho theory, these are the most concerning.

Bolan began to get a very cold feeling as he watched the data slowly scroll. The possibility that the United States had deployed "backpack" nuclear weapons in the Southeast Asian theater during the Vietnam War was still choice fodder for conspiracy theorists to this day. It was generally known that the Pentagon had considered the idea; what the exact targets might have been was again fodder for endless speculation, as was whether specific low-yield, low-signature weapons had actually been designed for the theater, or whether the powers that be had been contemplating already-in-production, standard, military nuclear demolition charges.

Some of the code words for the "in-theater" small nuke projects were known. Kurtzman had also managed to come up with several of Whitmore's code names used during his stint in Air America, and as an analyst for the CIA, where Whitmore's department had naturally been Southeast Asia. The code words designating the project and Whitmore's code names appeared together in several data streams.

Kurtzman had applied the words to Whitmore's library files and the disk from the Lancaster farm, and he was starting to get more hits.

Storing nukes in a prison. Hard to believe, Kurtzman typed.

Hard to think of a safer place, Bolan typed back. No prison gets raided unless there's a riot going on. It's an artificial, strictly controlled environment, almost no possibilities of leaks. Except for human rights groups, hardly anyone is monitoring the day-to-day activities of any specific prison. No government agency is, and if they are they're mostly just running surveys or monitoring political activity.

Which implies the warden and at least some of the staff are in on it.

Bolan considered his experiences with the Big U. That's a safe bet.

So how do we go in?

We can't. We have no proof. Duivelstad is a private prison. The warden is friends with the governor. We've got nothing and we're going to need a lot to get this place shut down and searched.

We could send in Able or Phoenix.

It was tempting to think of the Farm's two extraordinary action teams hitting Duivelstad in a combined raid. We're not authorized, and most of the guard and staff aren't in on this. They would resist, and then there's the possibility of it sparking a riot. We need more.

There was a pause on Kurtzman's side of the chat. So what are you going to do?

Both men knew it was a rhetorical question. Bolan gave the answer Kurtzman was expecting. I'm going to have to bust this thing wide open, force them to show their hand, or both. The good news is we've established the target list and the objective. I've got a lot to work with. Good work, Bear.

Thanks, but the objective has to be something more than just blowing down one of D-Town's walls and engineering the biggest jailbreak in history.

Well, that would be memorable, but I think Scott wants more bang for his buck. Literally.

Like how big?

Warden Linder wants money. Whitmore wants to die on some spit of sand in Southeast Asia, lying in a hammock with China white on tap in his arm.

And Scott?

He wants to irrevocably alter the American political landscape. I'm pretty sure he wants to do it by assassinating the President of the United States, and he wants to use a nuclear weapon to do it.

The Warden's Office

"HELLO, LINK!" WARDEN Linder smiled sunnily. It was a travesty on his face. He waved at a chair. "Have a seat."

Whitmore flinched. Zavala pushed him forward. Whitmore moved to the offered chair and tried not to squirm under Linder's overly intimate gaze. The warden was the one man on earth Whitmore feared. The warden had established their relationship early. He had learned of Whitmore's addiction, let him satisfy it for a few months uninterrupted, and then thrown him in the hole cold turkey. Whitmore had begged, screamed, soiled himself and climbed the walls for seventy-two hours with nothing to break up the hellish torment save a single serving of nutraloaf and a once-a-day hosing down of his cell and himself with the fire hose. At the end of it Whitmore had genuinely beaten his addiction.

Then Linder had let him out and shoved his arm full of heroin purer than Whitmore had experienced in decades, and started the addiction cycle all over again. The warden had mentioned once conversationally that Whitmore was too old to catch anyone's eye save for some of the oldest sissies looking for a husband to settle down with, but he was sure if he passed out the Viagra and gave them the proper motivation he knew some sickos in B Block that would take the case, and a man as advanced in age as Whitmore, and addicted to heroin, probably had enough bowel problems without that sort of attention.

Whitmore was a prisoner, a drug addict and a slave.

He was well liked in the prison. He enjoyed running the library

and teaching inmates how to read, or helping them earn their high
school equivalency diplomas. Several times a year Warden Linder
liked to let him get a little rocky, but Whitmore enjoyed a mostly
steady supply of junk of varying quality.

The man behind the desk could take all that from him in the
blink of an eye.

"You like movies, Link?"

Whitmore thought furiously. This was one of those weeks when
the warden had left him in need a little too long. It was often a
harbinger of the warden wanting something of him. "I do. Thank
you for showing *Casablanca* last week. It's one of my favorites."

"Mine, too." Linder took a small plastic bag and a cooking kit
out of his desk drawer. "Want to watch a movie with me?"

Whitmore trembled and sweat burst across his brow despite
himself. He dragged his eyes off the junk and the kit with diffi-
culty. "Of course, Warden."

Linder took a small penknife out of his pocket and pushed it
and the plastic bag across the desk. "You can snort one line now
to calm your nerves. I want you at your movie critic best for this."

Whitmore pierced the bag with the knife and poured and arranged a careful line. His need overcame his shame as he snorted
the line off the ancient wood. Zavala grunted in disgust. Linder
gazed on benevolently. "All better?"

Whitmore leaned back, craving more but calmed. "A bit."

"Well, watch this." Linder opened his laptop and clicked on a
film file. It opened showing Linder's office. Cooper sat in a chair
and a woman who could only be the lawyer known as "Cooper's
blonde" began to read him the riot act. A goon in a suit stood by,
looking imposing.

"I didn't know you had your office wired."

"Pay attention. Look at it like a CIA analyst. Is there anything
going on here I'm missing?"

Whitmore had been an excellent pilot and soldier until he had
been wounded and a little too much dependence on morphine
had led him to heroin. He had always been an excellent analyst.
He observed Cooper's meeting with the DOJ lawyer and then the
second one. "Run them again."

Linder hit the first film file once more.

Whitmore threw back his head and laughed. Linder wasn't exactly pleased at the sound. "What?"

"It's the oldest trick in the book!"

Linder placed his hand over the little bag of heroin. His voice went dead. "What?"

"They're blinking at each other in Morse code! Our captured pilots used to do this when the Cong tried to use them in propaganda films. I've seen the original film strips!"

"What are they saying?"

Whitmore went into genuine analyst mode. "They're good. You see how she keep running one hand through her hair and then the other? Turning her head? And look, Cooper is rubbing his temples again. They're trying to hide it without being obvious. I doubt there's much in the way of doublespeak in their conversations. The grilling is all distraction for the Morse code with the eyes."

"What are they saying?"

"Cooper just blinked 'hurt.' The woman just blinked 'out.' This was between the fights, so it must have been after the Wrecking Crew laid into Cooper, and she's asking if he wants extraction."

Whitmore took his hand off the heroin. "Very good, Link. What else?"

"He blinked 'no' and—" Whitmore laughed again. "You see how he keeps his head lowered? He isn't sure whether he's on film or not, but nearly all surveillance cameras are placed high to take in the whole scene, and he is acting appropriately. Cooper is a total pro. The woman is a talented amateur, at least when it comes to fieldwork."

"So we've been compromised."

Whitmore never took his eyes off the interview footage. "You have been penetrated, but Cooper still hasn't found the prize. That's why he's still here and the National Guard hasn't surrounded the perimeter."

"What else can you tell me?"

"Give me both files on a flash drive. They've managed to hide a lot of the conversation, but I bet I can extrapolate most of it."

Linder pushed a prepared flash drive across the desk and nodded at the heroin. "You go ahead and get yourself nice and high today. Tonight I want you working on it, and tomorrow I want a full report."

"I will, Warden, and thank you."

"You're a spook, Link."

Whitmore nodded. "I was."

"That blond DOJ bitch is coming again the day after tomorrow. I want you to help me reset the positions of the hidden cameras, and I want you watching the interview as it happens."

Whitmore stared at the heroin with ill-concealed longing, and another part of him was genuinely happy to be doing what he was best at. "Glad to oblige, Warden."

15

Bolan examined his handiwork. He'd had Patrick go retrieve the defense pencil from Kal. The soldier had invested some time in removing the sole of his left shoe with the surgical steel needle, then using the camouflaged weapon to dig a channel that fit the weapon perfectly in the hard rubber sole. He'd recoated the toes of both shoes with wood glue for fighting, and then applied just enough of what remained to reattach the sole on the left one. It was a dangerous gamble. Wood glue wasn't designed for holding rubber together. It was a brittle polymer and not intended to bend and flex with every step. If the soldier's shoe fell apart and the weapon rolled out at an inopportune time, there would be trouble. Bolan smiled grimly at his weaponized shoes.

He was in trouble now, and when everything hit the fan he was going to need to access with one good yank the fatal surprise the Cowboy had crafted for him.

Bolan slipped on his shoes. The upgrades made them stiff, but they had been stiff to begin with, and the soldier expected to be dead or breathing fresh air long before his prison issues ever got broken in. He took a deep breath and self-assessed. His legs ached; his back ached; his belly ached. The good news was that nothing was on fire anymore. Rather than pink, his urine was a sunshine-yellow from the partly indigestible prison food, the solid portions of which he could now hold down. Bolan chose to be a glass half-full kind of guy and gave himself an optimistic forty-seven percent fighting efficiency rating, and rising.

He wondered if that, a .22-caliber pen with one reload, and shoes glued to inflict the blues would be enough to take on an entire prison.

It was just going to have to be.

Bolan stepped out onto the tier. Patrick looked positively giddy and shot him the thumbs-up. He was clearly ready for Armageddon, or at least thought he was, and definitely wanted a piece of the action. Rudolpho the Elder stared circumspectly at Bolan and the shoes the soldier wore. The Mafia made man was hoping for some light at the end of the tunnel and was pretty sure he was asking for too much.

"You got another big date today?"

"That I do. You got another service appointment scheduled?"

Rudy gave Bolan a sly look. "Officer Renzo is about to experience connectivity issues with her tablet in, wait for it—" Rudy glanced at his watch "—five…four…three…two…one…."

A feminine voice snarled from C Block's floor level. "God-*damn* it!"

Bolan snorted. "Rudy, you rule the school."

"Thanks."

Officer Renzo stormed onto Tier 3 in a thundercloud of Sicilian fury. "Rudy!"

Rudy was nonplussed. "What have you done now?"

"Nothing!"

"Internet connection issues?"

"It keeps dumping me," Renzo complained.

Rudy raised an eyebrow. "What were you doing?"

Renzo's eyes narrowed dangerously.

"If I fix it I'm going to find out, anyways."

Renzo looked at the trio of cons before her and lowered her voice. "I was checking my profile on Pennsylvanianal Profession Singles, fuck you very much, and if that gets out among the population, you're dead."

Rudy sighed. "Those sites are no good. Everyone is exchanging information and links. Half the profiles on any of them are fakes to trawl for personal information or distribute viruses."

"Oh…shit," Renzo responded.

"Yeah, I'll look at it."

"If you do anything weird with it…"

"Do I look that stupid?" Rudy asked.

"You were stupid enough to get yourself sent here."

Bolan gave Rudy credit for taking that one on the chin.

"Do I look stupid enough to screw over a guard? I've got enough problems, Officer."

"I'll give you that, Rudy. But men in here get bored, and bored men get strange ideas."

"Nothing strange with you or any of your personal data, Officer Renzo." Rudy made the sign of the cross over his lips and kissed his fingers. "I swear."

Renzo smiled and handed over her tablet. "*Grazie, Rudolpho.*"

"*Prego.*" Rudy shot Bolan a shit-eating grin as Renzo wandered off none the wiser.

"You are slick," Bolan acknowledged. "I think she likes you."

Rudy let out a long sigh as the rearview of the Italian pulchritude disappeared down the steps. "In my dreams, and then I wake up and miss my wife."

Bolan reminded himself that both Rudy and his son were convicted felons.

The porcine sight of Officer Barnes mounting Tier 3 replaced Renzo. He smiled happily at Bolan. He liked girls, and good-looking ones kept coming to visit Cooper. "Let's go, Cooper! Warden's office! You have an official visitor!"

The Warden's Office

"LAST CHANCE, COOPER," Price snarled. The interview had been fairly short and sweet. Bolan could communicate through the library, and Rudy literally had a malfunction time bomb in any electronic device put in his hands. Barnes's and Renzo's computer problems were pernicious and persistent, enough that Rudy literally had a device a day coming in for the next week to allow Bolan direct communication. Price was mostly here because the meet had already been scheduled, she wanted to keep up appearances with Warden Linder, and she and Kurtzman both wanted an eyeball witness to make sure Bolan really was all right. Bolan and Price's Morse code had consisted mostly of "Are you all right?" "Are you communicating under duress?" and "Do you want extraction?"

Bolan signaled negatory on all counts, while Price kept up a steady stream of threats. "Marshal" Avery Roy stood staring like a stone Buddha. Bolan gave the appearance of sweating under the pressure.

Warden Linder looked over at his phone as it vibrated. He waved at Price to continue, and appeared to be checking a text. Bolan kept up his facade while Linder put one on. The warden wouldn't have made a good poker player. He was used to being in the power position and cruelly manipulating people. Suddenly putting on a poker face was out of character, and Bolan didn't care for it. The soldier could tell Price had picked up on it, as well.

Linder texted back and put down his phone. "I'm sorry, where were we again?"

Price gave the warden an exasperated look. "I was kind of hoping you and I were starting to become a team on this."

"This what?" Linder asked innocently.

Price gazed upon Bolan scathingly. "This one."

"Ah, yes."

Zavala stuck his head in the door breathlessly. "Warden!"

"Can't you see I'm busy?"

"We got real trouble in A Block!"

"Oh, for the love of—"

Everyone lifted their head as the alarm began to wail. It was literally a World War II air raid siren, and sounded as if the end of the world was on the way.

"Goddamn it!" Linder slammed his fist down on the table. "Lockdown! Zavala! Take Cooper back to his cell! Get Renzo to escort Agent Price and the marshal from the facility! ASAP!"

Zavala jerked his head. "Let's go, Cooper!"

Linder rose. "I'm sorry, Agent Price, Marshal Roy. We'll have to resume this meeting another day."

Bolan got off one rapid blink at Price, signaling, "Get out now."

"Move, Cooper!"

The soldier followed Zavala out. Boots thudded in the corridors. Nonessential personnel moved swiftly and calmly toward the gates. The soldier gave Linder credit for running a tight ship.

Zavala marched Bolan back to C Block and into his cell. He bellowed down to the floor, "Cooper accounted for!"

Barnes shouted back from C Block's gate in a surprisingly thunderous voice. "C Block accounted for! Lockdown!"

Every cell rattled simultaneously as doors slammed shut and locked.

"C Block lockdown confirmed!"

Zavala's smile was sickening. He failed to overcome his innately sadistic tendencies as he whispered through the bars, "Nice knowing you, Cooper."

Administration Section

"RENZO!"

Renzo, Price and Roy turned to see Officers Johnson and

Stewart marching up swiftly behind them. "What's up, RayRay?" Renzo asked.

"We have a potential riot situation," Johnson said. "The warden wants you up in the tower."

"Oh, for God's sake!"

"Lockdown hasn't been achieved in A Block. If this goes full blown, you're going to want to be in the tower with a rifle. Worse comes to worst, they can extract you through the top hatch by helicopter."

"Listen."

"You already told me no," Johnson advised. "You wanna try to tell the Force and every man in Aryan Acres no with nothing but a baton and pepper spray?"

Renzo chewed her lip.

Stewart rolled his eyes. "It's an order, if that makes it any easier to swallow, and besides, everyone knows you're the best shot with a rifle. We need you up top. We'll take care of the brawling if it comes down to it."

Renzo swallowed her pride and accepted her assignment. "Agent? Marshal? While you are in Duivelstad I'm remanding you into the custody of Officers Johnson and Stewart. They'll take you straight to Admissions, return your sidearms and escort you out the main gate."

Price shot Roy a look. "Let's get out of here."

Renzo broke into a run down the corridor. Stewart nodded at an exit arrow. "Follow me."

Price took out her phone. "I need to make a call right now."

"No time," Johnson admonished. "We have to get you out."

"I need just one—"

Price's eyes flew wide as Roy groaned and dropped to his knees. Officer Stewart was shanking him over the kidneys and liver like a sewing machine. Roy dropped and Stewart rose, grinning and brandishing a bloodstained spike of steel he had confiscated from a con long ago and kept in his throwaway weapon stash.

Price pushed a single button on her phone and threw it in Stewart's face. The Farm had been hit before. Price's life had been in danger. She wasn't a field operative but she had learned various self-defense moves. Price forked the first two fingers of her right hand and lunged forward for Officer Stewart's eyes.

Price's spear fingers never hit home.

A sledgehammer blow struck her just below her ribs. White fire lit behind Price's eyes, and she lost control of her limbs. Her attack turned into a collapse and she literally fell into Stewart's arms.

Delighted, he stroked Price's cheek with the bloody shank. "Oh, baby, I knew you wanted me the first time I saw you."

"GET ON THE horn, Rudy," Bolan ordered. "Now."

Sirens continued to wail. There had been one attempted riot during Warden Linder's reign. It had originated in B Block, and it had been ruthlessly crushed before it could spread outward. Men muttered on every tier. Some whooped and hollered. Others banged objects against the bars or threw toilet paper rolls in solidarity with whatever was happening, or just out of excitement.

Rudy looked up from furious typing on Renzo's tablet. "You're connected."

"Are Price and Roy out?" They each swallowed a gel cap–size transmitter before every entry into Duivelstad, which gave their location to the satellite Kurtzman had tasked above. The tiny devises also had the ability to monitor their basic vital signs.

Rudy grimaced at Kurtzman's response. "Your guy says negative. Roy is in the morgue section of the clinic and has assumed a temperature of 39.2° Fahrenheit."

Bolan frowned and took a long breath. "Where's Price?"

"I don't know. It's a part of D-Town I've never been in."

Bolan looked over Rudy's shoulder, and the sum of all fears manifested itself. "She's in the lounge."

"Jesus…"

"Tell Bear to open my door."

"He says he can't open yours without opening all of them." Rudy gave Bolan a leery look. "You want every cell in C Block open in a riot situation?"

"I have a key!" Patrick held up Bolan's length of flexible charges. "When I heard the siren I went and got it from Kal. He kept two for himself. I said okay. Oh, and I gave him his book back and told him what you told me to. That's okay, right?"

"That's all right." Bolan took the length and pinched off one of the charges. The cells in D-Town were electronically controlled, but a guard's key could override an individual cell. Bolan pushed his high-explosive key into the door and pressed down on the pin to activate it. The soldier stepped back as the flexible charge detonated and a jet of smoke and fire shot out of the lock. The whole block went silent at the sound.

The tracks rattled as Bolan flung back the door to his cage.

Cell Block C erupted as he stepped out onto the tier during lockdown and strode toward the steps. Rudy and Patrick followed.

"Hang back," Bolan ordered. He passed Kal's cell, saying, "You're going to have to make a decision."

Bolan kicked off his shoes and ripped open his left heel. He palmed his inner city defense pencil and stepped to the stairs. Zavala was coming up. The guard wore body armor and a helmet. He led with a ballistic riot shield, and held his baton cocked and ready for use. Zavala should have had a gun.

The soldier pushed his pencil's clip to arm it. Zavala hit the landing ready to crack skulls. Bolan dropped to one knee and put up his left palm, feeling a flash of pain run down his arm as Zavala crashed into him. Bolan rammed the pencil's push button into the instep of the guard's left shoe and squeezed the clip. The weapon made a snapping noise and Zavala screamed as the .22 round burst through the small bones of his foot. Bolan shoved hard against the riot shield as Zavala's pain and shock made him lift his left foot.

The prison guard toppled down the stairs, shrieking.

The stone vault of Cell Block C echoed with cheers as if it was the Hunger Games. Scores of cons screamed to be released. Bolan stripped Zavala of his shield, baton and radio, then cuffed him to the tier rail. The soldier reloaded his pencil as he marched down to floor level.

Officer Barnes stood behind the gate, the bars of which were sheathed inside and out with ballistic plastic. Barnes regarded Bolan in horror and shouted across the intercom. "Cooper! Stand down!"

"Open the door, Barnes."

Barnes's face set into startlingly hard lines. He drew a dark green Glock pistol from his holster and racked a round. "Cooper, go back to your cell."

Bolan shouted back behind him. "I need the guard's gate! Cell Block C!"

Barnes raised his pistol in both hands. "Cooper, don't!"

The entry gate was on a different circuit than the cell doors. Back in Virginia, Kurtzman's ghost in Devil Town's machine moved and C Block's gate rattled open. Bolan raised his shield as Barnes, to his credit, started shooting. The ballistic shield bucked, shuddered and spalled, but it was being hit with the small arms fire it was built to resist. The soldier stepped into the C Block gate room. Barnes got smart and aimed for his adversary's legs. Bolan dropped low and took two more shots to the shield as he closed. He rose and gave Barnes a Captain America–worthy blow with his shield. Barnes splayed back against the wall and collapsed to the floor.

Bolan took his pistol, Sam Browne belt and disappointing one spare magazine. He cuffed Barnes to the duty desk and then moved to the block control board. It consisted of a red light, a green light and a switch for each cell in C Block. All the lights were red for locked except Bolan's. The soldier hated to do it, but he flicked a switch and on the third tier a second sensor blinked from red to green.

Kal's cell was open.

Bolan unscrewed the lights and switched them. It wouldn't fool anyone for very long, but in a hurry, and an emergency, someone might not notice the green light was on the wrong side on a console of glowing lights.

Bolan gave it fifty-fifty that Kal would march downstairs and cripple him. "Rudy!"

Rudy appeared in the open gate with the Farm's tablet schematic of D-Town in hand. "Could you shout my name a little louder?"

"Shout out to key-master Rudy!" Bolan roared out to the block.

Only iron bars prevented C Block from doing the wave as they roared approval.

"You suck."

Bolan grinned. "I own you."

Patrick came through the gates as giddy as a schoolboy as he took in his tenuous lockdown freedom. "Awesome!"

"Tell the Bear I need a cascade of doors opening before me and locking behind."

Rudy typed, We're heading for the lounge.

"Yeah."

The door across the chamber rolled open under Kurtzman's ministrations.

"RayRay and Stu will be there."

Bolan checked the load in his new Glock. Barnes had gotten off seven rounds. The soldier switched in the fully loaded spare magazine. "I'm counting on it."

16

WARDEN LINDER DREW a .45 Colt Government Model from his drawer. He cocked and locked the pistol. "What's the situation?"

Schoenaur grinned. "Cell Block A has been compromised. The Aryans are holding it and making demands. They're holding two guards hostage. They haven't been harmed, as ordered."

"Good."

"RayRay and Stu have the Price woman in the lounge and are awaiting orders."

"Tell them I want them to get everything—and I mean *every-*thing—out of that woman, and I don't care how they do it, but make if fast. We're on a tight timetable."

"And when they're done?" Schoenaur asked.

Warden Linder spent a vain moment yearning to be in the lounge. "Leave her there, but with the door unlocked. When we lose control of the prison, let the cons have some fun."

Schoenaur laughed. At the same time his radio crackled, and he clicked it on. "Yo!" The captain's face fell at what he heard over his earpiece.

Linder didn't care at all for the change in Captain Schoenaur. "What?"

Schoenaur reached down and unsnapped the retaining strap on his revolver. "It's C Block. Zavala and Barnes are down. Cooper is out of his cell. So are the Rudolphos."

"What is the status on Z-man and Fatty?"

"Zavala has a foot wound. Apparently Cooper had some sort of zip gun that looked like a pen. Zav broke his elbow when Cooper threw him down the stairs. Barnes has a concussion."

"And?"

"And Cooper has Barnes's Glock."

Linder went to his office safe and unlocked it. He took out a Model 1928 Thompson submachine gun and clicked in a 50-round drum. When he had first taken over Duivelstad, the armory still had several of the ancient weapons racked. Like most prison-issue weapons, they had hardly ever been fired, and the Prohibition Era submachine gun was in nearly mint condition. Linder practiced with the weapon once a month and kept it lovingly oiled and maintained. He knew that if he ever actually lost control of the prison the inmates wouldn't keep him for ransom, they would visit unto him the indignities he had inflicted on them, upped a thousand-fold. He racked a round.

"What is the status in C Block?"

"Everyone else appears to be in lockdown."

"Where are the escapees?"

"Whereabouts unknown."

"I see. Inform Force of the situation. Tell him Cooper is on the loose and has the computer Mafia with him. Then tell RayRay and Stu."

"Where the hell does Cooper think he's going to go?" Schoenaur asked.

Linder took out a military surplus shoulder bag that contained four more loaded drums. "I'd say Cooper is coming for you and me, going for the Force, going for Link, and plans to rescue Price. Or all of the above, probably in reverse order."

"How the hell would he know we have Price?"

"How the hell did Cooper get into C Block's gate room, Rog? Fatty sure as shit didn't put out the welcome mat and open the door for him."

Schoenaur saw it. "He's in our system somehow."

"Somehow, hell. I want Rudolpho fucking crucified and his son raped by dozens before we blow this joint, unless someone shoots them first. Speaking of which, you got Renzo up in the tower?"

"Her and that rifle of hers are watching A Block."

Renzo was hands down the best rifle shot in Duivelstad and was one of two of D-Town's designated marksmen. "Radio her. Tell her Cooper and the Rudolphos have broken out of C Block. Tell her Cooper shot Zavala." Warden Linder smiled ugly as he played on Renzo's sympathies. "Tell her Cooper nearly beat Barnes's brains out of his head."

Schoenaur got on the horn.

Linder began removing banded stacks of U.S. currency and stuffing them into his briefcase. "Tell Renzo her orders are to shoot the escapees on sight."

BOLAN STRODE DOWN the corridor, shield and Glock in hand. He didn't need the Farm to give him a blueprint. He remembered being dragged down the sweating, turn-of-the-last-century underground passageway to Duivelstad's house of pain. Rudy and Patrick trailed behind him, until Bolan held up his pistol for them to halt. He could hear the sound of Price talking. Then she yelped.

"Shut up, bitch," Officer Stewart snarled.

Bolan rounded the corner.

"Here's your boyfriend now." Johnson laughed. "Goddamned Captain America himself."

Stewart joined in the hilarity. "You looking for this, Cooper?"

"RayRay," Bolan acknowledged. "Stu."

Price was a bloody mess. If there was any good news, it was that her bra and panties were still on. Stewart had his left arm under her chin and he held a shank to her right ear, ready to pith Price like a lab animal. Johnson took a two-handed hold on his Glock. "That's Officer Johnson and Officer Stewart to you, convict."

"I'm not a convict. I came here of my own free will, and I'm walking out the same way."

Officers Johnson and Stewart processed that information and didn't like it at all. Price bit her lip as Stewart pushed his shank against her inner ear. Johnson jerked the muzzle of his gun toward the floor. "Drop the gun, Cooper, and the shield."

Price blinked desperately in Morse code. DON'T!

Bolan blinked back HEEL, and hoped she got it.

The soldier's ballistic shield thudded as it hit the floor.

"And the gun. Toss it."

Price's face went grimly determined as she blinked. ON YOU.

Bolan's Glock clattered to the concrete, out of reach.

"On your knees, Cooper," Johnson ordered. "Hands behind your head."

Bolan dropped to his knees and raised his hands. His palm slid around the pen weapon he had clipped to the back of his collar, and he pressed his thumb to cock it. Johnson pointed his pistol at Bolan while he clicked on his radio with his free hand. "Warden, it's RayRay. We have Cooper, disarmed and on his knees. No sign of Rudy or his kid."

Johnson waved his pistol. "Hey, Cooper. Where are the Rudolphos?"

"In the library, taking over the entire Duivelstad computer system, and I told Patrick to kill Link. That young man is going to have to get himself a body if he's going to survive in here without me."

Officer Johnson's eyes bugged. "Oh Jesus…" He started shouting into his radio. Bolan jerked his right hand from behind his head and aimed over his knuckles as he fired the pen. He missed his opponent's heart, but Johnson faltered as a hole appeared just below his left collarbone. The soldier snapped his hand back to deploy the spike. Price stomped her heel into Stewart's instep with all her might, and he gasped as something cracked. Bolan flipped the pen in his fingers and threw. It was a weak throw and didn't penetrate into the brain, but Stewart screamed as about an inch of surgical needle sank into his eyeball.

"Fuck you, Cooper!" Johnson roared. "Fuck you!"

Bolan managed to scoop up his shield just as Johnson's Glock began thundering. The shield shuddered and bucked as the officer emptied his gun in rapid fire. Johnson didn't bother reloading. He stepped forward and slammed his size seventeen shoe into Bolan's shield. The soldier's legs hadn't recovered from his own visit to the lounge. Johnson outweighed him by a hundred pounds and the blow sent him sprawling. The rock and the hard place Bolan found himself between was his shield above him and the concrete below. Johnson put his entire weight behind each blow as he tried to stomp Bolan into oblivion. The soldier's arms failed and his shield fell to his chest.

"You think you're tough, Cooper? You're going back in the lounge!"

"Hey, fuckface!" Patrick shouted.

Johnson spun and put up his hands as the Rudolphos charged with Zavala's and Barnes's batons in hand. Johnson still had his right foot on top of Bolan. Patrick dropped low and slammed the expandable steel across Johnson's right kneecap. The guard's weight fell away. Bolan heaved up against the shield and Johnson tottered. Rudy took Barnes's side-handle baton in both fists and swung up for the bleachers. Teeth flew and Johnson's eyes rolled as he took the blow on the chin.

Patrick shouted in triumph. "Tim-ber!"

The ebony giant fell like a tree.

Bolan rose. Pain shot through his legs. His insides were definitely not happy, but nothing felt torn or was inflating with blood. He put a hand on the wall to steady himself.

"Rudy, take their guns, batons and cuffs." The soldier straightened himself and turned to Price. "Barb, are you all right?"

Unshed tears glittered in her eyes. "They killed Roy."

"I know. Patrick, go into the lounge and get her clothes."

Stewart kept shrieking. He clawed at his face, but couldn't stand touching the embedded steel. "Oh God! Oh God! Oh God!" Stewart's voice rose to an inhuman shriek as Bolan leaned down and yanked the shaft free. He retracted the needle and handed the weapon to Price.

"Hook this behind your back. Snap it to deploy it."

Patrick came out of the lounge with Price's torn skirt. She donned the garment, slipping the weapon inside the waistband at the small of her back. Bolan nodded at Stewart. "Take his shirt."

Patrick and Rudy stripped the mewling, half-blind guard. Price put on Stewart's uniform blouse. She also picked up the shank he had threatened her with. Patrick reloaded Johnson's pistol and Rudy checked the loads from Stewart's. "Where to next, boss?"

Bolan took up his Glock and shield. He stood over Stewart. "You both deserve to die. You want to live, Cyclops?"

"God! Yes!"

"What is the current status of D-Town?"

Stewart cupped his hand over his destroyed eye. "D-Town is in lockdown! The Aryans have A Block!"

"Under Linder's orders?"

"Yes!"

"Linder, Schoenaur, Link, they're getting out undercover of the explosion?"

Stewart coiled in on himself in fear. "How do you know about—"

"Yes or no!"

"Yes! The story is they're killed in the explosion!"

Bolan made an educated guess. "There are three weapons. One to blow down the wall and start the jailbreak. The Force had one in A Block and he's going to use it to hold what's left of the prison hostage. Linder and Force are taking the third one out of D-Town through the old tunnels."

"How do you—"

"Who's holding down A Block?"

"Rollin and Love! They got moved out of the infirmary!"

"The guards?"

"They have A Block in a cross fire up on the walls! Renzo is in the tower on marksman duty. She and all the guards have orders to shoot you guys on sight!"

Bolan nodded. "Patrick, cuff them. Put them in the lounge and lock the door."

Patrick was incensed. "But they—"

"I made a deal. Stewart's life for his cooperation. I consider RayRay part of it. Do it."

"Man…"

"Where to next, boss?" Rudy reiterated.

"I don't think the Big U has left yet. He's still cleaning up loose ends. But when he does, he's going to sacrifice his followers and have Link remotely detonate the weapon in A Block to add to the confusion."

"He strikes me as just that kind of sick son of a bitch," Rudy agreed. "But it couldn't happen to a nicer bunch of fellows."

"I think they have dial-a-yield weapons, probably from one to ten kilotons. They set one weapon at a kiloton, to knock down one of the main walls. But they'll have set the one in A Block at the max, a full ten. That will obliterate the structure, and at the very least drop B and D blocks, on either side, down on the inhabitants' heads. And we have friends there."

"Friends?"

"I got Chinese medicine from D, and Billy the C and Tavo are in B."

"You want to assault A Block and take their nuclear weapon?"

"That's the plan. You in?"

Patrick turned his new Glock over in his hand. "I am so in!"

"No, you're going to escort Price to the tower and try to get her to not shoot us when we move to B Block. Barb, do you have your phone?" Price rifled through Johnson's pockets and found her confiscated cell phone. "Good start having the Bear opening doors between you and the tower, and locking them behind you. Rudy, you in?"

"Blown up in a nuclear fireball or butt-raped by a hundred Nazis and then blown up?" Rudy shrugged. "Well, if that's the choice I'll take a little foreplay first."

Bolan smiled wearily. "You're a good man, Rudolpho."

Rudy turned to his son. "Patrick, take the nice lady and run."

"Link? I need your best guess," Linder growled.

Whitmore stared at his screen. "They're in the system. I can't detect their program. I swear it's a ghost. Whoever wrote the virus is a genius. But the proof is that doors are locking and unlocking apparently by themselves. On top of that we're losing security cameras."

"Can you override it?"

"I can't even pin it down or identify it."

"I'm tempted to break your thumbs, Link. You can't beat Rudy?"

"Rudy is more up-to-date than I am, and this isn't Rudy, though I suspect he has been instrumental in helping things along. Your system has been breached by a Pentagon-worthy cyberattack."

"You have nothing?"

"The security cameras are a double-edged sword. They're the only way for the enemy to actually look inside Duivelstad, but they are cutting them to cover Cooper's tracks. They've instituted random failures to try to confuse us, but if we surmise Cooper's mission, we can plot him by the camera failures."

"Nice." Scott walked into the library flanked by three of his best men. "Hello, gentlemen. My friends and I require guns."

Warden Linder nodded toward the computer table. Four more Thompson submachine guns lay loaded and ready with spare drums. Scott walked over and took up one of the weapons. It was shocking, but he actually had a beautiful smile, and it lit up the room as he examined the Tommy gun. "Warden, you are a man of taste."

"Whatever, we need to move. Your men are set?"

Scott nodded and slung a sack of drums over his shoulder. "My boys are ready to hold A Block to the death, or at least for an assault or two, and they have no clue about our lovely parting gift. What's this about Cooper being on the loose?"

Schoenaur scowled. "Him and the Rudolphos hacked the doors to C Block and busted out."

"What's the police presence at this point?"

"Local units have started to respond. State police are mobilizing."

Scott looked to Linder. "Should we get the party started?"

Schoenaur answered his radio, and the look Linder didn't like crossed the captain's face.

"What now?" Linder rumbled.

"RayRay and Stu aren't responding."

Scott sighed. "Our boy Cooper is moving fast."

Schoenaur's radio clicked again on cue.

"Tell me there's some good news," the warden suggested.

The captain shook his head. "I had Fleeger do a head count on C Block after they were sure it was locked down."

"And?"

"We missed it because only Cooper's cell was open, and some-one, I assume Cooper, switched the sensor bulbs on the board."

"What does that mean?"

"Kal's not in his cell."

Linder nodded. The die was cast, and it was time to get the hell out of Dodge. "Link, open C and D. Let's get this riot started for real."

"What about B Block?"

"The Puerto Ricans? I hate those sons of bitches. Bury them." Linder nodded at Link. "Light up the west wall."

17

Renzo glared over her optical sight as she scanned the yard and the spaces between the cell blocks. The Department of Homeland Security had handed out military weapons and equipment to state and local police for years, and jail administrators that had been clever had applied under the aegis of fighting terrorist cells in the prison system, and had fed at the trough. Renzo's rifle was a coal-black beauty of a current issue Colt M4 carbine with an ACOG self-illuminating optical sight, laser pointer and tactical light. She had named her carbine "Buddy." By Renzo's own estimation she and Buddy could hit an ant in the rear at four hundred meters, and that wasn't just her ego talking.

Renzo ran her eyes over A Block. The boys on the walls had their rifles and shotguns pointed at fortress Aryan Circle. Outside the walls more and more police cars were arriving, but the warden hadn't given the order yet to open the gates and let them in. At the moment Renzo couldn't have cared less about the Nazi pricks, the cops, the Big U or anyone else. She wanted payback for Barnes's brain. Renzo was hunting for Cooper. She scanned eastward. The son of a bitch had to come up sometime. From the tower she could take him even if he got outside the walls. "C'mon...." Renzo muttered. "C'mon...."

The windows behind Renzo shattered, and she ate linoleum as she was thrown off her feet, while the interior of the tower room shook and filled with white light. Instinct took over, and Renzo grabbed her rifle and leaped to her feet. She yawned at the ringing in her ears and blinked at the afterimages flashing across her vision. Then she turned, and her jaw dropped.

The west wall was gone.

The men who had been manning it were gone, as well. Renzo stared in shock at the huge crater and the tower of smoke rising in the air. Chunks of earth and stone began raining down from the sky. Massive chunks of wall had blown outward and crushed several police cars and the officers who had been watching from behind them. Renzo could dully hear the emergency siren howling back to life again. Something pattered the roof of the towers as if it was hailing.

Renzo's radio squawked. Captain Schoenaur shouted over the line. "Renzo!"

"Renzo!" she replied.

"The west wall is gone!"

"I see that."

"You all right?"

"I think so. The tower is a mess," she stated.

"We've lost control of the doors in C and D."

"Jesus…"

"We have to expect a massive breakout within minutes."

The sum of all fears was transpiring right before Renzo's eyes. "What are your orders?"

"For the moment stay in the tower. It's the safest place, and I want you reporting what you see." Schoenaur's voice dropped dangerously. "One other thing."

"What's that, Captain?"

"Shoot Cooper's ass."

Renzo shouldered her M4. "Copy that." Her ears were still ringing and she didn't hear the tower hatch open behind her.

"Officer Renzo?"

Renzo whirled. She saw Patrick Rudolpho with an issue Glock in his hand, and raised her rifle to pop him with a head shot. What stopped her was the sight of the Price woman bloodied and beaten, dressed in a Duivelstad uniform blouse and not much else. "Agent Price?"

The woman nodded. "Officer Renzo, we really need to talk."

"PRICE SAYS GO!" Rudy announced. Bolan and Rudy burst out of administration and ran across the open space for B Block. The grounds in D-Town were filling with prisoners. Some milled about, but most were surging for the blown-down wall. Bolan wasn't much worried by his fellow inmates. None would be willing to mess with the hero of the Hunger Games when he had a shield and pistol in hand. Most cheered as the soldier passed. Bolan waited for a bullet from the walls to hit him in the back.

"Cooper!" Rudy shouted. "Wait!"

"No time!" Bolan glanced back.

Rudy picked up a blackened and bloodstained pistol that had obviously belonged to someone who had been manning the west wall. Bolan nodded. "Let's go!"

The two of them broke for Block B.

A feminine voice shouted, "Cooper!"

Marilyn came running across the dirt. She was still beautiful, but was dressed for action in D-Town issue denims, and her hair was pulled back in a ponytail.

Bolan called over his shoulder to Rudy. "Entry gate to B Block!" The soldier reached the security door and it opened beneath his hand. He, Rudy and Marilyn lunged in and slammed the door behind them.

B Block's control room was abandoned. The guards had put the whole section in lockdown and gone to deal with A Block and the rioting Aryans.

"I'm kind of busy, Marilyn. What can I do for you?" Bolan asked.

"I'm with you."

"You don't know where I'm going," the soldier stated.

"You know what's going to happen to me during a riot?"

"I can imagine."

"Right now everyone is in shock. Fun time in this place should be starting at any moment. The safest place for me is with you," Marilyn told him.

"I'm going to assault Block A."

"Super. I hate those assholes."

Bolan took the spare pistol from Rudy. "You know how to use a Glock?"

"I love Glocks! I had a pink one on the outside!"

Rudy frowned. "Yeah, but did you ever use it?"

"A guy once paid me to shove it up his—"

Rudy interrupted the thought. "Too much information!"

Bolan went to the B Block control board and opened a single cell door. The soldier punched the button for the inner gate and went to Billy the C's house. The C hadn't made a move. He and Tavo sat playing checkers.

Billy took in Bolan and his companions. "You are in a world of hurt, amigo."

Bolan went straight to the point. "I need your tunnel."

Billy the C's face went blank with shock. "Cooper, you're dead."

"I need to get into Block A. The Aryan Circle has nuclear weapons. They blew the west wall with one."

"I heard it."

"They have a second one, and they're going to blow C Block, and B will fall right beside it. You and your people are going to get buried."

"You're going to take Aryan Acres?"

"I need to secure that weapon."

"You and what army?" Billy the C asked.

Bolan glanced back at Rudy and Marilyn. "I got the Rudolpho boys on my side, and Marilyn."

Billy the C stared at Rudy and the hottest thing in D-Town in poorly concealed derision. "*Vaya con Dios,* amigo. Good luck with that. And no, you can't have my tunnel."

Kal stepped out of nowhere. His hands were stained with blood. "Give Cooper the tunnel or I'll take it from you."

Billy the C stared long and hard at Kal. "That's fucked up, *ese.*"

Bolan gave the black warrior a hard look. "This might just be a one-way trip."

Kal held up his book. "You are actually promising me California?"

"Can I ask you a question?"

"Sure."

Bolan asked the one forbidden question within the entire U.S. prison system. "Did you do it?"

Everyone recoiled at this incredible breach of prison etiquette. Bolan was pretty sure it was a ballistic shield and a sidearm stopping Kal from killing him. One of these days pushing Kal was going to get him into trouble. So far it was saving his life.

Kal's jaw set and he stared Bolan straight in the eye. "No."

"I believe you."

"There was no DNA when I was convicted. Two of the lying-ass primary witnesses are dead. I don't care how good your lawyers are. I got nothing."

"Then it will just have to be a pardon."

Kal stopped short of exploding. "You think you can get the governor to pardon a black man convicted of killing four white folks? You know there's an election coming up?"

"Who said anything about the governor?"

Bolan had flabbergasted Kal several times during his incarceration. The soldier knew he had just topped himself. Kal stared at him. "You can get me a presidential pardon."

"The Man does owe me a favor, but you're going to have to crawl through a hole in the earth and help me secure a nuke."

"Who the hell are you?"

"I'm a guy who enters D-Town of his own free will, crawls through a hole in the earth and takes nukes away from Nazis. I believed you. You believe me?"

"Strangely enough, yeah."

"I'll go with them!" Tavo Salcido surged up from the checker-board excitedly. "I'll see to our interests."

"Interests?" Billy the C's face twisted. "We have no interests, *hermano!* D-Town's gonna fall! All I care about is my people not getting shot when the Pennsylvania National Guard retakes this place. I don't care what Super Cooper says. We stand down."

"So we either get blown up, or the National Guard takes D-Town and we all get transferred." Salcido held up his hands. "Either way, why do we care about the tunnel, boss?"

"Because he loves that tunnel. He worked hard on it." Bolan smiled. "And breaking up is hard to do."

Billy the C scoffed at Bolan. "You really want to pop up under Aryan Acres and get butt-raped by a hundred Nazi assholes, *chico?*"

"No, I want to kill a hundred Aryan Circle assholes and steal their nuke." Bolan shook his head. "I hate those guys."

Marilyn winked. "We all do!"

Billy the C was amused against his will.

"You want to go with these assholes, Tavo?"

"More than anything."

"Okay…" Billy the C and Salcido both grabbed the bunk the C had been sitting on, and heaved. It and the concrete it was bolted to slid back two and a half feet to reveal a dark hole below.

Bolan examined the exposed seam and admired the camou-flage. "Toothpaste and sand?"

"Every morning, *ese*. Every morning for ten years. I was doing push-ups against the bunk and I felt it shift slightly. Then I had me an idea. It took a year to cut through the concrete. But B Block is over a hundred years old. It was the first one built. Back when it was just one crazy man chained to the wall with a Bible in each cell. D-Town's designer? He wasn't ready for motivated boricuas on a mission."

"No one is," Bolan acknowledged. The soldier stared down into the hole. It was no concrete spider hole poured into the earth, or professional cartel smuggling tunnel propped up with supports. It was a mole hole in the dirt. Bolan wondered how much of it fell when the west wall was blown, and how much of it was ready to go at the slightest disturbance. He had been buried alive before and hadn't cared for it. "I'll take lead."

"Nobody move!" Renzo snarled. Patrick and Price were with her.

Bolan stared down the barrel of her M4. "Officer Renzo."

Renzo craned her chin at the tunnel. "You're shitting me."

"I would never shit a Sicilian," Bolan said. "I've had run-ins with them before."

"I just bet you have." Renzo stared at the hole again leerily. "The Nazis have a nuke?"

"You saw the wall."

"Yeah, I did. So when I have babies are they going to have two heads and stuff?"

"It was a demolition charge and blew the wall outward. One kiloton or less. The fallout should be minimal. When they blow the one in Aryan Acres, that will be more spectacular on a number of levels."

Renzo's eyebrows suddenly drew down in a V at Rudy. "Tell me that's not my tablet, *paisan!*"

Rudy gave the muzzle of Renzo's M4 a fatalistic look and shrugged. "'Fraid so. Officer."

"Bastard."

Officer Barnes bellowed and racked the action on a shotgun. "Nobody move!"

Renzo stared in disbelief. "Barnes?"

"Renzo!"

"They told me Cooper beat your brains out!"

Barnes didn't take his shotgun off Cooper. The entire left side of Barnes's face was swollen and purple. He gave Bolan a rueful look. "More like he swatted me out of his way like a bug. In his defense, I was shooting at him at the time."

"We're going to confiscate a Nazi nuke," Bolan advised. "Are you coming?"

"It's all over the prison that the Aryans have another bomb. I lost friends on that wall." Barnes's bruised jaw set. "I'm in."

"Give Tavo your pistol."

Barnes made a face. "You have my pistol."

"Give him your new one. I believe historically, during prison uprisings, some trusted prisoners were armed."

Barnes shook his head. "My trusted Tavo…"

Salcido took the pistol delightedly.

"Mr. C?" Bolan asked.

"Yes?"

Bolan nodded at Price. "Watch over this lady for me."

"The *senorita,* with my life," Billy the C swore.

The soldier held out his hand to Barnes. "Give me your tactical light." Bolan took the light and slung his shield around his neck by the sling. He found it awkward going down the hole. It was summer, but the packed dirt was cool and disturbingly crumbly. Bolan dropped the six feet to the tunnel proper, which was low but wide, and as dark as the grave. The soldier clicked on the tactical light, knelt down and began elbowing his way toward Aryan Acres.

Marilyn made a noise behind him. "Eew!"

"You all right?"

"On your six, Coop!"

Bolan reserved comment. It was going to be a long crawl, and several of his team members weren't in the best of shape. The soldier crawled. Puerto Ricans had crawled the path daily for a decade and packed the earth beneath him hard. The roof inches above, on the other hand, had a nasty habit of sifting down streamers of dirt for no apparent reason. You could time them by Marilyn's comments of disgust, but she stayed on Bolan's heels. He could hear Renzo swearing in Italian. Everyone else grunted or panted as the light behind them died out and only Bolan's tactical led them forward.

The cold and damp swiftly turned into a dripping sweatbox. The soldier passed the side branch of the tunnel that led to the old sewer system. He pressed on. It wasn't the worst hundred yards he had ever done, but it was close.

Bolan recognized Barnes making sounds of distress behind him and he sensed people stopping.

Salcido snarled. "Move, *Gordo!*"

Barnes wheezed and whimpered. The guard was out of shape, already exhausted, was under the earth in a tunnel that could barely fit his girth, had a concussion and was freaking out.

"I'll kill you!" Salcido shouted.

Kal spoke low. "Shit-can, that…"

"He won't move! I ain't dying down here behind his fat ass!" Renzo hissed. "Leave him alone!"

"He won't budge!" Salcido complained.

The entire line came to a halt.

Bolan contemplated the tons of earth scraping the top of his head. Trying to make Barnes crawl backward to the light of B Block would be impossible. There was no way to go but forward. Barnes required better motivation than Tavo's Glock against his backside.

The soldier roared in his sergeant's voice, "Officer Barnes!"

Barnes sobbed.

"Stick your left elbow forward!" Bolan ordered. He heard a whimper and movement.

The soldier's voice cracked like a whip. "Now your right! Use your knees!"

He could hear Barnes moving.

Salcido muttered, "About time, you—"

Bolan bellowed the cadence and moved forward. "You had a good home but you left!"

Marilyn of all people responded. "That's right!"

"You had a good home but you left!" Bolan called.

Kal laughed and joined Marilyn. "That's right!"

The line began moving again.

"You had a good home but you left!"

Everyone joined the call and response. "That's right!"

"Hump it, maggots! Hump it! Hump it! Hump it!" Bolan's voice rose to subterranean operatic heights. "I don't know, but I've been told!"

The line roared as a group. "I don't know, but I've been told!"

Bolan ad-libbed, "B Block tunnels are wet and cold!"

"B Block tunnels are wet and cold!"

The soldier called out cadences. The line responded. Bolan's assault team humped their way beneath the earth toward Aryan Armageddon as a unit.

18

BOLAN SLID UNWILLINGLY from the hole and found himself chin-deep in human muck. He rose as Marilyn splashed down beside him. "Eew!" she said.

The team extruded itself out of the tunnel one by one like people being squeezed out of a toothpaste tube into what appeared to be a cistern turned septic tank. Barnes gasped and slid like a corpulent otter into the filth as Salcido gave him unasked for help from behind. The Puerto Rican hit with a splash of muck. "The sewers leak in down here."

"No shit," Kal replied.

Bolan played his tactical light on the wall before him. Someone had spent a great deal of time working on it until he had figured out it was the wall to A Block and not the old sewers. It looked like a three-foot golf divot dug in stone. "Barnes."

Barnes looked as if he might start crying again. "I'm sorry, I'm so—"

"Officer Barnes, what am I looking at?"

Barnes regained his professional demeanor. "We're looking at A Block's basement. That's where they keep the emergency generator. In a situation they would have shut down main power to the block and would have shut down the generator remotely, as well. It's not normally accessible from the block, but if they have the guard station and the main gate, then they have the generator room."

"Rudy, ask for a geothermal on A Block. Is the generator on?"

Rudy wiped his hand on the least filthy part of his shirt and typed. The rest of the team once again stared at Bolan in awe.

"Yeah," Rudy replied. "Bear says definite heat signature, well within the range for an industrial diesel generator."

"Kal, you got those charges I gave you?"

"I do."

Bolan eyed the chipped, three-foot-circumference crater that had been dug in the ancient, crumbling concrete. "Put both in the middle, but don't push in the pins."

Kal placed the charges while the soldier made a five-point star around the edge of the excavation. Bolan put his thumbs on two of the detonator pins and Kal followed suit.

"Marilyn," Bolan said, "do you want to have some fun?"

"This girl was built for fun!"

"Put your thumbs on those pins, but don't push yet."

Marilyn took position. Bolan nodded. "This is a boricua tunnel. You want some of the action?"

"Definitely, *ese!*" Salcido put his thumb on the last pin. "On three?"

"On go," Bolan ordered. "Go!"

Everyone pushed their pins and jumped back. The seven charges flashed like very unsafe fireworks and the stone chamber echoed. The smoke cleared. The divot was blackened and had six deeper pockets in it, but there was no hole.

Marilyn cocked her head. "Well, it was fun."

Bolan grimaced. He was running out of time. "Tavo, I need you to go back and get whatever kind of digging tool Billy the C has."

Salcido shook his head defeatedly. "The biggest thing we have are screwdrivers. It took ten years, amigo."

Kal ran his hand over the cratered stone. "We cracked it."

Renzo gazed heavenward for strength. "Are you packing a sledgehammer I don't know about, Kal?"

"I am." Kal took two steps back, roared and threw the most powerful back-kick Bolan had ever seen. Kal's foot shot through the blackened hole the double charge he had personally detonated had created. He retracted his foot and kicked three more times. Chunks of masonry fell away and light from the generator room spilled into the chamber. No bullets came streaming out at them. Salcido and Barnes began heaving at the edges and widening the hole. Kal stepped back and took a deep breath.

"That was amazing," Bolan declared.

"I think I may have broken several bones in my foot."

"Walk it off," Bolan suggested. "Unless you want to crawl back."

"Oh, hell no."

Salcido and Barnes moved aside as Bolan stepped forward. The soldier slammed his ballistic shield into the hole three times to widen it, and crawled through. Most of the basement was taken up by the dull green, car-size bulk of a very old diesel generator and attendant fuel bunker. The generator thrummed away. The Aryans hadn't been expecting a subterranean attack and apparently had heard nothing through the thick floor above and the sounds of sirens and shouting. Marilyn took her role of covering Bolan's six seriously and appeared at his left elbow.

"So we cut the lights?" she asked.

"Can you see in the dark?"

"You'd be amazed at what I can do when the lights go out."

"Every squad," Bolan said, "has a comedian."

"Comedienne," Marilyn corrected.

"Yes, ma'am, and no, we're not turning off the lights."

Bolan's team filled the basement. The soldier gave everyone his or her assignment. "We take the guardroom, slam every cell shut from the control panel and put A Block in real lockdown. With luck we'll trap a few hostiles in their cells. If we're really lucky, they have the nuke stashed in one of them with guards outside, and we isolate it. I'll take point with the shield. Barnes, I want you behind me with the scattergun. Renzo, you're right behind him, but forget us. I want you and your rifle watching the tiers. Grease anyone who's armed. Rudy, I can't run a tablet and fight at the same time, and you're our only link to our outside resources. You're hanging back. Patrick, I'd ask you to guard your dad, but I can't spare you. You and Tavo are the second wave when we get in. I need to locate the bomb and take it. I need you two watching my flanks and capping anyone who gets froggy."

The young Mafioso was out of smart remarks. To his credit he gave Bolan a serious look. "I have your back."

"We both have your back," Salcido agreed.

"What about me?" Marilyn asked.

"Patrick and Tavo have my flanks, and you are on my six and the guardian angel watching my ass."

Marilyn did a Monroe-worthy simper. "I can do that!"

"Kal, they'll have men guarding the control panel and the front gates. Grab a gun as quick as you can."

The soldier nodded at his team and moved to the basement steps. "So let's do this." Bolan had good reason to bet the Aryans were outwardly focused. He moved up the stairs to the guardroom. "Rudy, is the basement door locked?"

Rudy checked the Bear's program that was checking everything in Duivelstad. "Nope!"

"On go." Bolan put his Glock in his waistband and his hand on the door. "Go!"

Bolan flung open the door and drew his pistol.

A bare-chested, heavily inked skinhead stood by the block control console wearing a pair of guards' Sam Browne belts crossed over his shoulders like Pancho Villa. He also had a .38 duty revolver in each hand. That told Bolan the convicts had more than just the guardroom officer's Glock. Someone had let them dip into the armory.

"Freeze," Bolan ordered.

Pancho Skinhead didn't freeze. He went gunfighter with the weapon in each hand. The con never got his pistols up. Bolan put a hole through the swastika inked on the skinhead's forehead. The Aryans guarding the main gate shouted in alarm. More shouts came from within A Block. "Barnes! Lockdown! All cells and the main gate room!"

"On it!"

Barnes ran to the control panel and punched a button. Kal picked up the two fallen revolvers and reloaded them. The door that led from the main gate to the guardroom rolled shut, trapping the Aryans guarding the gate. Bolan was hoping they were the ones with the heaviest weapons. Barnes threw the main block switch. The warning buzzer sounded and every light on the cell control began blinking. Shouts of consternation came from A Block as every cell door rolled shut. Every light on the panel went from green to red as the doors locked. "On me!" Bolan ordered.

The team assaulted A Block.

Some cons shouted in rage from the cells, but far too many were on the ground floor and outside. Bolan estimated he had a good seventy-five opponents before him, and way too many of them had guns. A bullet spalled against Bolan's shield and then another. Two Aryans were firing revolvers as fast as they could pull the triggers, and cons fell into a screaming shooting wedge behind them. The soldier aimed around his shield and took the leading men with a pair of double-taps. Barnes's shotgun blasted, and another Aryan screamed and fell.

The revolvers and shotguns the cons had were antiquated. A tactical center in Bolan's mind deduced that Warden Linder had never thrown anything away when his prison armory was upgraded, and had kept a secret stash of weapons. As antiquated as the firearms were, buckshot and .38 Specials had probably killed more people in the U.S. than any other calibers.

Bullets thundered against Bolan's shield. He put three more men down. Convicts twisted and fell. Marilyn, Salcido, Kal and Patrick began unloading. The battle for A Block had turned into the gunfight at the O.K. Corral. Both sides just stood and shot at each from spitting distance. A rifle bullet punched straight through Bolan's shield and cracked an inch from his ear. "Renzo! Sniper!"

Bolan heard the crack of the carbine behind him and a man with a scope-sighted rifle fell from the third tier. The Aryans surged forward to overwhelm their opponents. The soldier's weapon clacked open on empty, and he knew he wouldn't get the chance to reload. The battle was about to go hand-to-hand.

Renzo stepped forward and flicked her carbine's selector lever. She had no illusions about what would happen to her if her team lost. "Let's rock!"

Renzo emptied her magazine into the mob.

The thunder of the carbine firing on full-auto thundered against the block walls. Men screamed and fell. Others tried to turn back, or threw themselves down. The Aryan formation began to break apart as men scattered. A space opened in the crowd. Rollin stood there wearing nothing more than a bandage, like a diaper. Sawyer Love stood beside him, armed with a revolver. Both men aimed at Renzo as she reloaded.

Bolan raised his shield and charged.

The soldier's shield vibrated and shuddered when Rollin unleashed a 50-round drum into it. Love threw his smoking revolver at Bolan and stepped forward. He grabbed the shield and ripped it out of his grasp. Bolan let him. The soldier slammed the butt of his empty Glock into Love's chest right above the heart. The man dropped dead for the second time by Bolan's hand.

Rollin slapped a fresh drum into his Tommy gun.

Bolan took a page out of Love's book and flung his empty Glock into Rollin's face. The Aryan's head snapped back as he took over a pound of metal and plastic in the teeth. Bolan dropped to one knee and spear-handed Rollin in the bladder.

Rollin fell, vomiting as if shot through the bowels. Bolan rose and ripped the Thompson from his hands. The Aryans rolled over the soldier like a wave. He saw stars as a fist hit him in the back of the head. Hands clutched and tore, and fists struck him from every direction, while others tried to pull him down. Bolan hunched and just managed to rack the action on the Thompson as two different pairs of hands grabbed the barrel to rip the gun from him.

Bolan squeezed the trigger.

Two bursts were enough to clear the space in front of him. Bolan surged against the hands grasping at him and twisted to his left. Men screamed and fell as the soldier held the trigger and his attackers fell away. Bolan spun to his right and fired two more bursts to give himself elbow room. The soldier heard Renzo's rifle spraying again, and more of the Aryan mob seemed to be running in all directions. It was a terrible risk, but Bolan lunged forward and vaulted up onto one of the tables.

He threw a glance backward and saw that Kal, Salcido, Marilyn and Barnes were down. Patrick and Rudy stood by Renzo as she reloaded, but none of the Aryans were shooting anymore. Most had flung themselves to the floor. One of the nice things about automatic weapon fire was that it had that effect on people. Others had run for their cells in blind panic, only to find the doors barred to them.

Bolan fired a short burst into the air. "Everyone on the ground! Hands behind your head!" The soldier used the refrain from the yard that every inmate had been trained to respond to. "We resume shooting in five, four, three, two—" Bolan scanned the block. Everyone on floor level had dropped or been dropped. "Rudy! Open the left-hand cells on floor level!"

Rudy went into the control room and the cell doors rolled open.

"Everyone who can walk get in the cells! Now! Keep your hands where we can see them!" The ambulatory Aryans rose and shuffled toward the cells. The dead lay scattered everywhere and the wounded moaned among them. "Lockdown!"

The cell doors rolled shut once more.

"Rudy, open Unit 1, floor level, then see to Barnes! Patrick, police up the weapons and put them inside! Renzo, cover him! Shoot anyone playing possum! What's our status?"

"Barnes has one through the shoulder and one through the leg. Kal's a mess. Tavo and Marilyn are gone."

Bolan stared down at Rollin, who lay clutching himself in a pink-tinged puddle. "Where's the bomb?"

"Fuck you!" Rollin groaned.

"Tell me or I'll shoot you in the stomach and ask someone else."

Rollin groaned in real distress. "The Force's house! Last door on the right! Floor level!"

Bolan stepped down off the table. He took up the bag of ammo drums and reloaded the Thompson. "I need the last cell on the right! Floor level! On my signal!" The soldier stepped through the sea of bodies and strode to the end of A Block. He stopped in front of Scott's cell with his Thompson leveled. No one was home except for a nuclear weapon.

Most nuclear demolition charges Bolan had encountered looked like small suitcases. This one was shaped like a medium-size cannon shell, which told Bolan it had been designed to be dropped from a plane, carried in a backpack or, indeed, shot from a cannon. "Rudy! Open her up, and I need you!"

The door to Scott's cell rattled open and Rudy came at a run with Renzo's tablet in hand.

"Put the camera on that for the Bear."

Rudy tapped an icon and turned on the speakerphone and the video function.

"Bear, A Block is secure, but we have a lot of dead and wounded."

"Do you have the weapon?"

Bolan nodded at Rudy, who aimed the tablet at the bomb.

"Do you see what I'm seeing?" Bolan asked.

"Oh, I see it," Kurtzman replied. "That has got to be one of the rumored Vietnam nukes."

"How do we stop it?"

"That is serious 1970s retro technology. Get me a closer look at the nose."

Rudy squatted on his heels and ran the camera over the area. Bolan examined it, as well. The nose was a separate unit from the body, like the fuse of a cannon shell, only slightly longer and more complicated. It looked as if it could be twisted in several places and multiple gradients and numbers lined the seams.

"All right, from what I can tell, you set it like you would a cannon's fuse. All the gradients and numbers seem to be aligned sequentially. Nothing is out of sequence, so I'm willing to suggest the weapon isn't set for an impact detonation and that it's not on a timer.

"So it's waiting for someone to phone it in."

"Exactly. And since we're talking the 1970s it will be a radio transmission."

"You got a bird that can jam across all frequencies?"

"I have one that can jam most frequencies, but I had it tasked with scanning across most frequencies in case you tried to send out a radio signal."

"Jam as far across the spectrum as you can, keeping a 1970s detonation signal in mind."

"You've just had a prison fight, a wall blown down and hundreds of escaped convicts. That is going to play hell with police, fire, rescue and the National Guard."

"A ten-kiloton surface detonation will be worse."

"Well, there is that."

"Can your bird scan and jam at the same time?"

"It can."

"Look for the detonation signal."

"That is going to be very short. It will literally be your needle in the haystack."

"But I'm betting Scott will push the button several times when he doesn't hear the big boom."

"Nice. I will see if we can pick it up and get you a triangulation."

"Thanks, Bear."

"What are you going to do?"

"There's no evidence Linder or Scott left by the main gate. I think the old sewers must link with the sulfur mines. I'm going back down."

"I lost you on the tablet when you were in the tunnel."

"I know. Download the ground-penetrating radar imaging to me. We'll go from there. Linder is a strong man, but he's not at fighting weight, and Link is an old man. They'll be loaded down with the nuke, weapons and the money I suspect they're lugging out. They won't be moving fast. That's why the bomb hasn't gone off yet. They're nervous about lighting it up while they're still underground."

"That's as solid an assessment as I we think we're going to get. The Pentagon is scrambling together a team to defuse the weapon."

"I'll keep A block in lockdown until they arrive. I'll make contact again when possible. Striker out."

Bolan ran back to his team. Salcido's face had been ruined by a shotgun blast. Marilyn's was still beautiful, but the pattern of buckshot on the left side of her chest had broken her heart forever.

Barnes was gasping and pale, but Patrick had bound up his shoulder and leg fairly professionally.

Kal lay on his back, clutching a wadded shirt over the bloody bullet hole is in his stomach. "Did you disarm it?" he gasped.

"We put it on quiet time. I give it a good eighty percent chance it won't go off before guys arrive who can take it apart."

"That's the best odds anyone ever had in D-Town."

"Oh, it gets even better."

"How's that?" Kal asked.

"You're gut shot. You can linger for days."

"You're an asshole."

"I gotta go."

"Hey, that presidential pardon. You really mean that?"

"You mean to go back to California?" Bolan asked.

"Leaving L.A. was the biggest mistake I ever made."

"Then if I'm alive by next year, I'll look you up. We'll surf Redondo," Bolan told him.

"The first beer will be on me."

"Deal." Bolan turned to Renzo. "You're in command of A Block. Keep it in lockdown until the Feds show up, and don't let anyone in Scott's cell until the Pentagon boys arrive."

"I don't surf, but if you're alive around this time next year I want dinner."

Bolan smiled. He owed Renzo. "One condition."

"What's that?"

"Lend me your rifle," Bolan said.

Renzo sighed and handed over the weapon and her four remaining magazines. "His name is Buddy, and I want him back."

Bolan tossed the Thompson to Patrick. "Merry Christmas. Try to keep your bursts short."

"Sweet!"

"Rudy, grab a shotgun and two flashlights. We're going back down."

19

BOLAN STRUGGLED BENEATH the earth, which sought to reclaim its own. Moving back along the path from A Block, he found the branch that led to the old sewers turned from a fork in the road to a buttonhook from hell under the earth. Trying to crawl it backward would be impossible for exhausted men. There was no choice but to try to turn around at the junction, which was a question of inches and angles; and the underworld was not forgiving human frailty. The beatings Bolan had suffered had sapped his strength, and the bruising had taken a terrible toll on his flexibility. He was stuck fast, and the pride of B Block was coming dangerously close to becoming his grave. He set down the tactical light and sank his fingers into the earth. "Patrick!" Bolan said through clenched teeth.

"Yo!"

"Push my feet!"

"Umm…okay!"

He felt Patrick's hands close on his feet, and the young man pushed. The soldier tried to go with the pressure and draw his knees up. The act of folding up like a cricket to get his legs around the corner did nothing good for his internal injuries. Bolan grimaced with effort. Soil sifted down. "Harder!"

Patrick coiled himself and shoved. Bolan groaned as his knees came closer to his chest. "Harder!" Patrick shoved as hard as he could with what little leverage he had. A shout tore from Bolan's throat as he convulsed his body to break the logjam. Then his feet scraped the tunnel wall and his legs suddenly uncoiled behind him. He flopped, half in and half out of the fork in the tunnel. The soldier lay in the earth on his side, gasping like a fish.

"You all right?" Patrick asked.

Rudy's voice came from behind. "Is he all right?"

Bolan ran a mental check of himself. The Mack Bolan machine

was running at a low forty percentage of fighting fitness. His insides hurt, but he didn't think he'd ruptured anything.

"You want some water?" Patrick inquired. "I brought some water."

"That'd be good."

Bolan felt a plastic bottle prodding him in the leg. He reached for it and gratefully poured some of the precious liquid onto his face. He took several long breaths and then several long swallows. The water felt a little uncomfortable going down, but he didn't get the pressured, nauseous telltale feeling that presaged internal bleeding.

"Thanks." Bolan passed the bottle back and gingerly twisted onto his stomach. He crawled to where he had shoved Renzo's carbine, and crooked it in his elbows, then moved forward to make room for Patrick and Rudy. "Come ahead." The soldier couldn't see behind him, but he heard Patrick twisting himself around the junction with the pliancy of youth, and in one-tenth the time it had taken Bolan.

"C'mon around, Dad!"

Bolan kept moving ahead. Behind him a steady stream of swearing ensued as Rudolpho the Elder pitted himself against the hairpin corner from hell.

"You got it, Dad! Grab my foot and pull! Pull!"

The scrabbling and swearing suddenly subsided into gasps. Rudy called out in exhaustion, "I want a presidential pardon, too, Cooper! In fact, I want two of them!"

One corner of Bolan's mouth quirked despite his own exhaustion. He broke the holiest law of prison etiquette for the second time in a day. "Did you do it?"

Rudy muttered something under his breath.

"I did!" Patrick volunteered. "Caught red-handed!"

One of Bolan's grunts of effort turned to a snort of amusement. "That's very honest of you, Patrick."

"Isn't that the point of a pardon? Being forgiven?"

"You freely admit all your sins?" Bolan asked.

"I cannot tell a lie!"

"Oh, really?"

The young man's voice grew serious. "Not to you, Cooper. You helped my father, and saved me from a life of butt-piracy at the hands of a man whose nickname is Rolling Thunder. I may be young, and I got caught, but my father raised me right. I understand a debt of honor."

It was too bad Patrick's father hadn't steered the young man clear of the Family business, but it was the Family business, and Bolan had to give the young man points for maintaining a positive attitude in a very bad situation. "You all right back there, Rudy?"

"You know, I thought I was going to enjoy this *Great Escape* bullshit."

"You freaking out?"

"A little. I'm really starting to hate being here. I can feel it pressing down and closing in."

"You're doing great, Dad!" Patrick encouraged.

"Rudy, take the water, pour some on your face, take three deep breaths, then three swallows, and start crawling. It's a straight shot from here. We'll get you out of the cold ground and into a nice filthy sewer system."

"I can't wait."

Bolan began kneeing and elbowing forward. He could sense that the tunnel was sloping downward slightly. The crawl was interminable. It had taken them fifteen minutes just to get around the bend. "Rudy!"

"Yeah!"

"How many bars we got down here?"

Rudy laughed raggedly. "Mr. Cooper, I regret to inform you that you are outside your coverage area."

Bolan lifted his chin as he crawled on, and sniffed deeply. He had never been so happy to smell human waste in his life. "Hey, Rudy!"

"What!" Rudy's voice was tinged with irritation. Bolan would take anger over fear any day.

"Guess what I smell?"

A measured amount of hope crept into Rudy's voice. "The nutraloaf you ate last week?"

Patrick laughed.

"Give the man a cigar," Bolan acknowledged.

"You just get me to Shit Creek, Cooper. I don't need a paddle. Just get me out of this endless goddamn grave."

"Done!" Bolan followed his nose toward effluvium. What was left of his team had been through hell, but they were still salty. The end game was close at hand. Bolan's light played on concrete and an open hold ahead. His hands met stone where the Puerto

Rican tunnelers had breached the sewer, and he reached the smell at the end of the tunnel.

Bolan stuck his head out and played the tactical light around a far more spacious tunnel. It was the typical poured-concrete cylinder of a sewer section. A bit of raised walkway girded both sides of the sluice. Bolan held his light on fresh footprints on the dry walkway. They were scuffed, but the soldier made it two pairs of boots and two pairs of convict shoes. That made it Warden Linder, Link, Schoenaur and Scott.

Bolan eased himself out the tunnel and his bare feet gratefully met solid stone. "Come ahead."

He gave his two teammates a hand out, and all of them straightened and stretched. "Which way?" Patrick asked.

The soldier pointed at the prints. "They head that way, and that way also leads to the old mines."

Bolan turned off his flashlight, flicked on the light mounted on Renzo's carbine, and broke into a run. "Let's move."

The Hills

THE WARDEN TOOK a deep breath and looked down at his castle. From his vantage point in the hills he could take in the entire tableau of D-Town's downfall. Smoke still rose from the demolished west wall. Well over a hundred state and local police vehicles formed a cordon around the prison, and a sea of news crew vans formed their own parking lot out in the field. Three police helicopters orbited the sky over Duivelstad.

Linder sighed. He had really enjoyed his run as warden and firmly believed in the line from John Milton's *Paradise Lost,* "Better to reign in Hell than serve in Heaven." He had made Devil's Town earn its name, and had enthroned himself as Lucifer. He thought it was fitting that Duivelstad would end burning in radioactive fire.

Linder held out his hand. "Give it to me." Whitmore handed over the detonator. The detonation device was simply a D-Town issue, multiband tactical radio. "The frequency is set?"

"You can transmit anytime," Whitmore confirmed.

Scott finished pulling on the clean civilian clothes Schoenaur had secreted there at some previous time. They had all changed. Schoenaur had shaved off his mustache, and both he and Linder wore state police uniforms. Whitmore wore a windbreaker and chinos and looked like a librarian. Scott wore a suit and sunglasses and looked downright distinguished. The Aryan crime lord laid his Thompson submachine gun lazily across his shoulder and grinned down at his former home. "This should be interesting."

Schoenaur looked at the detonator in his former boss's hand and then at Whitmore. "Can we watch it go up, or will we go blind or something?"

Whitmore was still shaking from his trip through the sewers and the mines. "The weapon is inside A Block, so the initial flash will be contained."

Scott was mildly disappointed. "No mushroom cloud?"

"Well, it's only five kilotons, but if you've never seen one live, it should be spectacular."

Scott sighed happily. "Good." When he assassinated the President of the United States, his entourage and everyone else with several city blocks, he definitely wanted a mushroom cloud. He wanted that mushroom cloud front and center on every newscast and on the front page of every newspaper in the world. "Warden?"

Linder clicked on the radio, held down the transmission button and punched in 6-6-6 on the keypad. The four men gazed down into the valley expectantly. Law enforcement light bars continued to flash atop vehicles. Choppers continued to circle the sky. The warden punched in the detonation code again. "Is there some kind of delay?"

"No." Whitmore stared down at the prison complex worriedly. "It should have detonated immediately."

Linder punched in the code a third time and then handed the radio back to Whitmore. "Are we on the wrong frequency?"

Whitmore checked the setting and punched in the code himself. "No, everything is correct. D-Town should be gone."

Linder turned a baleful eye on the old man. "Link, I'm very disappointed with you."

Whitmore shuddered in open fear beneath Linder's gaze.

Scott cocked his head in reflection. "You don't suppose our boy Cooper happened to storm A Block and defuse that firecracker, do you?"

Whitmore grasped at the change in conversation. "I can't imagine any way for him to do so. Even if he somehow got past all your men, the only way to diffuse the weapon would be to disassemble it. That's takes special tools." He toed the backpack that held his belongings. "And I have the only set outside the Pentagon."

Schoenaur took out his radio. "Should we try mine?"

Linder continued to glower at Whitmore, but nodded. "Give it to him."

Whitmore took the radio with shaking hands. He set the frequency and sent the signal several times. "Something is wrong."

Schoenaur snatched the radio back. It had been screeching with guards and staff trying to get hold of him, but that had ceased when he went under the earth. "You want me to call in to see if anything has changed inside?"

Linder nodded. It was a small risk. "Do it."

Schoenaur clicked on the guard frequency. "Renzo, sitrep?" The former captain jerked his head back at the blast of static he got in return. "Jesus!" Schoenaur turned down the volume and tried again. All he got was static. "Boss?"

Whitmore punched buttons on the other radio and got half a dozen short bursts of static. "We're being jammed."

"What?"

"Across the spectrum. The tacticals, the police and emergency bands? Everything. No one down there can send or receive, either."

Schoenaur scowled. "How the hell do you jam everyone's radio?"

"You would need one hell of a powerful transmitter locally."

Scott laughed aloud. "Or a military electronic warfare satellite."

Linder, Schoenaur and Whitmore stared.

The Aryan chief shook his head in admiration. "Cooper isn't Special Forces. He's goddamn James Bond, or a reasonable facsimile."

Linder spit in disgust. "Link, weren't you supposed to be some kind of hot shit CIA guy? Why didn't you figure this out?"

Whitmore stammered. "I—I…"

"I'll tell you why, because you're a goddamn degenerate hophead, that's why. Never trust a junkie, never depend on one."

"Please, Warden…"

"You're shaking, Link. You need to fix?"

Whitmore couldn't keep the eagerness out of his eyes. "Warden, I—"

"Force, you figure you know how to set the weapon yourself?"

Scott nodded at Whitmore. "I paid attention in class."

Linder nodded to Schoenaur. "Rog, give Link his fix."

Whitmore suddenly found his wrist engulfed by one of the most powerful hands in Pennsylvania. The old man cried out as Schoenaur squeezed. Whitmore's fingers curled into an involuntary fist and the veins across his hand stood out in high relief with the pressure. Schoenaur held up a hypodermic needle. "Sweet dreams, Link."

"Please! God!" Whitmore shrieked. "No!"

Schoenaur stuck the needle into the vein between Whitmore's ring and little finger and injected. He left the needle in Whitmore's hand and let him go. The old man staggered back a step. His eyes fluttered as the hot shot surged through his bloodstream and pure heroin pulsed through his brain. Whitmore's eyes rolled back in his head and he fell like a boned fish into the weeds.

Linder spit on the dead man. It was most likely the last time he would get to degrade a convict. He jerked his head toward the entrance to the mine behind them. "Rog, throw him down the shaft. Scott?" Linder nodded toward the van with state police markings. "You're driving."

The Computer Room, Stony Man Farm, Virginia

"Got him!" Akira Tokaido threw his fists skyward in victory. "Short burst, low power radio transmissions! The dumb-ass tried to send the signal five times!"

Kurtzman rapidly typed orders to the satellite two miles above Pennsylvania tasked with listening to Duivelstad. "Zeroing in." He watched his screen as the satellite tracked the signal and his computer laid out a map grid. The signals originated in the hills, just to the east of Duivelstad.

"He sent again!" Tokaido glowed with scorn. "Man, what a dumb-ass!"

"We have a location. Mack's instincts were right. The transmission origin is just outside one of the old sulfur mines. I need eyes on. Get me imaging."

Tokaido ordered the satellite whose job was to stare at D-town to use its high-resolution imager and zoom in. "I have two individuals and a van. Sending you the video stream."

"Two?" Kurtzman frowned at the window that popped up the gray images in the feed. "Mack said he thought there would be at least four. Definitely Linder, Schoenaur, Scott and Whitmore."

"Maybe they split up already?" Tokaido suggested.

"That wouldn't be good." Kurtzman pondered. "There are scores if not hundreds of inmates loose in the hills. There will be dragnets and roadblocks everywhere. The only way Linder and his crew can get through is if they pass themselves off as law enforcement. Pull the imaging back."

Tokaido zoomed out. "There's only one road that leads up to the mine. I don't see any vehicles on it. Nothing going cross-country. Maybe there was a double cross? Linder and Schoenaur killed Scott and Whitmore? Or vice versa?"

"Possible…"

"Should we send in the cavalry?" Tokaido asked. "Or at least alert them?"

"If we alert law enforcement, we no longer have a say in the situation. I want to at least wait until Mack surfaces and makes contact."

Tokaido enumerated the worst-case scenario. "What if he doesn't? What if they already fought it out down below and Team Linder came out on top?"

"Even if that's true I'm not sure we want to initiate a standoff. I don't think Linder is normally the suicidal type, but he sure as shooting doesn't want to go to prison. He might just set the weapon off in spite, and if it's Scott? That man is one of the top dogs in American white supremacy. He might just enjoy going out in a radioactive blaze of glory. Better to let them run to ground and think they're safe. Then we can have Able Team launch an assault by surprise."

"So we just wait and see?"

"We wait for Mack, and we track that van if it moves."

BOLAN CLIMBED. SOMEONE had recently reinforced the vertical shaft's ladder with fresh rungs of new wood. Linder had hired someone to dig a fairly sophisticated smuggler's tunnel that connected the abandoned sulfur mine to the old sewer system. Bolan highly suspected that particular someone and his construction crew were probably dead and rotting in one of the abandoned side shafts.

The soldier hauled himself ever upward. It was better than squirming beneath the earth, but climbing a hundred feet of ladder wasn't doing him any favors. The saving grace was that he was climbing toward fresh air and there was light at the top of the shaft.

The light suddenly occluded and Bolan saw Schoenaur.

Bolan was thirty feet below, in the vertical shaft's well of darkness, and he knew Schoenaur couldn't see him. The guard captain had Lincoln Whitmore slung across his shoulder like a sack of potatoes. Schoenaur shrugged Whitmore off and tipped him into the shaft.

"See you in hell, Link!" Schoenaur said before he disappeared.

Whitmore's body came tumbling down like a rag doll.

Bolan hugged the ladder and hissed down at his teammates. "Hold on!"

The soldier watched the corpse bounce off the walls and thud and clatter against the ladder. Bolan rammed an arm out as Whitmore dropped. His palm hit flesh and he tried to deflect the dead man to the other side of the shaft. The old man's foot brutally clubbed Bolan in the shoulder, and he nearly lost his grip on the ladder. Patrick stifled a yelp.

Whitmore continued his descent and disappeared in the darkness. The thuds of his bouncing path down the shaft ceased a few seconds later. Bolan had already started moving again, and he climbed for all he was worth. He reached the top and unslung Renzo's carbine. The entry shaft was wide and had tracks for mine cars. Bolan broke into a run toward daylight. He could feel his legs failing beneath him, and his lungs burned. He could hear an engine turn over out in the sunshine. The soldier redoubled his efforts. Patrick had already caught up and easily ran by his side.

The two of them burst out of the mine.

The soldier had spent an hour beneath the earth, and the sunshine slammed into his eyes with whiteout intensity. Bolan staggered and dropped to one knee. He shouldered his weapon and brought the carbine's optical sight up to his streaming eyes. He could make out the blurry shape of a van driving away at speed halfway down the hill.

Bolan lowered his weapon.

"Shoot!" Patrick shouted. "Why don't you shoot?"

The soldier took a ragged breath. "Because if I don't take out the van, they get away and know we're right behind them. Then it's anybody's guess what they might do."

Patrick saw the wisdom of it. "So we let them think we're still in D-Town, and that they got away clean."

"And we hope to hell my people are tracking them." Bolan

looked back as Rudy emerged from the mine, squinting and grimacing. "Rudy, are my people tracking them?"

He held up the tablet. Kurtzman's voice came on over the speaker. "We're tracking them, Striker."

"Bear?" Bolan looked down on the sea of flashing lights in the valley below. "I need a car."

20

"I NEED YOUR CAR." Bolan smiled at Officer Alison Ottewalt in a friendly fashion. The soldier had a very attractive smile, but he knew it was shining out from a barefoot man in prison garb caked from head to bare feet in dirt and nearly every substance a human body could excrete. He was also smiling from behind a rifle. Deputy Ottewalt was built like a feminine fire hydrant in khaki. Bolan almost felt bad. With radio communication down, Kurtzman had broken into the streams of emails and texts shooting back and forth between law enforcement down at the scene, and sent Ottewalt on wild-goose chase up to the old mine. She had barely put her cruiser in Park before she found Bolan and Buddy in her face.

She gave Bolan a steely glare. "Convict, you will never make it out of this valley."

"Actually, I've never been convicted of anything."

Ottewalt openly scoffed. "Every con says he's innocent."

"I never claimed to be innocent. I said I've never been convicted of anything."

"Then why are you in D-Town?"

Bolan looked out toward the prison. "To stop this."

"Yeah? You did one hell of a job."

"Oh, that's just one wall. The real plan was to turn the entire facility into a smoking hole in the ground."

The deputy grudgingly looked back toward Duivelstad. "I suppose your two friends have never been convicted of anything, either."

"Guilty as charged," Rudy admitted.

Patrick nodded. "And as the day is long!"

Deputy Ottewalt shook her head. "You'll never get out of this valley."

"We will if you drive," Bolan countered.

"I refuse. Do your worst."

Rudy whistled. "She's got sand."

"You best commence shooting." Ottewalt took her hands off the steering wheel. "I'm drawing my sidearm in three seconds."

"She said 'commence shooting,'" Patrick said in admiration. "That was cool."

Bolan nodded. "Rudy, put Deputy Ottewalt in touch with Officer Renzo, video chat."

"Three seconds to drop your weapons," Ottewalt warned. "One…"

Rudy tapped some keys and handed the tablet to Bolan. Renzo popped up on her phone. "Cooper!"

Ottewalt's hand went to her holster and the Beretta holstered there. "Two…"

Bolan gave Renzo the short version. "Listen, Linder, Schoenaur and Scott are in a van. They killed Link. They have the third weapon. They don't know we are onto them and I have satellite tracking. I need a car, and I need you to convince Deputy Ottewalt to assist us." Bolan held out the tablet to Ottewalt. "It's for you."

Ottewalt stared at the tablet as if it were a snake.

"You can draw if you want. Gentlemen, drop your weapons."

Bolan and the Rudolphos disarmed and took a giant step backward.

Ottewalt took in the beleaguered looking corrections officer in the video chat window. "Officer…?"

"Renzo! I'm in Duivelstad! Listen up!" Renzo read Ottewalt the riot act. Everyone in Pennsylvania law enforcement knew who the Force was. Most knew Schoenaur's reputation, and every citizen in the state knew the Big U. Renzo played her phone's video camera over the wounded Barnes and Kal, and the small ocean of bodies in A Block. She neatly summarized the entire situation, and Bolan particularly admired her closing remark, "Decide what side of history you want to be on, Deputy."

"I need your car, Deputy," he reiterated. "And I need you."

Ottewalt stared incredulously. "I'm supposed to disobey orders, abandon my post and go chase a nuke with three convicts?"

Bolan sighed. "I told you, I've never been convicted of anything."

"Those two have, and they're armed."

"They were armed, and I kind of deputized them."

Ottewalt looked as if she was getting a migraine. "Oh, and do you have that authority?"

"No." Bolan grinned again. "But you do."

"I can't believe this. And if I say no, you three are just going to surrender?"

"No, those two will. I can't."

"You won't?"

"I said I can't, but I absolutely refuse to fight law enforcement. I will attempt to escape and evade and continue my mission."

Deputy Ottewalt's head seemed seconds from exploding.

"Deputy, we're running out of time," Bolan prodded.

Renzo chimed in from the chat window. "Shit or get off the pot, Deputy!"

Ottewalt rolled her eyes again, but this time it was with disbelief at herself and the apparent reality failure occurring all around her. "I don't exactly know how to deputize anyone. We never covered it at the academy."

"Well, just say something."

"Oh, for the love of…" Ottewalt squeezed out an oath under pressure. "Do you swear to uphold and defend the Constitution of the United States against all enemies foreign and domestic?"

Bolan nodded. "I do."

"Definitely," Rudy agreed.

Patrick was nearly beside himself. "Awesome!"

Deputy Ottewalt watched the end of her law-enforcement career flash before her eyes. "Get in."

PASSING THROUGH THE roadblocks proved to be no problem at all. Duivelstad was in full riot status, and the United States had just suffered the biggest jailbreak in its history. Rumors of a massive explosion were spreading like wildfire. Local, state and federal law enforcement and increasing numbers of National Guardsmen were everywhere and fanning out in all directions. A uniformed deputy in a cruiser flashing her lights was waved through checkpoints literally without slowing. Bolan, Rudy and Patrick stayed low. Bolan knew Linder was using the same trick. The soldier watched the Farm's satellite feed on the tablet.

Kurtzman spoke across the feed. "They're on I-81 heading east. You need to get on the highway."

Ottewalt breezed through the checkpoint at the on-ramp to I-81 and used the opportunity her lights and sirens gave her to step on the gas. The Crown Victoria's police modified V-8 engine roared like a beast.

Bolan considered his limited ways and means for the mission. "What have you got, Deputy?"

"What do you mean?"

"You were responding to a reported prison riot. You bring along any party favors?"

"I have a tear-gas launcher in the trunk and a patrol rifle."

"How many gas masks?"

"Just the one."

That narrowed the tactical applications, but it still put another arrow in a very lean looking quiver of options. "You have any spare .223-caliber ammo?"

"I brought six boxes, and have six spare loaded magazines."

"Bring any extra 9 mm?"

"Two boxes."

"I need to borrow a bit when we stop, so me and the boys can top off our magazines."

"Like I'm going to say no at this point," Ottewalt muttered. The deputy stared off into the distance. "You know, I enjoyed being a cop. I'm going to miss it."

"You're not going to lose your job, Deputy," Bolan assured her.

The deputy wasn't buying it. "Oh? And just how am I supposed to explain this, again?"

"You don't. In fact, you probably won't have to. My people are already working on your situation."

"And what does your people are working on my situation mean, exactly?"

"Assuming we survive the next hour or two, you will most likely receive a glowing letter of commendation from the Justice Department, the Department of Homeland Security or both, for your valor and voluntary assistance in a matter of grave national security. The details of which will be mostly redacted, but it will look awesome on your service record, or your résumé, if you want to aim for the big leagues in your career."

Bolan had received a lot of dumbstruck looks in his life. The Duivelstad mission was breaking all previous records. Ottewalt returned her attention to the road. "I have this feeling that you've actually done this before."

"Actually, this one has pretty much been a new one even for me," Bolan admitted. He gazed out the window and saw the lines of hills fly by. Traffic was extremely light and nearly devoid of emergency vehicles. Outside the radio jamming zone citizens were being asked to keep off the roads and stay in their homes. "But this last part here? Yeah, that I have done. I always take care of my team."

"He's going to get Kal a presidential pardon," Patrick offered. "But Dad and I suck. We're guilty, and have to pay for our crimes."

"So why did you two volunteer for a suicide mission, then?" Ottewalt asked.

"Deputy, have you ever been in Duivelstad?" Rudy asked in return.

Ottewalt smiled for the first time. "Something about fresh air, sunshine and a ride in the car?"

"Something like that, and not getting blown up."

"Deputy?" Bolan asked.

"Yeah?"

"You've already done me a huge favor by getting me and my team out of the cordon around Duivelstad."

"What are you saying?"

"I'm saying that the Aryan Circle has a nuke. They're going to be willing to kill to keep it, and most likely light it off rather than lose it. If you can get us close to wherever they run to ground, you can drop us off and run, try to get a piece of Blue Mountain between you and the detonation."

"That is a mighty tempting offer." Ottewalt locked her big brown eyes on Bolan's blue ones. "But do you remember that oath I made you escapees take up at the mine?"

"I do."

"Well, before I put on this badge, I took it, too."

"Officer Ottewalt in the house! Large and in charge!" Patrick pumped his fists. "Winning!"

"I warned you…"

"You warned me about 'awesome!' I said 'winning!'"

"No, I'm warning you about 'large and in charge….'"

"He's a bit irrepressible," Bolan stated.

"I noticed."

Kurtzman spoke over the chat window. "Linder has left I-81. Breaking north."

"North?" Bolan gazed at the map on the tablet. North of the satellite tracking was the equivalent of a Pennsylvania little Big Empty.

"North!" Ottewalt's eyes flared with the lightning bolt of inspiration. They were already traveling at well over the speed limit. Bolan was pushed back in his seat as Ottewalt stomped on the gas. "Oh, that son of a bitch!"

The Computer Room, Stony Man Farm, Virginia

"North?" Tokaido stared quizzically. North of that stretch of I-81 there was very little in the way of roads or major towns, and few highways. "He's pulling off, apparently into—"

Kurtzman suddenly sat up straight in his wheelchair. "Frackville!"

"Is that some kind of *Battlestar Galactica* reference?"

"No…"

"So what is the significance of the charming borough of Frackville, exactly?"

Kurtzman had been crunching a great deal of data on Pennsylvania's correctional facilities the past few days. He began touching points on his screen and lighting them up on his map and Tokaido's.

"Frackville is home to the Corrections Department and the maximum security State Correctional Institution. The United States Prison Bureau is just ten miles south, in Minersville. Schuylkill County Prison is about equidistant in Pottsville, and Columbia County Prison is about twenty miles north.

"It's like corrections central. Who knew?" Tokaido said.

"Linder does. He's been the warden of Duivelstad for more than two decades. He has spies and connections throughout both state and federal corrections. I bet a lot of people on both sides of the bars in all of them owe him favors, and I bet he knows where a hell of a lot of bodies are buried. I suspect he'll have all the help he needs to lay low, get his retirement finances collected, and facilitate his safe transportation out of the state and out of the country."

"He's taking Lehigh Avenue north, and he's turning!" Tokaido zoomed the imager. "He's pulling into a warehouse! He's inside! We no longer have eyes on the target."

Kurtzman pulled up the address and hit his communications tab. "Striker, target has gone to ground in Frackville."

"I know," Bolan replied. "Give me the address."

SCOTT DROVE INTO the warehouse. He rolled past four guards with Uzi submachine guns. The men nodded at him respectfully and with awe. Scott nodded back. "Gentlemen."

He stopped the van and killed the engine as the warehouse door rattled down behind him. Two very dangerous men stepped out of the shadows. Warren Coburn's head gleamed in the overhead lighting, but that was because he was bald rather than a skinhead. In cargo pants, a pink dress shirt and wire-rimmed spectacles, he looked like a middle-aged banker on casual Friday. He had long ago forgone the outward trappings of the supremacist movement and was one of the Aryan Circle's most deadly undercover operatives. Assassination and arson were his specialties. He had earned his CPA certification, had a thriving small practice in Allentown and moved a lot of illegal Aryan money.

William "Wild Bill" Monahan on the other hand was a mountain of a man with the long hair, grizzled beard and leather-and-denim regalia of an outlaw biker. The affable giant played Santa Claus during his club's toys for sick children drive. The self-same Santa had once dismembered three men alive with an ax. He had commemorated the act with the tattoo of a bloody fire ax with the Roman numeral III beneath it. Wherever he alighted for any length of time he had an ax nearby. One lay on a crate close at hand in the warehouse. Coburn was practically a myth in Pennsylvania crime circles. Wild Bill was a genuine legend.

Scott leaned his head out the window and grinned. "Greetings, brothers!"

The three men all bore the same Aryan Circle branded over their hearts.

Scott, Linder and Schoenaur piled out. Schoenaur's hand stopped short of hovering for the fast draw. Aryans and former Corrections personnel stared at each other. Scott was positively jovial. "Brothers, may I introduce Ulysses Linder and Roger Schoenaur."

Monahan's laugh boomed off the warehouse walls. "The Big U himself!" The big man shoved out his hand. "You know, I've spent a significant portion of my life hoping to never meet you. Pleased to make your acquaintance!"

The tension broke and they shook hands.

Monahan gave Schoenaur's right paw a dubious look and his own hand hovered. "I don't know…I've heard stories about this…"

"Wild Bill's a card!" Scott laughed.

Schoenaur slapped his hand into Monahan's and shook. "You're on the right side of the bars, Bill, and I'm retired."

Coburn shook hands with both Corrections men, but his eyes were calculating. "You're a man short."

"Link sort of failed to live up to expectations," Linder growled.

"Waste of good heroin if you ask me." Schoenaur spit. "That shit was one hundred percent pure."

"Heroin was how the old fuck entered Duivelstad, and heroin was how he left," Linder said. "I admire the irony of it."

"Goddamned poetic," Monahan agreed.

Coburn shot Scott a look. Business was business. The Aryan Circle played by certain rules.

Scott nodded sadly. "I don't like breaking a deal, either, Warren, but Link just didn't live up to his end. He was supposed to light that candle and eliminate all traces. Duivelstad is still mostly standing. Now, none of us here assembled would talk, but old Link, he was indeed a degenerate hophead. A couple days without a fix and it wouldn't take much more than a stiff breeze to roll him over."

Coburn eyed Linder and Schoenaur. "Then we're keeping Link's share of the money, and his junk."

Scott shrugged casually. "Oh, let's just split it four ways and part company as pals."

"You can keep the junk," Linder offered. "We don't have the time to worry about trying to move it."

"I'm amenable," Monahan said. "Speaking of business, what do you say, Ulysses? You bring that big bad bitter pill we heard tell about?"

Linder unslung the canvas bag from his shoulder and set it on a crate. He unzipped the bag and the five men contemplated the thermonuclear weapon.

"Shee-it." Monahan shook his head wonderingly. "You really fucking delivered, Force."

Scott nodded at Linder and Schoenaur benevolently. "Had a lot of help, Bill."

"Speaking of which," Linder said. "You bring the money?"

Coburn set three briefcases next to the bomb. "As agreed. The new IDs and documents are inside and we have two clean vehicles out back." The killer opened one case and swiftly began sorting the banded stacks of Whitmore's share into four equal piles.

"You guys hungry?" Monahan asked. "We got a barbecue in the back. We can burn you a steak and open a jug of something."

Coburn snapped out his phone and stared at his incoming text. "Hoder says there's two gnarly-looking clones outside with Thompson submachine guns."

"Who's Hoder?" Linder asked.

"Our guy on the roof," Monahan answered. "Who are Tweedle-dum and Tweedledee going *Untouchables* outside my door?"

"My guys outside," Linder replied. "The Totts twins. They're good people. Reliable. I've used them on jobs outside D-Town before. You want to let them in?"

Scott regarded Linder drily. "A little extra insurance?"

"Never hurts," the ex-warden replied.

Monahan shrugged. "Well, hell, I brought enough beer for everybody. There ain't no reason to go outside tonight except maybe to get caught. Let's party!"

21

"SITREP, BEAR," BOLAN said. The soldier crouched behind a garbage bin about a block away from the warehouse with a frontal view of the target. "Any change in target status?"

"Striker, the van is still inside," Kurtzman reported. "No verification on how many got out of it. No individuals have left through the front or the back. We had two armed men entering about half an hour ago. Be advised there is a man on the roof."

"Status of roof sentry?"

"He appears to be alone, and reports in with his cell phone. He has a rifle. Be advised, thermal imaging shows a bright heat source within the warehouse near the rear entrance."

That raised mild alarm bells with Bolan. "What kind of heat source and how hot?"

"It's a mostly a steady five hundred degrees above warehouse ambient. Frankly, my best guess is they're cooking something on the grill. We're not getting much in the way of smoke telltales, so I'm thinking the Aryans are using propane."

Bolan's stomach growled in response. He was running on fumes. "How is Barbara?"

"She has left hospital and is back at the Farm. The beating took a bit of a toll on her. She's resting against her will, but wanted me to tell you that Billy the C was a perfect gentleman and charming company."

"And the nuke?"

"I got word from Renzo. Some very serious suits from the Pentagon showed up and after about twenty minutes left and took the device with them. A Block has been cleared. I got a report from the hospital. Barnes is going to be fine and should be able to resume work in six to eight weeks. Your pal Kal has been stabilized. He had a lot of internal bleeding, but he has been moved out of surgery to the ICU. His prognosis is excellent."

"What's his prognosis for parole?"

"You spend a lot more time talking to presidents than I do. I don't know, excellent?"

"I told Kal he and I would surf Redondo same time next year. Tell the Man at the top I intend to keep that promise, even if I have to break Kal out."

"I don't think he'll be surprised. Be advised you have someone closing on your six, and Ottewalt has signaled Patrick is on approach."

"Copy that." Bolan smelled Patrick before he heard him, and it wasn't the stench of their trip through the sewers. The young man squatted on his heels and presented a take-out bag. The scent was almost maddening. Bolan raised an impressed eyebrow. "Meat loaf?"

"Cracker Barrel takeout, Cooper! I told Deputy Ottewalt that I figured after three days of nutraloaf you needed to get back on the horse. She got on the stick while you ran your recon."

"You are the wind beneath my wings, Patrick." Bolan tore into the ketchup-smeared half brick of take-out meat loaf with his hands.

"I put ketchup on top. That's all right, right?" Patrick asked. "You like ketchup?"

Bolan spoke around a crocodile-worthy wad of meat. "Ketchup is good."

"And I told her you needed coffee." Patrick handed out a take-out tall. "I figured you needed coffee."

Bolan took the cup of joe gratefully. "I needed coffee."

"I told her to put a shitload of sugar and cream in it."

"A shitload is pretty appropriate right about now, Patrick." Bolan ate meat loaf and drank coffee. He knew he had injuries that would take weeks to heal. The soldier didn't want to contemplate what percentage of fighting effectiveness he was at currently, but whatever it was he could feel it being braced and buttressed as he ate.

"Where're Deputy Ottewalt and your dad?"

"They sent me in on foot with the food. They're hanging back in the cruiser until you decide on a plan." Patrick tucked into some steak fries. "So what's the plan?"

Bolan licked his fingers clean and sipped coffee. "Nothing left to do but assault."

"Could we wait for the cavalry or something?"

Bolan thought of Able Team and Phoenix Force. "I know some guys, but they're currently deployed elsewhere. It would take too long to put together a Special Forces team, and I don't want local or state law enforcement turning this into a siege. It would go from standoff to assault, and if that happens I think we all go up. We have to go in with what we have. Now or not at all."

Patrick contemplated that. "How many do you figure are inside?"

"We got a lookout on top with a rifle. Have to figure on Linder, Schoenaur and Force. Figure they met at least one or two guys inside, and they have a couple guys for security. Two more arrived half an hour ago, so at least ten, most likely heavily armed. Possibly more."

"Two to one odds at best."

"We will have surprise on our side. Just like A Block."

"We lost some good people on A Block."

"We did, but there we were outnumbered seven to one. Now we're better armed and can pick how we hit them."

"So how do we hit them?"

Bolan had worked every angle a hundred times. "The key to everything is taking out the sentry on the roof."

Patrick's budding tactical mind considered the problem. "We don't have any silenced weapons. What are you going to do? Climb up the to the roof and Hunger Game him or something?"

"Given the circumstances, that's how I would normally play it. But the fact is, Patrick, I'm just about done." Bolan gave an honest assessment. "I'm not climbing anywhere tonight."

Patrick bit his lip and nodded. "You want me to do it?"

Once again Bolan found himself admiring the young man's grit. "That's very kind of you, but we have to do it silent, and we have only one shot at this."

"But we can't do it silent. You said so yourself."

"Right, so we have to do it as quietly as possible, and that means we need a new plan."

Patrick gave Bolan a wry look. "I think we're fresh out of giants, swordsmen, holocaust cloaks and wheelbarrows, Cooper."

Bolan smiled wearily. "That we are, but we do have a teargas gun, a police cruiser—" the soldier returned Patrick's look "—and a punk hoodlum."

Patrick stopped mid–French fry. "Punk hoodlum is cold, Cooper."

BOLAN SLID A CS tear-gas shell into the single shot, 37 mm grenade launcher's breech and snapped it shut. The battery on Renzo's tablet was dying, with no way to recharge it, and that and Ottewalt's cell phone were all Bolan's team had in the way of tactical communications. Rudy crouched behind him with his commandeered D-Town riot gun ready. Bolan spoke into the chat window. "You two ready?"

"Copy that, Cooper," Ottewalt responded.

"Ready," Patrick said.

"Go."

Bolan waited while his assault came together at a walking pace. Three blocks away Patrick was deploying out of Deputy Ottewalt's cruiser and heading toward the warehouse. Bolan had removed the buttstock of Patrick's Thompson submachine gun, effectively turning it into a giant machine pistol, and one he had concealed in a carry-all from the back of the cruiser, along with his two spare drums.

Deputy Ottewalt spoke across the link. "Patrick deployed. Swinging wide, ETA ninety seconds on reestablishing Patrick."

"Copy that." Bolan turned to Rudy. "If it all goes south, we hit that door. Kill anyone in your way. Whatever happens, secure the nuke. Got it?"

"I wish my son wasn't here."

"Me, too, and right about now so does he. But I'm proud of him."

"So am I."

"We're all volunteers on this one, Rudy."

"We took an oath," Rudy agreed.

"That we did."

"Cooper, I know you can't get us a pardon, but if we don't make it, my wife—"

"It's already taken care of," Bolan affirmed. "You have my word."

Rudy slowly nodded. He had a loaded Glock in the front of his waistband and another in the back. In his hands he held a 12-gauge, and he had a pocket full of spare shells. "Then let's do this."

Bolan slung Buddy. He took up the 37 mm and put two spare gas grenades in his shirt pockets. "Well, all right then." The soldier spied Patrick walking down the alley toward the warehouse. "I have eyes on Patrick."

"Copy that," Ottewalt responded. "I have eyes on. On your signal."

"Copy that." Patrick wandered up the street like a young man who had jumped out of a boxcar and found himself in the wrong town and on the wrong side of town. "Kid's a natural," Bolan commented.

Rudy grudgingly admired his son's gall. "That's one way to describe him."

Bolan kept most of his attention on the man on the roof. "The sentry sees him. He's phoning in." The soldier shouldered his launcher. "Here we go." Patrick walked past the warehouse, the sentry tracking him with his rifle.

Bolan spoke low. "Deputy, you are go." The soldier saw the sentry hunch down as Ottewalt slowly rolled her cruiser down the street. "Bear, status on sentry."

"He's on his phone."

Ottewalt pulled her cruiser up behind Patrick. She flashed her lights and blooped her siren twice as she screeched to a halt. The sentry rose and aimed his rifle, pressing his phone against his ear with his shoulder as he reported what was going on outside. Deputy Ottewalt got out and gave Patrick a professional hassling. Without prompting, she suddenly grabbed her radio, spun and ran to her car, as if she had just received a major incident call. Patrick ran as if God on high had given him a get-out-of-jail-free card. Ottewalt hit her lights and siren full blast, and her tires screamed on the asphalt as she pulled away.

Bolan stepped out of the shadows and into the street. Timing now would be everything.

A rifle or pistol shot was a high decibel crack that was unmistakable, while 37 mm grenade launchers were only rated for tear gas and rubber buckshot. They made a low thump that sirens and screeching tires might mostly hide. Ottewalt tore down the street. The sentry lowered his phone and raised his rifle to track Patrick. He jerked when he caught sight of Bolan stepping into the glare of the streetlights.

Bolan raised Ottewalt's grenade launcher and fired.

The launcher shoved against the soldier's shoulder. Its low-decibel half bloop–half thud sounded as loud as doomsday to Bolan. He could only hope it was masked or confused with the sound of sirens, revving engines and screeching tires for the men within the warehouse. None of that changed the fact that a tear-gas grenade weighed half a pound and the launcher threw it at over a hundred feet per second. Bolan caught some luck and the roof sentry flew backward as he caught the grenade in the teeth. Gray gas began billowing from the rooftop. Bolan snapped open the launcher's smoking breech and reloaded. He dropped the weapon on its sling and took up Renzo's carbine.

"Sentry is down and not moving," Kurtzman reported.

"Copy that. Ottewalt, take position," Bolan ordered.

"Copy that, ETA thirty seconds."

Bolan motioned his team forward. "Let's move."

The soldier marched across the street with Rudy on his six. Patrick stopped his headlong flight and Bolan waved for him to join them. The young man ripped his Thompson out of the bag and racked the bolt. Ottewalt cut her lights and sirens four blocks up and swung back around wide to take the back door. Rudy and Patrick both jumped as the sentry above let out a gurgling scream of agony.

"Jesus!"

"Shit!"

The light behind the peephole in the door occluded as the guard in the office looked out at the sound of the scream. Bolan put a burst through the door, then shoved his foot into it. The door to the warehouse office bounced against the guard behind it. The soldier gave it a second kick, and the door broke off its hinges and fell atop the fallen sentry. There was no time to wait for Ottewalt. Bolan took point. Like most warehouses, the office had a wide window giving a panoramic view of the main storage bay, where men were shouting and unlimbering weapons. The office window shattered in a cascade of glass as Bolan put a burst through it into the closest man with an Uzi. "Covering fire!"

Rudy's shotgun hammered and Patrick cut loose as Bolan put his shoulder into the office door and rolled behind the cover of a forklift. The Rudolphos dived through the window. Rudy took cover behind a trio of industrial barrels and Patrick a pallet of crates. Bullets began flying in all directions. Bolan heard Scott booming orders. "It's Cooper and the Rudolphos! Screw them! Out the back! Go! Go! Go!"

An Uzi-armed man with a ponytail lunged for the back door. It was an emergency exit and by code had to open outward. The Aryan bounced off it as if he had run into a brick wall. Ottewalt had parked her cruiser against the door. The orders Bolan had given her were simple. None shall pass.

A blast from Rudy's shotgun bounced the man against the door again, and this time he left a massive red smear as he slid to the floor.

Bolan popped up just beneath the driver's seat of the forklift and caught sight of a redheaded man with a Thompson submachine gun scuttling from one pallet of crates to another. The soldier put three rounds into the man's chest and dropped him.

"Lem!" An identical twin of the man rose screaming from behind the cover his brother had been running for, and began unloading at Bolan. "Lem!" Sparks flew off the forklift like fireflies as the soldier dropped back down.

"Walking fire!" Scott bellowed. "Swarm them!"

It wasn't a bad tactic, given the confines of the warehouse, and the enemy had a lot of Thompson submachine guns with 50-round drums. Bullets began sweeping the interior office window and hitting the forklift like hail. There was almost no way to get a shot off.

Bolan dropped Buddy, unslung the gas launcher and sent a grenade blind over the forklift. He quickly reloaded and fired off another. The Aryans shouted and swore in consternation. It was a gamble. The gas would interfere with Bolan and his team, as well. But the enemy was going to eat it for a good handful of seconds before Bolan and the Rudolphos would, and the soldier had been exposed to war gases and continued fighting before. The Aryans came forward, spraying on full-auto. The other redheaded twin came in screaming and holding down the hammer.

He fell as a pistol cracked five times from the office.

Bolan risked a glance back and saw Renzo in the window. She shot another man with an Uzi. Schoenaur popped up, took an extra heartbeat to aim and sent Renzo staggering and falling out of sight with a .357 in the chest. Bolan sent a burst the guard captain's way, but he had already dropped behind cover.

"Rudy!" Bolan shouted. "Patrick! No one gets out the front!"

Bolan moved out from behind cover. He took six huge, deep breaths and then moved into the gas. He hunted the sound of coughing. He heard it and moved to his left. A bald man in a pink shirt rose and fired a burst from his Uzi into the barrels Rudy was behind. Baldy moved forward and stepped into Bolan's line of fire. The soldier stitched him with a burst and dropped him.

"Got you, motherfucker!" A giant came out of the gas weeping, coughing and blazing away with a MAC-10 submachine gun in one hand, like a giant pistol, and waving a fire ax in the other. Bolan put three rounds into the big man and Buddy ran dry. "I got you!" the giant screamed.

The gas ruined his aim and bullets drew a line across the floor as Bolan rolled out of the way. The soldier had to breathe, and his lungs made fists as he breathed in gas. The giant tossed his spent weapon and raised his ax in both hands like some Viking of the Apocalypse. "I got you! I got you!"

The ax rang off the concrete an inch from Bolan's head as he dodged. Bolan drew his D-Town Glock and fired up into the man.

The giant staggered backward as he took shot after shot center body mass. Bolan kept squeezing the trigger. The soldier ran out of options as the slide slammed back on a smoking empty chamber. Wild Bill Monahan toppled like a human landslide to the warehouse floor.

Bolan rose. He heard a cough behind him, but his injuries and the gas filling his lungs made him a second too slow.

Bolan found himself staring down the barrel of Schoenaur's .357.

The sadist said nothing, but he took a suicidal heartbeat to smile in victory. Bolan's left hand struck like a snake across the top of the revolver and squeezed. Schoenaur's six-gun had been modified into a fast-draw weapon. The hammer was bobbed, so that meant it wasn't cocked. Schoenaur instantly squeezed the trigger, but in Bolan's grip that meant the cylinder wouldn't turn. The former guard captain took another suicidal heartbeat to try to yank the weapon free. Bolan took the opportunity to punch Schoenaur in the throat. He buckled with the blow and Bolan felt cartilage crack as he did it again. The soldier ripped the revolver out of Schoenaur's palsied grip as the man fell choking and dying.

Bolan tucked the revolver into his belt and reloaded Buddy.

A pair of Thompsons began ripping off long bursts. Linder began screaming and coughing. "You know who I am? I'm the Big U!" The former warden punctuated each outburst with a burst of bullets. "I'll put every last one of you in the boneyard!"

It sounded as if Linder had lost it. Bolan rose and leveled Renzo's carbine. Linder caught sight of him through the gas. "Cooper!"

Bolan fired. So did Rudy and Patrick. Linder flapped like a ruptured bird with Thompson submachine guns for wings, and fell before the firing squad. The Executioner dropped back down and his team followed his example. "Patrick, check on Renzo! Rudy, hold position!"

Scott shouted from behind the cover of a huge crate. His voice was ragged from the tear gas. "Cooper!"

"Surrender, Force!"

"I have the nuke!"

"I know!" Bolan called back.

"I was paying attention when old Link explained how the weapon works!"

"Wouldn't expect anything less, Force! Now give it up!"

"It fuses four ways! One is by radio signal—nice job on jamming the one in D-Town, by the way!"

Bolan ignored the compliment. "Surrender!"

Scott ignored the order. "The other three fusing methods are proximity, impact and timer!" These were all things Bolan already knew, and he had a sinking feeling that he knew where this was going. The soldier moved at a crouch to a stack of crates. A dead Aryan lay behind them, still clutching his Uzi. Bolan nodded back at Patrick and Rudy, and they began moving in from the sides. Scott lectured on. "Now, I'm not sure what good proximity would do me, and as for impact? Well, Cooper, I've watched you work. I really don't want to have to be slamming the goddamn thing against the floor, hoping it goes off while you go kamikaze on me."

"Force, don't make me come over there and take it from you—"

"You assholes are fine right where you are!"

Rudy and Patrick froze.

"Any of you make one more move toward me and we all go up!" Scott snarled. "Which leaves the timer. Just so you know, I set it at thirty seconds as a fail-safe. All I have to do is twist two fusing rings! Then we are half a minute away from a thermonuclear Frackville, and there will be nothing either you, me or anyone else will be able to do to stop it. That leaves you with two big questions, Cooper! One! You doubt I'll turn those rings?"

Bolan knew Scott would. "No."

"Do you want me to turn these rings?"

"You know I don't. What do you want?" Bolan asked.

"Nothing, just a head start. Who's out back?"

"A cop named Ottewalt. She deputized us."

"Nice. You're going to have to order her to stand down."

"They'll catch you. You'll never get anywhere near the President."

"Probably," Scott conceded. "But first, they'll have to catch me, and I'll use Ottewalt to get me out of town."

"So I just let you go and that's it?"

"Well, sorry to say, I don't trust you, Cooper."

"I'm sorry to hear that."

"So you're just going to have to stand up and let me shoot you."

"I'm not sure I approve of that plan," Bolan said.

"Cooper, we both know I don't want to detonate in Frackville, but we both know I will. I walk out of here, Frackville never knows how close they came, and you just have to bet your life that your people are better than mine and can track me down and take the weapon before I do something exciting with it."

Bolan considered his dwindling options. Rudy and Patrick shot him questioning looks from behind cover. Renzo was most likely bleeding out in the office.

"There's about four thousand souls in this town, Cooper, and not much surrounding it for miles!" Scott prompted. "Maybe Frackville is an acceptable sacrifice for you!"

It wasn't. Bolan stood.

"I'm afraid I'm going to need the Rudolphos to stand up as well!"

"Rudy!" Bolan called. "Patrick!"

The Rudolphos rose. They were clearly shocked and horrified, but Bolan had to give them full marks for conspicuous bravery as they stood up in the face of certain death.

"Fuck," Rudy declared.

"Lower your weapons!" Scott ordered.

"You heard him," Bolan said.

His team lowered their weapons. Scott rose with the nuke cradled in his left arm. In his right hand he held a gleaming stainless-steel revolver. He held it loosely and kept his bottom three fingers on the bomb's fusing rings. "Lose the weapons! You first, Cooper!"

Bolan tossed away Buddy the carbine and the gas launcher.

"And the pistol!"

Bolan tossed Schoenaur's revolver.

"Now you, Rudy!"

Rudy glanced at his son and gave Bolan one desperate look. Bolan shook his head.

Rudy bitterly tossed away his shotgun. He relinquished his two pistols and stood with his fists clenched in helpless rage.

"Now the kid!"

Rudy's voice shook with everything he would never have the chance to tell his boy. "Son…"

Patrick's voice broke. "Dad!"

Scott dropped back partially behind cover. "Don't fuck this up!"

Bolan spoke calmly. "Patrick?"

"What?"

"Don't fuck this up." Then Bolan barked out in his sergeant's voice, "Shoot the barbecue!"

Scott's reddened eyes flared.

"Shoot it!" Bolan ordered. "Now or not at all!"

The Aryan's eyes flicked to the grill three yards away. Once the firefight had started no had bothered to turn off the barbecue. It was still on high, and a pair of steaks were burning into briquettes and sending black smoke to mix with the tear gas. Scott clamped his fingers on the fusing rings.

Patrick shoved out his Thompson and put fifty rounds through the barbecue.

Bolan dropped behind the crates as the propane tank went off like a bomb. The heat and pressure blew over the crates he was using for cover in a wave, and buried him. That was a blessing as the skylights blew out and shards of glass the size of kitchen knives rained from the ceiling. Bolan ignored the ringing in his ears as he pushed free of the crates. He stripped the Uzi from the fallen Aryan and rose.

Scott stepped out of the smoke.

He was a mostly skinless, hairless, clothesless, blistered thing. His whole body was swathes of lobster-red and charcoal-black. Blood leaked from his eyes, ears and mouth. He still clutched the nuke. It seemed his hands had been seared to the metal cylinder. A piteous howl came out of the burned pit that was Scott's mouth.

Bolan put a 3-round burst through Scott's face and ended the Aryan Circle man's suffering. The soldier winced as the nuke clanged against the floor, but nothing nuclear happened. The good news was the propane blast had dispersed most of the tear gas. "Rudy!" Bolan called. "Patrick!"

Rudy rose unsteadily from behind cover and tottered toward his son. Patrick sat in the middle of the warehouse. His face and arms were nearly totally black, but as he opened his eyes and yawned, that appeared to be mostly from smoke. His eyebrows were missing, as was the first inch of his hairline. His mouth opened and closed several times.

"I think he's trying to say 'awesome,'" Bolan guessed.

Patrick flopped back and stared up into the shattered skylights. "That was awesome. Admit it."

"I admit it," Bolan told him. "*You* are awesome."

"Finally." Patrick coughed. "Some recognition."

Bolan staggered to the office and hit the button for the main warehouse door. The remaining gas began to billow out into the street in a low fog. He groaned as he limped into the office. Renzo had a bloody hole in her shoulder and she had stuck her finger in it.

"This is going to hurt," Bolan rasped. He dragged Renzo from the smoke-and-gas-filled office and out to the curb. Ottewalt came pounding around the corner. "Oh, shit!"

"Medical kit!" Bolan ordered. "Stat!"

Rudy came out of the warehouse with his son leaning on him heavily. He shot Bolan a grin. "We did it."

Bolan considered the Rudolphos and their actions. He glanced back into the main warehouse. "You see that van?"

"Yeah."

"I bet there are two suitcases of money in it, and probably Schoenaur's uniform. "Put it on and drive for Lake Erie. Leave the guns. Pick up Renzo's tablet from the alley on the way and find a place to charge it. By the time you reach Erie my people will have contacted you on it. They will tell you which ferry to take, and have you cleared for customs."

The Rudolphos just stared.

"You're a hacker and an embezzler, Rudy. Your son is a hoodlum. Your United States privileges are revoked. Try to straighten up and fly right." Bolan jerked his thumb northward. "Now get the hell out of here. And call your wife. She's probably worried and probably needs to buy a plane ticket."

Bolan turned back to Renzo before the Rudolphos could say anything.

"So how did you find us?"

"I called my iPad with my phone and used the Where Is My iPad? GPS app. I figured you might need some backup."

"Your talents are wasted in Corrections, Renzo."

"Yeah, we need to talk about that."

The van pulled out of the warehouse. Rudy waved. Bolan waved back. Ottewalt reappeared with the first-aid kit from her cruiser and began applying a field dressing to Renzo's wound. "It doesn't look too bad. I've seen worse."

"Hurts every time I cough." Renzo coughed.

Patrick walked out of the warehouse and set Buddy at Renzo's feet and the nuke at Bolan's. "It was all stuck to him and stuff." He held out three Rolling Rock beers. "The cooler survived. You looked like you could use one."

Bolan took the beer and twisted the cap off with an effort. "Thanks."

"Well, later!" Patrick limped to the van and jumped in. The Rudolphos pulled away.

"Later." The soldier wiped the sweating bottle across his brow. He took a long pull and nearly coughed it up. Bolan decided to just press the cold bottle against his head for a moment while he admired the sea of flashing lights deploying into Frackville off the highway. The state police van carrying the Rudolphos drove right past them.

"Hey, Cooper," Renzo groaned. "Shit or get off the pot."

Bolan held out the beer. "Trade you for your phone."

"It's a deal."

The soldier took the phone, picked up the blackened nuke and rose creakily. The moment Renzo had called her iPad, Kurtzman had invaded it, Bolan knew. He tapped in a number from memory and Kurtzman popped up in a window immediately. "Striker!"

Bolan took a left at the alley and began walking out of town toward the reservoir. "Bear, the nuke is secure. I need extraction."

Every inch of the Executioner's body hurt like hell, and he knew that it would take more than a couple weeks of solitude and R and R to get back into fighting shape. But did he have the time? A warrior's work was never done; another mission always loomed large.

But then again, tomorrow was another day.

* * * * *